# DAYS LIKE THESE

Roy Calley

Bloomington, IN  Milton Keynes, UK

authorHOUSE®

*AuthorHouse™*
*1663 Liberty Drive, Suite 200*
*Bloomington, IN 47403*
*www.authorhouse.com*
*Phone: 1-800-839-8640*

*AuthorHouse™ UK Ltd.*
*500 Avebury Boulevard*
*Central Milton Keynes, MK9 2BE*
*www.authorhouse.co.uk*
*Phone: 08001974150*

*First published by AuthorHouse 5/16/2007*

*ISBN: 978-1-4343-0388-2 (sc)*
*ISBN: 978-1-4343-0389-9 (hc)*

*Printed in the United States of America*
*Bloomington, Indiana*

*This book is printed on acid-free paper.*

# Days Like These

It's on days like these....when the wind sings its tune, when the rain offers its deluge, and when the greyness suffocates the very life... you can feel it. It's on days like these that the stillness can strike at the heart and overwhelm the mind. It's on days like these that the dreams and nightmares take hold and worry the very essence. Thankfully, days like these don't happen often, but when they do.......

# CHAPTER ONE

*"Beauty is beautiful when it is looked at in the right way"*

It was a saying that had been with Caroline her entire life. Her Father had taught her from her earliest years that she should look for the beauty in everything. No matter what the circumstances and no matter where the position, there would always be beauty if you were prepared to seek it out. It may not be immediately apparent and it may quite often take time to see, but if you looked with an open mind and a trained eye, and more importantly, you looked in the right way, you could find beauty in just about anything. His belief had not come from any strong religious faith. He never attended a church or a chapel, but he had a strong moral sensibility. It was a kind of unstructured mixture of Christianity and magic, which seems to be found amongst most country people. The saying had stayed with her always, and soon after her Father died, she had a small-framed plaque made, with those very words engraved on it. It now took pride of place above her bed, so that with the rising of the sun she could read it, and with the ending of the day she could read it. It always comforted her.

Many people would describe Caroline as beautiful. She was 37, but looked a decade younger despite the constant toil of looking after two young children and a demanding husband. Her long blonde hair, crystal-blue eyes and a stunningly engaging smile gave her the kind of attention from male admirers that most women pretend not to care for, but many yearn after. Her figure was petite and slim, her personality equally attractive as her looks, but her total devotion to her family, and in particular to husband Tom, meant that never a man would get as close to her as he would secretly wish. There was a near perfection about her. She was beautiful in body and spirit. She looked for beauty all around her and she gave out beauty in almost everything she did. Caroline was happy and content in her life. There was nothing she would change about it, even if it were possible.

They had met quite by chance. He was a travelling sales-representative with a firm of stationers and she was a part-time help in a small local bookstore. She had loved books and reading for as long as could remember, and after failing to live up to her parents expectations at school, she had immersed herself in knowledge gleaned from books. She'd started an Open University course in the evenings in a bid to reclaim some of the early promise suggested to her by her high-school teachers. The chance to earn a little extra money during the day, and surround herself with books was something she couldn't miss out on. After a month or so she started to notice the salesman who called every Tuesday, always smartly turned out with an unusual but pleasant taste in cologne. He seemed to linger in the shop for much longer each time he visited, and then after about six weeks he'd asked her out. It was only her second date since splitting with her childhood sweetheart Patrick and she wasn't sure how to behave. Patrick had grown into a wild young man after his parents had been killed in a car crash and had effectively driven Caroline away. She had neglected her studying and failed most of her exams, much to the obvious and open despair of her Mother and Father. Since then she had tried to ignore the charms or temptations of the opposite sex, apart from a blind date set up by a 'friend' that had gone disastrously wrong.

She instantly liked Tom though. He seemed an honest man, always attentive and caring when they were together. He had been born in Lancashire and had that way of talking and behaving that only exists in that part of the country. He had been incredibly old-fashioned in some ways, especially when it came to taking care of her when they were out. She was never allowed to pay her way, and she secretly thought that his idea of a perfect wife was to have someone who would attend to his every need. She found soon that he was a gentle and tender person in their intimate moments, and in no time they were in love and engaged to be married. Both sets of parents got on famously and it was certain they would marry. When they did, the event was as wonderful as anyone could imagine. She looked radiant in every way, and many people commented on how beautiful she looked. He was handsome and strong and it was clear they were in love and would live happily ever after. The first few years were a bit of a struggle financially, but once Tom changed careers and became involved in the insurance sector, then the money started to flow in. The small semi-detached house was soon changed and upgraded for a larger detached modern house on the edge of a huge rambling estate, the extra bedrooms handy once the children arrived.

Now they lived in a 17<sup>th</sup> century thatched-cottage in a small hamlet called Little Hanwick. It was inevitable they would live somewhere like that. It had the 'chocolate-box' beauty that so typified rural England, and when Caroline had first set eyes on it six years ago, she knew they had to move there. It was small, only three bedrooms, a small bathroom, living room, reception hall and an oak-beamed kitchen with the added attraction of an Aga. It was white-stone walled and had a garden that ran around the entire circumference of the property. It was set back from the road and was pleasantly hidden by a huge Corsican pine tree that overhung the front of the cottage. To the rear of the garden was a large field where cows grazed and sheep spent their days wandering aimlessly as only sheep can. It was far too expensive when they bought it, but it was beautiful, and Caroline had to have it.

The village of Little Hanwick can also be described as beautiful. If a stranger were to arrive unprepared it would be of no inconvenience to them, as set before them is the archetypal village scene, complete with immaculate green and duck pond. There is a four hundred year-old stone-built church, more cottages uniform in character and splendour, a village store and a welcoming public house. The village straddles the only main road in the area, although more like a country lane, which winds its way through the adjoining forest and then disappears into the distance to connect to the next hamlet. With a population of only 76 (and counting due to the landlord and landlady of the public house suddenly finding themselves with child once again), there is little chance for the locals to conduct their lives with a great deal of privacy. Any newcomer will of course be instantly noticed. There is a comfort in this as it helps to maintain the security and well-being of the community, but of no use to the city-dweller who imagines that relocating there will be the quiet and solitary existence that they have so craved.

For Caroline, Tom, Adam, Shelley and George the rather too large Labrador, each and every day was an idyllic existence. George guarded the family, ate too much and chased rabbits. Shelley saw each waking hour as a new adventure with new and exciting things to experience. Adam had that air of a five year old who was now beginning to blossom with the help of his new teacher at school, Tom went to work each day by car to the town to work as an insurance advisory (a job he adored nearly as much as he was adored by his wife), while Caroline spent each day glorying in the essence of her surroundings and constantly looking for new sources of beauty with which to enhance their lives. It was a perfect existence, but Caroline had a secret...

\*         \*         \*

If you were to look at the woodlark, it may not look beautiful to the untrained eye. It is a small bird with streaky brown and white colours, which offer perfect camouflage in its natural environment. To the experienced and passionate ornithologist it represents the beauty and majesty of nature, but to the less aware, it offers no more than a passing distraction. What cannot be argued over though is the beauty of its sound. The 'titloo-eet' it cries is stunning in its simplicity and as melodious as a chorus of angels. It is this cry that awakens the good people of Little Hanwick at the same time every morning. It is constant and repetitive and refuses to observe the early morning sensitivities, instead choosing to embrace and glory in the dawning of a new day. Long before the rest of its kingdom awakens, long before the village opens its sleepy eyes, the woodlark impatiently calls out. It stands alone at the edge of the forest in an area of heather, preening its feathers and views the scene dispassionately. Its arrival suggests all is as it should be in the World.

It is the second cry that awakens Caroline. She blinks her eyes briefly and quickly rises from the bed silently so as not to disturb Tom. He will sleep for another half an hour at least, enough time for her to have made his breakfast and have it waiting for him on the kitchen table. It has been this way for as long as they have been married, and she would not have it otherwise. Outside the sun is beginning to rise, heralding another glorious summer's day. Shafts of light are beginning to find their way through the fabric of the bedroom curtains, falling on the wrought-iron bed they have shared throughout their wedded life. The atoms of dust shimmer in the sharp focused light. A quick look at the plaque, *"Beauty is only beautiful when looked at in the right way"*, a smile and she quietly leaves the bedroom and makes her way down to the kitchen. In the next room the children sleep soundly. They will be woken as Tom prepares for work, and then it will be their turn to have the full attention of Caroline.

The kitchen is quiet, only the gentle snoring of George disturbing the early morning serenity. As a family pet there is no better, but as a guard dog there is no worse. He only wakes from his slumber once the sound and smell of his breakfast being prepared reaches him. Even the scurrying of the resident field mouse across the bare floor as it leaves its evening repose and makes its way towards the hole in the skirting board to the great outdoors refuses to disturb him from his sleepy stupor. A much loved pet of 9 years, but a truly useless deterrent against any unwelcome guests.

The morning routine is familiar. Breakfast is the same every day. Two fried eggs, bacon, mushrooms, tomatoes, toast, orange juice and hot coffee. It has never changed in their entire married life as Tom has always insisted that breakfast is the main meal of the day and would not consider for one moment facing his day without the full fry-up. Hardly healthy, but as Caroline has often remarked upon with a playful squeeze of his midriff, it hasn't harmed his waistline. Annoyingly to those who spend their time moving from one extreme diet to the next, Tom was the kind of person who could never put on any weight, even if he tried. For Caroline though, there is no such extravagance. She has always started the day with a glass of orange juice and a bowl of cereal, and of course the most important part of her routine. The moment she can pull open the kitchen blinds and drink in the beauty of the scene before her. It is always a moment she cherishes as the first shafts of sunlight temporarily blind her before her eyes become accustomed to the light, and then gradually she can behold the sheer majesty of nature all around her. The bluebells and white-blossom, the gentle swaying of the trees, the white mist of the early morning dew as it covers the greenery of the rolling fields and hills, the chattering of the birds, the constant darting of the grey squirrels as they forage for whatever titbits they can devour. It was all so beautiful. Closing her eyes she allowed the sun's rays to tickle her face and bring warmth to her body, still shivering gently from the shock of leaving a warm bed. Steadying herself against the kitchen sink, she silently swayed with the rhapsody of the silence of the moment. It was, as always, a perfect start to the day.

Of course it didn't last long, it never does. Tom's stocky frame getting out of bed and his stuttering early-morning movements upstairs immediately brought her out of the ecstasy that she had briefly been enjoying. A quick glance at the wooded kitchen table to check that everything was as he expected, breakfast waiting, coffee hot and steaming, a napkin perfectly folded, the chair pulled out so all he had to do was sit and eat. Nothing too strenuous for her darling husband before he went to his place of work. As he moved

6

around upstairs, she busied herself with tidying the kitchen of dirty pots and pans, opened the window partly to allow the freshness of the outside world to take away just a few of the less than pleasant cooking smells, and shooed George into the back garden.

*"One person can't change the World, but you can change the World for one person"*

It was another one of those sayings that she'd kept in her mind and tried to live by. She couldn't remember where she'd heard it first, or by whom, but it was one that seemed to be apt in her marriage. No matter what it took, she would always make Tom happy, and this familiar routine every morning was her daily way of showing how much she loved him. Even if he took it, and indeed her, for granted, it was something she did without complaint or hesitation. When her Mother had visited a couple of years ago, she had been almost horrified at the level of servitude Caroline had shown in her marriage. It had been most un-modern, something which she may have expected to have shown with Caroline's Father in their early years, but in this day and age? Haven't women moved on from that era? Caroline's ears had been deaf to such suggestions though and she had carried on regardless. She loved Tom and cared for and cherished him. It was what she did and would always do. Besides her Mother was no longer around was she, so what did it matter?

His large frame filled the kitchen doorway. He stood there immaculate in his newly-washed and ironed shirt (prepared by Caroline the night before), a flower-patterned tie and black chinos that gave an air of smartness but casualness too. Black shoes set off the effect. He didn't move but stood there staring at his wife.

"Morning darling". She stopped the wiping of the draining board with the tea towel and went to embrace him. He stood there and just stared at her. A gaze of confusion and mild amusement crossed his face. Then he smiled. She looked at him and smiled back. "What's wrong?" she almost laughed out. She saw him grin broadly and wondered why. "Why are you laughing at me?" she giggled.

" Because Caroline, you silly girl....." he went to hug her, "You have forgotten to get dressed again. You have been walking around the house completely naked" He put his arms around her soft body and held her tightly. She giggled again and then pulled away looking down at herself. "Oh dear, so I have...." She just hadn't realised and the warmth of the morning had not made her notice. She had come downstairs, fed the dog and made Tom's breakfast, but had completely forgotten to get dressed.

"I had better go upstairs and put some clothes on" It had happened once before, but she had put that down to the mixture of the heavy wine and the warmth of the evening. It was a long time ago too. She giggled again at Tom with a mixture of amusement and embarrassment and left him to eat his breakfast while she returned upstairs. Silly Caroline, she thought, I really must make a note of that later.

It was later, much later in the day, after the children had been washed, dressed and driven to school. After the tidying had been completed and after the dog had been walked through the woods, it completely dawned on her. The life she led was complete. It was wanting for nothing. There was not a single thing that she could think of that she might want or need if she continued. Sitting in the wicker chair outside the kitchen door in the garden as the sun blazed down and warmed her face, she knew that everything was as perfect as it could be. Sipping the iced tea that she had bought that morning on an impulse and found surprisingly agreeable, she came to the realisation that there was something more. She just needed to find it. The sound of the woodcock amongst the rusty shades of oak trees in the nearby wood briefly interrupted her thoughts. In the distance, unseen by Caroline, a tall slender fallow hopped into the meadow opening, whilst a grass snake slithered its way to the stream. All images of beauty and perfection, but to Caroline they were no longer enough to satisfy her. There was one more thing...she knew that she had to find it.

# CHAPTER TWO

There was little of beauty in Ben Fuller's life. For his entire 13 years on this cruel, unforgiving World, he had seen nothing but human misery, despair and deprivation. Raised in a squalid two-bedroom flat on the eighth floor of a high-rise block in the inner city, his life was born to a struggle and would continue until the day he could break free. The environment that surrounded him, from the foul-smelling, urine soaked stairways that led to each floor of the block, covered in teenage graffiti that refused to give in to successive cleaning operations, right to his damp, dark, barely furnished bedroom that he shared with his younger brother Dale. It gave out the aura of decay, desperation and the sheer futility of a life that was never given a chance from the moment it left the comfort of its mother's womb, to the moment that it would be predicted to end in a drug-addicted saturation. Ben's life had been mapped out for him by the inconvenience of his circumstances. Parents who had many years before surrendered all too meekly to the constant temptation of substances that they could not, and now would not, abandon, leaving Ben, an unexpected and unwanted arrival, to effectively take control of his own life. In a way that was what could be the saving of him. Teachers at the primary school had long since given up any hope of making a difference, restricted by the apathy of education councillors and the lack of suitable funding from central government to implement even the basic of standards. If any young child wanted a glimpse of a better life, there could be no reliance on the two

constants that most children take for granted, parental love and
affection coupled with the steadying influence of education. Ben,
like those around him, had to find his own way.

Sadly Ben was incapable of finding his own way. Older peers whose
lives were tainted by the inescapable drudgery of inner-city life surrounded
him. He tried to break free, but the invisible shackles that appeared to
tie him to his destiny continued to hold him back. At the age of 13 he
wasn't fully aware of what lay ahead, but he was pretty convinced that
whatever it was, he didn't want a part of it. The only teacher he had any
respect for at school, Mr Adams from English, had once written a note
at the end of one his essays. It was a saying gleaned from someone quite
famous many years ago, and although he couldn't understand it fully, he
knew that it had been put there for a reason. Mr Adams, the only one
who took any notice of him, was trying to tell him something. He would
read and re-read it, but still couldn't totally fathom it, but he knew it
meant he had to take notice. It was written in red ink underneath a 9
out of 10 mark and said..

*"Nothing splendid has ever been achieved except by those who dared to
believe that something inside of them was superior to circumstance"*

One day he would understand what it meant. Not this day though.
This one had started like the one before, and the one before that, and
indeed virtually every one of his days. The sound of a baby crying from
the next flat which the paper-thin walls could hardly muffle. That was
the sound that usually woke up Ben and his younger brother. There
was no breakfast waiting for him in the kitchen before his school day,
and certainly no-one to make it. His mum and dad were usually deep
in a night-before drug and alcohol hazed sleep, which neither would
normally wake from until well past midday, only to immediately start
the whole process again. Ben had to scavenge around the nearly bare
cupboards for anything at all, normally a chocolate digestive biscuit
or two and maybe a glass of milk, if of course either had been bought.
Not quite the century-old image of a child walking to the mill seriously

underfed and under nourished, but not far from it. He often wondered on days like these how poor Dale coped without a full meal inside him. He was seven years younger and hadn't gained the streetwise experience of Ben yet. After all, if there was no food or money in the flat, there were plenty of full shops that he could steal from, something that he had done on a regular basis. Thankfully today though he probably would not need to. He had found a couple of pound coins in his mum's purse before leaving the flat and that would be more than enough to stop off at the chip shop after school. He reasoned, quite correctly, that both his parents would be completely unaware of this. If he had enough money left over, he would bring back some chips for Dale. He liked to look out for Dale.

School was not a particularly welcoming place, set as it was deep in the heart of the council estate where he lived. A fashionless, unremarkable building which had long since passed the time of showing its age, and was now deep in need of renovation. Graffiti decorated the walls, the grey coloured annexes had little more room than a standard portakabin, while the frontage would deter any respectable parent. The interior fared little better, a testament to years of council neglect. What frills and fancies had been added to the usual school layout had been due entirely to the care and compassion of any teacher that had stayed beyond their usual term contract. Each class was over-subscribed. Too many pupils, too few teachers. A recipe that could hardly lead to success. This was the inner-city hell that had been demonised in the 80s and 90s, but now hardly raised a whimper from government circles in the millennium. These were the places that middle-class England chose to ignore, the kind of places those well-meaning words were spoken about, but so little action was taken on. The places that bred the drug-pushers, thieves and criminals of the future. The places that bred the 'underclass' as they had become known. Well that was the general perception anyway. Not every boy or girl left Peterson comprehensive as a potential axe murderer, but if anyone was to move on to bigger and better things from this lowly starting point, they would have to fight a lot harder than most. Ben had promised himself, even at this relatively immature age of 13, that he would be one of those who would break away. Unfortunately, it wasn't always that easy.

He actually liked school. It was a break from the largely ugly environment of the flat, but he liked the process of learning. He had always been inquisitive and a yearning for knowledge had at times caused more than a little tension with some of his friends, but he was strong for his age and knew how to take care of himself. One comment too many from a teasing school pal had occasionally resulted in a bloodied-nose or a blackened-eye, and the offender hadn't teased him again. He had a particular interest and indeed burgeoning talent in English. Writing essays was one of his solitary joys, something that was quickly seized upon by Mr Adams, who had almost despaired of finding a pupil who would be capable of writing his or her name down the same more than once. Ben was a talent, and one he wanted to flourish. They had become almost like friends, with teacher and pupil spending time alone in the classroom well after the final bell so that they could talk of storytelling, essays and prose. Peter Adams had decided that Ben would be the pupil that would succeed, no matter how far behind his starting-point was, and he would make sure he played a hand in it. It wasn't easy though……

*     *     *

"Look it's easy, it's not like you haven't done it before is it?" The deceptively soulful eyes bore deep into his own weakening his resolve by the second. "All you have to do is stand and watch. We'll be out within a couple of minutes and the job's done. You get a tenner, yeah?"

The older boy, Pete, was standing tall above him in his own intimidating way. It was another job for Ben, one that he really didn't want to be involved with. It was only a newsagent on the Charley estate, miles away from his flat so no one would know, and it only meant him standing outside on lookout while Pete and his mate, who he had never spoken too, went in and quickly did it. The newsagent distracted by the greeting card stand being toppled over, the till opened and the cash pocketed. Both Pete and his mate would be out within two minutes and could be looking at maybe a hundred quid, Ben would get a tenner just for standing there. Easy really and he had done it at least half a dozen times before, but each time had made him more and more nervous. They'd collared him as he left the school gates and had followed him halfway home. He was the only who could do it as he was the only one they could trust. He was clever. Remember the time before last when an old lady was about to enter the shop to buy herself some bread and he'd pretended that he knew her? He'd confused her by saying that they had met in the town a few weeks ago and he'd offered to carry her bags. She obviously couldn't recall, but he was so convincing that she eventually smiled and gave him a fifty pence piece to buy himself a present. She was still smiling when the baker came tearing out of his shop screaming at the two youths who were fleeing in a frenzy of taunting, expletives and self satisfying shouts. She barely seemed to notice the young boy run after them without even saying thank you. "That was just brilliance", Pete had said. "That's what we need".

Ben had vocally refused them as loudly as he could so as to attract the more attention, but it had been of little use. In this area, very few people took notice of others' business. He had tried to distance himself physically, but they just continued to follow him along the road. They knew where he lived. He had no choice, he realised that. They were too big and overpowering and he knew that to deny them would just cause more trouble. This had to be the last time though. With the predictable air of resignation he nodded his head in agreement and looked to the heavens. The sky was earthly grey with a few molten lead clouds waiting to unleash their torrent. There was a darkness that pervaded the air and a stillness that could numb the mind. A drop of rain fell on his cheek. It was almost beautiful, but the darkness and the stillness felt like it was beginning to tear at his heart and invade his mind. Days like these were happening a few too many times.

# Chapter Three

The only thing of beauty in Sara Palazzo's life was her young daughter Verity. Abandoned by her husband at the moment of pregnancy, Sara's life had been and continued to be a relentless struggle against all of life's evils. Living in the rented flat supplied by the housing agency, with few friends and even fewer acquaintances, a solace in drink was found every evening. Cheap red wine became a friend that would visit unannounced and would not leave until the late hours.

Sara was 24, but looked much older. The last three years of bringing up her child had aged her dramatically, yet it had not always been that way. The love that she had felt for the father of her daughter was all-consuming with a passion that had threatened to overwhelm both mind and body. They had met in her days at college where she was in the second year of media studies. A bright, vivacious and witty girl, she had always been popular with fellow students and tutors alike, her personality hiding the fact that she had not been blessed with good looks. It wasn't that she was ugly, far from it. She just wasn't particularly attractive. An almost characterless face that was dominated by what is described as a 'roman-nose'. High cheek bones and wide eyes quite often gave her the look of permanent surprise, which could cause amusement and confusion at the same time. She had quickly become used to the fact that she was always the last to be asked out for a date, and then very rarely asked again, and in fact had almost gloried in the knowledge that her life would be independent from the expected peer pressure of commitment, marriage and long-term love. She had grown to look at life in a different way and had become happy with her role in it. Then she had met Elio. An Italian who had come to Britain to further his English. He was stunning in looks and personality with that typically Sicilian wildness so loved and admired by impressionable young girls…of which Sara was definitely one. It was a whirlwind romance. Not so much swept of her feet as taken in a full force gale of lust, desire and want. She couldn't quite believe her fortune as each day she opened her eyes and looked upon this living Adonis who had taken possession of her mind, body and above all her heart. Friends, when not whispering amongst themselves about how mis-matched they were in the looks department, constantly reminded her that he was more than something special, and she had to be more that something special to keep hold of him. Cruel taunts driven for the most part by green-eyed jealousy, but truthful words too. Yet her lingering doubts were dispelled by the offer of marriage. This beauty of a man, this lothario, this wonderful dark-haired dream, who she hardly knew anything about except that he was from a land of romance, had asked her to marry him. She could hardly say no…. in fact she could hardly say yes quickly enough. Her parents were delighted, and secretly rather relieved. Her friends, if they could be called that, were outwardly and publicly congratulatory, but inwardly and privately despairing. Sara was just overwhelmed. She stopped her media studies. She moved out of her parents' house and the two of them bought a lovely little apartment in the heart of the city, and she prepared for married life. It hardly lasted six months.

The arguments began early. At first she assumed it was the Latin temperament, but that soon gave way to a realisation that the love he professed at first was a typical means to an end. The man wasn't for marrying. The man was for enjoying life to the full and with an English wife he could enjoy life even fuller in the knowledge that this was to be his home. He stayed out at night more, coming home later each time. Soon he stopped coming home at all. The tell-tale signs arrived early. The secretive phone calls that ended the moment she walked into the room. The smell of a new cologne that had not been worn before, even the almost ridiculous smudge of lipstick on the collar. It had become that obvious. When she was announced she was pregnant, there was hardly a glimmer of emotion in his eyes. That night he went out and just didn't return. She never saw him again. She also never saw the eight thousand pounds he withdrew from her account the next day ever again. She was left totally alone and with few prospects. She tried to trace him, even at one stage employing the services of a particularly expensive but utterly useless detective agency. They worked for three months without a single sighting or a lead and then charged her the rest of her savings. Her parents were kind and understanding but in no position to help financially and so she said a tearful and reluctant goodbye to the apartment she had put so many dreams into and had moved to the seaside with the new love of her life. Her beautiful daughter Verity. That is where Sara lives. Lonely, withdrawn, on the verge of alcoholism, but with the single-eyed determination of so many other single mothers. She would look after her daughter and ensure that the result of her unhappy union would never feel unloved or uncared for. No matter what she had to do, she would do it. Unfortunately she had been forced to do it a few too many times recently.

At first she did it once and only once so she could pay a bill. It was as unpleasant as imagined. A suggestion by a so-called friend, and once bitten she was hooked. It was only for the money and for no other reason, but in a strange and exciting way she felt as if she was in complete control of any man who desired her. Prostitution was always a last resort, and for her it certainly was, but in an odd and unexplained way, it gave her back the self-esteem that had been so cruelly snatched away from her by the Italian romeo she had foolishly loved. The money was great. It certainly helped the schooling fees for Verity and anything else that was required, but she soon realised that to earn the really big rewards, she had to take it a step further, and like any drug you get addicted to, it eventually turns round and destroys you. A particularly sickening evening with a group of young and very drunk men had finally made her realise that she had to walk away from that way of life, including the financial rewards. Unfortunately a less that sympathetic landlord had made a point of checking her recent history, and when the latest rent demand had been ignored and not actioned, he had suggested his own way of payment. It wasn't that she hadn't had these moments before, but there was something more than distasteful about the over-bearing middle-aged man, whose body odour made her retch, and whose bedroom habits were too repulsive to be spoken and thought of. He was a particularly repugnant creature, but in her current situation she had little choice but to go along with it, and after all she had been with so many other men who had physically appalled her. It was something that she just had to do.

It was the day that Verity had walked into the bedroom when she was entertaining him that made her realise that this was a way of life that she had to walk away from. The child was too young to understand, but the look in her eyes when she saw her mother that way would be something that would haunt her for many years.

For his part, and to his credit, the landlord, all sweaty and out of breath, had attempted to make light of it and even had pretended he had been playing a game with the child's mother, but Verity, even at her tender age, hadn't believed him. As he left in an unseemly hurry, he had shot a worried and almost apologetic glance at Sara as if to say "Don't let her understand". Sara herself had immediately pulled on the discarded clothes and ran to her daughter.

"Hello my darling," she had said in a worried tone. "Shall we play hide and seek?", but her daughter had sensed an unreality in the scenario and not answered. It took Sara most of the rest of the day to glean some positive reaction from Verity, and take away the dullness from those once-sparkling eyes, but when she finally did, they had spent the rest of the day playing together like all mothers and daughters. It had been though, a salutary lesson and one that Sara was willing to learn.

The landlord, maybe out of a sense of duty, or maybe out of shame, had called the next day to see her. He'd knocked on the front door, the one that hid her and her daughter away from the despair of their surroundings, and had smiled when she had answered. "I want you to know that what happened last night should never happen again".

"Thank you", she said, rather taken aback by his presence. She managed a weak smile and stared at him. He was a physically ugly man. Late forties, balding and very overweight. His way of dress was unflattering in the extreme. A too tight shirt that accentuated his portly figure, and trousers that hadn't seen a pressing iron since the day they were made. It was a most undesirable effect.

"There shouldn't be any reason why your daughter should see you doing those things". He glanced beyond Sara into the sparsely decorated room towards where Verity was finishing her breakfast of cereal. Verity looked away when she saw him in the doorway. "I have a suggestion".

Sara stood there and didn't answer. There had been little kindness in her life for too long now and she certainly didn't expect any from this man. He caught her stare and held it with his own before continuing. "The point is…" He started to blush, as if what he was about to say was not going to come easy to him. "The point is…" he tried again. "Look the point is, you are a very nice girl and you have given me the pleasure and…..and I have enjoyed it" He looked away as Sara's stare bore into him. "I am willing to help you if let me".

"Why?"

The directness of the question unsettled him even more.

"I think you have a bad time in your life and I think you need some help"

She stared at him even more. Her face showed no emotion, no trace of her thoughts. She looked deep into him and tried to see what was there.

"My suggestion is this" he blurted in a seemingly desperate way. She looked harder into him as if she was trying to delve deep into his soul. "I am a single man. I have never been married. I'm not great in the looks department, but my heart is in the right place. I am financially secure. I make a lot from this building and I've got two other blocks on the other side of town. In fact I've got so much money that I actually don't know what to do with it"

She stood there and continued to say nothing, but she felt like saying, why not spend it on some new clothes, or why did you use my body, why not let me off until I could pay the rent? She wanted to say those things, but she didn't. She just continued to stare at this man who was visibly wilting under her intense glare.

"I need a partner" It was said with such force and conviction, and she realised instantly what it was he was suggesting. "I have not had too much experience with *ladies*" The word made her smile inwardly. Not too many men had referred to her as a lady recently. "….but I like you and I think I could make you happy…if you would let me". The last five words were said in a pleading way and he met her stare once more. It held for a few seconds before he turned away and looked toward the floor. His eyes focussed on a lone wood beetle that was making its leisurely way across the floor toward the threadbare carpet that covered the centre of the corridor. He gave an involuntary shudder, maybe from the sharpness of the morning air that had permeated through the windows, or from the desperately uncomfortable circumstance he found himself in. Looking up again at Sara's face, he smiled at her. A thin and nervous smile. She didn't return it, but just continued to stare back.

"What do you think?"

She looked deep into him once more, almost so deep to see into his soul. She showed no recognition of his awkwardness. It was almost like secretly she was enjoying this physical and mental power that she was subconsciously exerting over him. He shuffled from one foot to the next and turned to leave when she answered. "Thank you, I will tell you tomorrow "

With that Sara closed the door and walked back to her daughter who was drinking the last drops of milk off her spoon. She patted her newly-combed hair and kissed her forehead gently. "Today is a better day", she whispered. Outside in the corridor, Frank Bolton stood and stared at the peeling paintwork on the now closed door and wondered what he should do next.

# CHAPTER FOUR

Thursday 13th June:

*"Today I discovered what it was that I was missing. The realisation that there was something else has been with me for so very long, and this was the day that I finally understood what it is that I need to make my life as complete as it ever could be. It will take me sometime to reach that level, but when I do it will be so wonderful. Everyone will see me for what I am and they will rejoice in that. I stand on the verge of a great discovery and it excites me greatly. I give thanks for this feeling of excitement. Wouldn't it be so wonderful if everyone could experience this?*

*Tom looked nice today. Must buy him another shirt like that. Adam was a bit clingy with me. Have to keep an eye on that. Doesn't Lorraine look awful with that new hairstyle?"*

Caroline sighed quietly to herself and gently closed the red-leafed diary. At the end of each day she sat down at her dresser and wrote the day's entry. It had been something she had done since she was a child and the attic was almost overflowing with numerous books of all shapes, sizes and colours erratically dated for 30 years. Tom was obviously aware of his wife's strange obsession with recording each day's activities, but he had never pried and had never commented. At the end of each evening, usually after the daily bout of lovemaking that was such a feature of their idyllic marriage, Caroline would sit at her dressing-table with the faint glow of the yellow lamp so as not to awaken Tom, and compose her thoughts to be transferred to paper. It had to be done every day and not a day could be missed. It wasn't quite obsessional but was certainly an addiction she couldn't break free from.

She allowed herself a few moments to reflect on the glory of the day in the tranquillity of the night. Only Tom's gentle but persistent snoring could be heard, but in a way for Caroline it was a rhapsody of movement in which to itemise the day's events. This of course had been such a special day, but had been negated by the usual domesticity that was now a part of her life.

The children had been fed.

"Why can't I have chips?" Adam had looked genuinely hurt when his mum had told him that he would have to eat spaghetti bolognese, especially as this morning she had promised chips and fish fingers. She had said he could have it if he's been good at school, and he had been good. He tried to tell his mum but she didn't really take much notice.

"You are having spaghetti and that's all there is to it". Caroline had little time for the daily tantrums of her son. At least Shelley was quiet tonight, and in fact was hardly ever any problem at all, but Adam could be so wearisome at times. "You will eat it all up and you will like it. I have spent a long time making your tea so start being a little more grateful" Adam pulled a face and sat quietly as his mum put the plate on the oakwood kitchen table. "Do you understand?"

"Yes mummy", but Adam didn't understand. As he spooned a mouthful of spaghetti he thought about unfair it was. His favourite food in the whole world was chips and fish fingers and his mum had promised him this morning that he could have it if he was good. So unfair. Shelley had hardly said a word and had sat there quietly and slowly as she ate hers. Neither of them knew that in fact Caroline had spent precious little time in preparing the food, but had bought a tin from the food market this afternoon and all she had to do was heat it up on the aga. It would be different for Tom though as she would spend considerable time ensuring that his meal was everything to his liking. Both Adam and

Shelley got on with the job of eating and eventually finishing their tea, both in almost total silence.

The children were then bathed.

"Will you stop splashing your sister please?" Carline was becoming more and more exasperated by Adam's bad behaviour. Bathtime was always a chore she disliked, mainly because the children looked upon it as a time for play and not a time to wash away the grime and dirt that accumulated from the day. It was always at the worst moment too when she had a keen eye on the clock knowing that Tom would be on his way home and she just had to be ready to greet him. The children could never understand that the last thing she needed at this time of the day was the two of them splashing and having fun. She just needed them to bathe quietly and make their way to bed with a glass of milk and biscuit. Shelley wasn't the problem. She was quiet, sat there opposite her brother in the sunken ceramic bath. In fact Shelley was always quiet. It was Adam who just wouldn't behave.

"Yessss" Adam screamed as he threw the bar of soap into the bathwater for the third time with such force that the bubbles flew in all directions, soaking not just he and the unsmiling Shelley, but the walls and bathroom floor. The water oozed over the side of the bath and started to drip down the side, eventually soaking into the dark blue bathmat like a sponge.

"Stop it!!" screamed Caroline as she rushed towards Adam. "I will not tell you again". She was angry and Adam was aware that when mummy was angry he had better stop it. He sat there silently and looked at his little sister, who still hadn't said a word. Caroline looked at the two of them and allowed her anger to subside and then calmly said. "Now get out of the bath the two of you, and go in front of the fire and get dried. I will bring you some milk and biscuits and tuck you in bed"

Adam looked at his mummy and then his sister, before turning to look at his mummy again. "What about daddy? Will he come and tuck us in?"

"Your daddy won't be back for an hour yet, you know he has to work hard. He will come and say goodnight to you when he gets back. Now do as you are told"

Then the children were put to bed.

That in fact wasn't quite as difficult as expected as the two of them were so very tired following their exertions at bathtime. Shelley yawned loudly and closed her eyes, while Adam tried for as long as possible to stay awake, but the onset of the darkness and the warmth of the bed soon overcame his resistance, and very soon he had drifted away into a restful sleep. It was early evening, and Caroline still had time.

Each night she had conducted the same routine. In the very brief hour before Tom's return she had quickly run herself a lavender scented bath, covered herself in Tom's favourite perfume and draped herself in red silk flowing nightdress and gown. It always looked good for Tom. He'd told her all that time ago when she had first worn it and so had continued to wear it each and every night in readiness for his arrival. She's always had a sumptuous dinner ready for him too and this evening had been no exception. Whilst at the food mart in the village, as well as picking up the tin of spaghetti for the children, she had also picked up some nice fresh lemon sole. It was that that was slow cooking on the aga for his dinner. A bottle of nice white wine was chilling gently in the fridge, and she was warming gently for her husband. If only all married couples could share the happiness that her and her man shared each and every waking day, the World would be such a happier place. *"One person can't change the World, but you can change the World for one person"*. She had done that for Tom and would continue to do that for as long as she was alive, and tonight was going to be even more special. Today she had found the answer to her previously unanswered question. It was going to be a special evening.

\*              \*              \*

She smiled to herself and quietly turned out the table lamp. The room was then basked in the faint rays of the moonlight cascading through open curtained window. Her eyes slowly grew accustomed to the light and before crawling into bed alongside her sleeping husband she looked up at the plaque above the bed. The words could not be made out clearly but she knew them by heart. The words *beauty* and *beautiful* could be discerned, but the rest melded into the greyish-white haze of the retreating moonlight. She knew them by heart and she knew what she now had to do.

*　　　　*　　　　*

The headlights caught the glare of the fallow deer stood in the centre of the road. The eyes shining like beacons in the murky haze. Tom wasn't driving fast and was thankfully aware of the poor creature in front of him as he slowed to a virtual stop. It mattered not to him that his journey home was slightly delayed. In fact as he carefully manouvered around the fearstruck animal, he inwardly wished there had been an even more serious delay. Each night was becoming the same. His colleagues had teased and laughed him to scorn when he had told them of his problem. Some had shown the green-eyed jealousy that was expected when such a thing was discussed in public, and none of them could understand why he should regard it as a problem. Surely better this way than not at all? As each night came he found more and more excuses to leave the office a little later. Another appointment he must arrange or keep. Another batch of paperwork that really must be finished this evening, or the sales accounts from last month needed to be updated. Janet found it odd and amusing, but knew as a woman that there was a deep-rooted problem somewhere that Tom was not willing to discuss with her. Maybe he will one day.

So again Tom left a little later and drove home a little slower. If there was a longer route he could take, he would. Each mile that he got closer to the cottage his heart sank just a little deeper. The dryness in his throat would increase as the hamlet came into view and the heartbeat would grow faster as the cottage became visible. Leaden feet as he got out of the car after parking it on the driveway and an inner wish that he could enter the front door and find the place quiet and dark. Everyone in bed fast asleep, but not tonight. As he put the key into the lock and turned the key he could hear the strains of The Carpenters from the CD in the living room and smell the unmistakable aroma of the now all-too familiar evening meal. Stepping into the warmth of the porch and taking off jacket and shoes he said weakly and without too much enthusiasm, "I'm home". Maybe tonight would be different, he thought, and for a very brief moment when there was no answer he believed his prayers may be answered, but then the kitchen door opened and his heart sank even further.

# CHAPTER FIVE

PC Henrose hated this estate. He hated patrolling it every night when he was put on this particular duty and from the moment his shift started there every second seemed like a minute, every minute like an hour and every hour like a day. It wasn't necessarily the people who were forced to live their existence in the drab, concrete surroundings, but more to with just that. The drab, concrete surroundings. They gave out an air of decay and depression and a suggestion that there was nothing more to life than this miserable existence. He felt enormous sympathy for anyone trying their hardest to eke out a respectable living in this inner-city hell that had become the Charley estate. There were too many drug pushers, too many pimps and their poor put-upon prostitutes, too many people living on the periphery of normal society, and too few people in positions of power who were prepared to make a difference. Maybe it will always be like this, he thought as he parked his patrol car at the foot of the stairs leading up to number 39. Maybe this is the future for a certain section of society who have never really been given a chance.

A group of young children, maybe aged 10 to 12, but certainly older in their ways, eyed him suspiciously. The police were never welcome here and he would normally travel with a colleague when assigned to a task in this area, but cutbacks as ever had meant there too few police for too many crimes. He didn't feel threatened this evening though as the rain that had started as a drizzle during the late afternoon was now turning rapidly into a torrent. There would not be too many people around in this kind of weather, only the young kids who were skulking in the doorways to keep dry, and they certainly wouldn't want to cause any trouble on a night like this. At least the rain freshened the air, but it couldn't wash away the stench from the stairwell leading up to the third floor of the tenement block. Nothing could ever get rid of that until the whole housing block was demolished. He said a silent prayer of thanks that he didn't have to experience this on a daily basis.

The door of number 39 was like all the others. Painted white which had faded through the years and an iced-glass front that had the inevitable cracks. The doorbell didn't work so a hard tap on the window was enough to alert the occupants. Of course it took some time for them to actually answer, especially as flicker of the living room curtain had meant that someone inside had looked before opening and had seen a burly policeman standing there. Jim Henrose stood there patiently all too aware that Chippy and Mary Fuller were cleaning the flat before he could be let in. Cleaning not in the usual sense of the word, but more to do with hiding the various drug-connected implements that they were convinced he was there to discuss. Eventually the door was opened by the smallest margin and a gaunt female face, hollowed eyed and long black and rather unkempt hair looked through the gap. "Yes?"

"It's about Ben, your son".

*           *           *

"This is not the first time he has been spotted like this. The shopkeeper said that he had been seen at another branch in Wolling. They circulate posters between the different shops and his description is on all of them. It's becoming a habit and a nasty and dangerous one at that". Henrose looked at the two people sat opposite on the threadbare settee in front of him. Sitting in the hardly-furnished living room with the dinghy couch and too uncomfortable chair that he had been lead to, he wondered how anyone could live in conditions like these. The wallpaper was peeling from the damp that came from a lack of insulation, the floorboards were bare apart from an extremely old and tattered rug that age had destroyed and the television in the corner was clearly not for this world for too much longer. The only other item of furniture was a once-valuable table that now had too many scuff marks and stains for it to be of any worth. He hadn't seen any of the other rooms in the flat, being lead from the hallway directly into the living-room, but he could imagine they would be similar. There was a musty and rather unpleasant smell that hung around, rather like dampness when the windows had not been opened for far too long, and the coldness of the place didn't seem to come from just a lack of heating. He felt he wanted to get out of there as soon as he could, but his professional training had conditioned him to far worse. He also knew that somewhere in the flat there was another child, Dale, younger and more vulnerable and he needed to know that everything was okay there.

"He can be a bit of handful at times, I must admit". It was Chippy who had spoken. A tall and once-handsome man, who had now allowed the years of drug abuse to alter his features so that he no longer had the youthful vigour that had made his so attractive in his younger years. He was called Chippy because he once held a job as a carpenter for around two years, before deciding the life wasn't for him. He still had a talent for woodwork, but now very rarely the desire. "…but he's no worse than any other kids 'round here".

"The point is Mr Fuller, is that he is getting himself more and more in trouble, and unless you take a stand you will be seeing more and more of me in the future". They both looked at him with a faint of horror, but there gaunt and almost expressionless faces said more than words. "There is nothing we can do at the moment, but from what I can tell from his teacher, he's a bright lad and could have a decent future if he is steered along the right path. Do you understand?". He looked from one to the other and saw nothing. They stared back and he quickly realised that in fact there was little he could do in this situation. "How do you both fill your time during the day?". It was a leading question especially as he knew that the two of them spent it normally in a cocktail mixture of drugs. "Neither of you are working are you?".

"It's not a crime is it?". The reply from Chippy was more defensive than aggressive, but he realised that this was not a situation he needed to handle badly. "We try to get work, but there's nothing 'round here is there? The kids get fed, the bills get paid, we look after ourselves see…."

"I do see, and I am just concerned that Ben is going to school on a daily basis"

"Oh yes", this time it was Mary who spoke up, her voice raising a slight octave as the nervousness caused her to tremble a little. "Whatever you think, our Ben is good at school. I keep telling 'im that he's got to be good at school then he can do summat wiv himself". The tremble had made her talk just that little bit quicker.

"You have another son, don't you Mrs Fuller?".

"He's in the back", came the quick reply. "Do you wanna see him?" It was almost a challenge and one he really wanted to take. They led him into the back bedroom, as sparsely decorated as the living-room, but at least had a bunk bed and a few toys that suggested a level of care. Dale was sat there eating from a plate of chips, tomato sauce around his mouth, a glass of fizzy drink to his side. In the corner was an old television that was tuned to a cartoon from an equally old, but effective, video machine. Inwardly Jim breathed a sigh of relief that the child, and indeed both children, appeared to be looked after. Maybe not the textbook parenting that we all strive for, but certainly better than he had expected when he had first set foot in the flat. No need to get the social services too involved just yet. Jim turned to the two and said in a quiet but firm tone, honed to perfection from years of being in the police force. "There is nothing else I can do now, but I strongly urge you both to talk to Ben and steer him away from this path. He has fallen in with a few bad 'uns and it doesn't take much for it to become too late. I'm sure that is not what the two of you want…is it?". There was no response, but a thin smile from Mary as he turned to leave. As he approached the front door she caught his arm. "He turned quickly to face her, conditioned immediately for trouble, but she had a different expression this time. "We will try, I promise". It seemed a desperate plea, but also there was a feeling that there was a genuine feeling of hope. Maybe Ben, and indeed Dale, might just have a better future after all.

# CHAPTER SIX

The next day Sara made her decision. It actually hadn't been as difficult as she had imagined, and surprisingly it hadn't taken anywhere near as long as she expected. It was almost as if she had been waiting for a moment like this, no matter how improbable. After closing the door on the landlord, and putting Verity to bed, she had then turned to her eternal friend, the half empty, but still half full, bottle of red wine. Between them they had thought about the future, and what it was she would let herself in for. Her options she realised were extremely limited. With a young daughter to bring up with a small income, if at times any income at all, there seemed little prospect of moving on with her life, and also giving Verity the future that she so deserved. She so desperately didn't want to move back into the circles that she had been forced to inhabit in recent times, and this man could be changed. He was too old, he was too fat, he was too crude, but he could be changed. Frank Bolton looked at her in a way that few men had and certainly the first since Elio. The thought of Elio brought the familiar tug at her heart and the knot in the stomach. No matter how many months, weeks, days, minutes and seconds had passed since he walked out, the pain would always return, never to say goodbye forever. It was like a constant reminder of her foolishness, and the belief that she could enjoy the happiness she could see in other people around her. This man could help dull the pain though and could give her and her daughter a future, a financial future at that....so she made the decision.

\*　　　　　\*　　　　　\*

She stood at his doorway, Verity at her side, and waited for him to answer. She had put on a hint of extra make-up and a fetching black trouser-suit, whilst dressing Verity in a new patterned frock that she had bought last weekend, despite not really being able to afford it. Her daughter had been quiet when told where they were going, down the two flights of stairs to the landlord's flat, but had been re-assured by her mum that it was okay and that Mr. Bolton, or Frank as she would learn to call him, was a friend and was going to take care of them.

Frank has spent the evening and the next morning wondering what on earth he had done. This was a woman he hardly knew except in a purely impersonal physical sense, and yet here he was effectively offering her a lifetime commitment. Was he mad? Yes he felt he was at times, but there had been too many days in his long and lonely life when he had looked at others in their quest for happiness, and just for once had desired to take the same route. There had been no-one, since his dear mother had departed, and for too long he had found solace in the never ending search for financial gain, and his growing stock of jazz records. He was a man and a man had needs, of that was no doubt, and the girl upstairs had been willing when the suggestion was made, but he soon began to realise that this was someone who he really didn't want to share with anyone else now. What to do? It was only one answer, but the best one. He would propose a deal to her. It seemed so simple when he played it out in his mind but Sara's impassive and almost amused look when he confronted her had taken away his will power and self belief. Too late now, as he waited for her return. Time to be made a fool of.

The door opened slowly, as if years of suspicion had meant that each and every visitor had to be checked thoroughly before any admission could be gained, but on seeing Sara and Verity, Frank Bolton opened the door wide and smiled a smile that welcomed them instantly. He too had made more of an effort with his attire, a clean and crisp white shirt, open at the neck, and a razor sharp-pressed pair of clean, if rather old-fashioned black trousers. Sara looked him up and down and smiled inwardly to herself. On the surface though her face remained impassionless and it was that that made Frank lose his composure a little and the smile faded. "Hello, I wasn't sure if you would come down. Would you like to come in?", stepping aside he allowed the two of them to enter, neither saying a word, Sara still as stony-faced as she had been the night before. His flat was surprisingly tastefully-decorated in pastel colours that belied the man who lived there. There were two rather expensive sofas sandwiching an exotic Persian rug, with a large plasma TV in the corner. In the background she could hear the soft strains of a jazz CD, suggesting that there was more to this man than she had originally thought, meaning of course this would be so much easier. It actually filled her heart with a supreme sense of optimism, but she was not willing to share that just yet with him. She was prepared to make him work a little hard for her and her daughter, if that was what he really wanted.

"Please sit down, can I get you both a drink? Coffee? Maybe a soft drink for your daughter? I've forgotten her name, I'm really sorry, I really should know shouldn't I? I'm sorry but my flat isn't all that tidy, years without a woman's touch if you see what I mean, not that I'm just looking for a woman to tidy the flat, far from it, in fact I can be quite domesticated when I want to be.....", the monologue continued unabated as Sara and Verity sat themselves down on the sofa facing the window overlooking the trees in the garden outside and which occasionally if the wind allowed, gave a glimpse of the sea in the distant. She felt like laughing at this 48 year old man trying so desperately to impress a female half his age with the burden of a young daughter too. It made her feel good though. ".....and I just didn't think that you would come. Let me get that drink. Coffee and a coca-cola wasn't it? " . It wasn't as Sara hadn't said a word, but it would be welcome. He disappeared into the kitchen and she sat there quietly taking in the surroundings. It was pleasant and she could make a few adjustments to make it better. Verity sat there without saying a word, but the look of confusion and mistrust meant more than words. Sara looked down at her daughter and gave a warm but brief smile. "Its okay, don't worry". She squeezed her hand and Verity smiled back. Although her decision hadn't been that difficult, she knew that once she had confirmed it with Frank Bolton, the hard part would come next, how to win her daughter over to the situation.

He returned with the drinks and handed them to Sara and Verity. Then he sat on the sofa opposite and looked at them. Sara took a sip of the coffee, realising that in fact he hadn't asked whether she preferred milk and sugar and had just added it anyway. In a way that said a little bit more about the man she was about enter into an agreement with. She said nothing and stared back at Frank. He sat there looking extremely uncomfortable. Outside the sounds of the sea waves crashing against the harbour walls could just about be heard above the gentle beat of the jazz CD in the background. It gave a relaxed air to what was a rather unusual circumstance. Frank cleared his throat and looked at Sara intently. "Have you come to a decision?". There was a quaver in his voice suggesting a nervousness that he was determined to hide. Sara nodded and finally spoke.

"Yes, I have. I thought a lot about it last night and I eventually decided."

She looked at Verity and then to Frank and saw the pleading in his eyes. It gave her a power that she hadn't had for some time, and in a way it excited her again. " I have decided that I will take you up on your offer", she could almost hear the audible sigh that he tried so desperately to hide, "but there are strict conditions which you must adhere to otherwise it will not work". His eyes gave away his eagerness to hear more and he nodded at her expectantly.

"Firstly, if you are willing to take on me and Verity then please be aware that my loyalty will always be to my daughter before anything or anyone else…"

"Of course that goes without saying" he interrupted

"She is the only reason why I am agreeing to this at the moment". She looked down at Verity, who was sat there now a little bored, and squeezed her hand once more. "She is my life, and if I cannot give her the life that she so deserves, then I am willing to put my trust in someone who can". She looked up at Frank and saw him catch her daughter's eye and smile. That was encouraging, although she couldn't see whether Verity had smiled back. That would wait for later.

"There will be no talk of marriage or indeed any kind of commitment until I am totally sure of your intentions. For the first three months I will continue to sleep in my flat upstairs with Verity, but will gradually spend more time here." She looked around the apartment slowly "...and I think I can make a difference". Frank sat there not sure what to do or say but just listened. This was a little more than he expected in many ways, but so far it was going according to plan. She continued.

"Obviously for those first three months there will be no intimacy of any kind". With that she stared directly into his eyes, but he just nodded and agreed. If he was disappointed by that he certainly wasn't showing it. "There is a huge age gap between the two of us and I am not totally certain that you have thought it through as completely as you think. Maybe I will become a trophy for your arm, or maybe you will become bored of me, or even more likely I will become bored with a man who is a quarter of a century older than me, but for the time being I am willing to agree to this arrangement". He sat there and smiled. "I have no problems with any of that".

"There is one final thing though"

"Go on"

"I should now live in my flat for rent free. After all you should not expect to charge your girlfriend to live with you should you?"

He smiled a huge smile back. "My girlfriend...what a lovely expression. Of course you shall live rent free. You will realise very quickly that my intentions are totally honest. I will take care of you and your lovely girl. There will be no problems as far as that is concerned, and..." he looked at her again with a steely expression, "...I am willing to wait the three months."

34

"Good. Now Mr Bolton, I am sure you would like to toast our agreement with something a little better than coffee. I notice you have a wine rack in the kitchen. Maybe a glass would seal it?"

"Of course, I will go and open the bottle." With that he got up and went to the two of them. He patted Verity gently on the head and then leaned over and planted a tender kiss on Sara's right cheek. "You will not regret it"....and that was that. Suddenly a union of two people was made. It wasn't conventional, but if it worked it would be beneficial to both, and who is to say that is wrong?

Outside the spring air suddenly changed. The freshness of the day was replaced by a heaviness that appeared almost instantly. The white clouds transformed in the blinking of an eye and became dark and ominous. In the distance a clap of thunder could be heard, and the hovering seagulls suddenly grew restless. They flapped their wings in agitated insistence and flew in separate directions. The rain that had kept away returned with a vengeance and suddenly opened its downpour on the streets below. The scene had changed. In the apartment, protected from the elements of nature's worst, three people, one unwittingly, embarked on a course that they believed could bring the happiness they so desired. These are the moments that change the course of a person's life.

# CHAPTER SEVEN

The next morning the woodlark was absent. There were no early morning cries to help waken the inhabitants of Little Hanwick. The sun broke through the early morning mist of a spring day, and the fallow deers woke from their sleepy slumber. The daffodils opened their yellow petals and embraced the warmth, but the woodlark didn't appear. It was not noticed by anyone, except Caroline, and its absence hardly caused a murmer of recognition amongst the creatures of the forest.

Friday 14th June:
*"I heard no sound this morning. Its absence completely confused me and made my preparations for the day late and far too hurried. Where is it? How can it just disappear like that without any warning? It has upset me deeply and taken away a piece of the beauty that I so long for. I must find something to replace it as soon as possible."*

It had caused Caroline a huge problem. No cry had meant a few extra moments in a light sleep before suddenly waking and realising that her morning was not what it should be and had been for so long. Everything was late and she had spent all of the first part of the day frantically chasing after it. Those extra moments in bed had deprived her of the morning beauty she looked forward to each day. She had not had the time to embrace the day through the kitchen windows and breathe in the freshness of the morning dew, nor had she time to gently prepare the morning's breakfast for her beloved husband. There was hardly time to take a look at the plaque on the wall and for that she grew angry. Her anger was taken out on the children and the morning was a maelstrom of abusive words and frantic actions. Tom had left in a hurry and she felt so very guilty, while the kids were packed off to school without so much as parting kiss or word. The absence of the woodlark had completely thrown the world into a spin and she had to use all of her powers of self-discipline to slow it down and get her day back on track. It wasn't until around midday that she managed it.

*　　　*　　　*

She stood in the kitchen and stared out of the window and beheld the breathtakingly beautiful countryside before her. It was the moment that should have happened when she started the day, but no matter, it will do now. She looked at the dozens of different type of flowers that were enjoying the sunshine on the still damp forest floor and closed her eyes and prepared for the time ahead. The beauty of it made her tingle all over and excitement of it made her breathe that little more deeply. She felt her body rotate with the motions of the moment and just for an instance allowed herself to imagine. The thoughts that ran through her head became insistent, a rhapsody of beauty that all but overpowered her. They ran through her mind and then took over her being, delving into her innermost parts. They caressed her and teased her as she opened herself completely to their touch allowing them to probe her every nerve and sense. No human touch could compare to their exquisite feel as they danced against her, breathlessly. She opened herself fully and allowed them to fill her completely. The delight was all-consuming and nothing could stop the moment as it reached the point of no-return. She had to steady herself against the kitchen sink as the feeling took over losing herself deeper and deeper into the waves as they spread over her whole being. The ecstasy she felt was something she was becoming so accustomed to and she could only feel sympathy for those around her who could only wish for such moments. It ended with a silent groan and a sigh and a flush of blood to her pretty features. Opening her eyes she looked deep into the forest and saw the creatures looking straight back. They stared at her accusingly as if they knew where she had been and where she was about to go. They looked deep into her eyes and down deep into her soul and they wondered what it was that made these things happen. Sara stared back and then turned away dismissively. They could not change her destiny no matter how hard they tried.

Crawling along the kitchen desk top was a spider making its way from the open sugar bowl to the web it had weaved from the window blinds to the wooden shelf that held the many condiments used in Caroline's daily meal making during the afternoon. She had seen the web grow over the past few days and had carefully avoided touching it so as not to disturb its repose. The spider though would leave soon and make its home elsewhere, somewhere away from the beauty that was the thatched cottage. For the spider beauty was just circumstance. There was nothing it could see that would distinguish one from the other. Caroline didn't want it to leave, so she opened the drawer and picked up a nail. The nail was pushed into the soft wooded top and to that she attached a piece of string, gently tying a bow so that it could not be released. That part was easy, the next not so. She captured the spider and then proceeded to attach the string to one of its legs. This took quite some time as the spider refused to stay still and unfortunately its skittiness resulted in the loss of at least two of its legs. That wasn't a problem though as she had read that spiders can survive with only four, and she was pretty sure that they grew back in time anyway. Eventually she completed the job and she watched with pride and love as the spider tried to make its way away from its predicament, but all of the time was slowly wrapping itself around the nail until it could no longer move and was trapped there. It would stay there for the rest of its life, which wasn't going to be that long. Caroline then got on with the next part of her day.

*         *         *

Tom sat at his desk in the open office and stared straight ahead, not seeing anything. He had been like that for quite some time and his appearance had started to worry some of his colleagues. Sat opposite was Janet, pretending to be busy but all of the time keeping a guarded eye on her boss. She was 34, slim, dark haired, an engaging smile, and never been married. She loved her job as a secretary in one of the country's most established and respected insurance companies and outside of work had kept herself fit and healthy with long walks in the countryside and regular visits to the gym and squash. Most of all though she was in love with Tom. At first she had thought it had been an infatuation following a particularly destructive affair with a former school friend, but as the months and then the years had passed, and she had been Tom's secretary for three years now, she had realised that her feelings had taken on a new intensity. He was married, and happily so, so she never let him know the way she felt. Even one weekend when they had gone away for a sales seminar in Scarborough, and he had got quite drunk in the evening, she had said nothing. She respected him greatly and also had a deep moral sense of being for the pretty wife whose framed picture sat on his desk. She also knew that no matter how attractive she thought herself, and she knew that she had a sexiness that appealed to men, there was no way she could ever compete with the lady that smiled from the photograph each and every day. Who could blame Tom for being so passionately in love with this woman? So she had become a friend to Tom, not just a secretary, and that at first was enough for her. Occasionally she felt he had looked at her in a more than a professional or indeed friendly way, but maybe that was her vivid imagination. At the moment though he wasn't looking at anything.

He had driven into work with a deep sense of foreboding. He couldn't exactly understand why, but he knew it had something to do with Caroline. How had it come to this? There was a time when he almost worshipped this woman, when he would do anything to make her happy. She in turn had made his life so special that each and every day had been a new awakening. The life they had planned, and the life they were living was completely without any ill-will or despair. Every day was a honeymoon, but something had changed. Was it him, or was it that Caroline didn't change? She had continued to act as if each day was her first with him, and it started to become overwhelming. There was no relaxation or respite from the outward feelings of love, lust and desire that she felt for him. Even after the children had been born, it never changed. She focussed herself entirely on Tom and it started to smother him. He had fallen into deep water, the type that he had been warned of, and found himself unable to keep afloat. She was dominating his every act and every act she performed was for him. It had become unnatural. She saw beauty in everything and rejected anything that didn't give her pleasure. The thing that seemed to give her pleasure more than anything was Tom, and he knew that he should feel so very grateful for her, but it was now too much. As he sat at his desk, with the usual pile of quotations, sales graphics and targets to sift through, he wondered how on earth he was going to change his life.

"Tom?". He was startled back into the moment by Janet. She knew him well enough now to call him Tom and not Mr Patrick. "Is everything okay?"

"Yes", he lied. "Sorry I was daydreaming a little. Miles away."

"You have been like this all morning, is there anything I can do?". In a way that was a personal plea, but she knew he probably wouldn't see it that way.

"Oh, I'm fine, just a few things on my mind. Been having difficulty sleeping and one of the children has the flu so have to get up all night with them. Silly isn't it?". He smiled a weak smile at her and she knew he wasn't telling the truth." I tell you what you could do for me." She looked into his eyes deeply and wished. "You could get me a nice cup of coffee. That would wake me up and then we could get on with these quotes that have to go out tomorrow". He looked at her and she smiled brightly and got up to walk to the kitchen. Inside she was secretly cursing that this man could still only see her for coffee making when she so wanted to be more to him.

As she turned away the hem of her black skirt caught against the fabric of her tights and for a fleeting moment a shapely thigh was exposed before she set it free. It was unintentional but in a way quite deliberate. She wondered whether Tom had noticed. As she walked away Tom looked up and admired the way she moved. He had noticed, and just as importantly, had liked what he saw.

*     *     *

The next part of the day saw Caroline go on a mad cleaning spree throughout the cottage. She hadn't planned it but after coming across a ball of dust on the kitchen floor, she decided within herself that the whole house needed to be scrubbed clean. She started by disinfecting the floor itself before scrubbing and then polishing the work table. That was followed by a complete grating of the aga and dusting of all the walls, ceiling and curtains. Following the kitchen she then attacked the living and dining room with the same vigour and enthusiasm and that was followed by the bedrooms and bathroom. It was an exhausting business but one that Caroline revelled in. It took most of the afternoon too, but it didn't matter as she kept her inner self amused by singing her favourite songs, and by the time the whole cottage had been spotlessly transformed, she had sung just about every song and lyric that she could remember from her short but happy life. Sadly it meant that the time had evaded her again, especially after this morning, and it meant that the children would have to be given a lift home by Lorraine once more, but she didn't mind. It would give her the opportunity of telling her how dreadfully awful her new hairstyle looked. Honestly, Lorraine...that woman!

*"I so used to like Lorraine, but her demeanour and outlook on life is so against my own that I can bare to stand in front of her nowadays. Still, she has been good in looking after the children when I have had more pressing duties. Shame about the spider, but I did warn it not to try and leave."*

By early evening she had caught up with herself and the night spread before her. The children had been returned by a clearly harassed Lorraine who seemed to be quite upset that she had been forced to bring them home once more. As Caroline had explained though, she was coming this way anyway.

"I just don't know why you are making such a fuss. You take one sugar don't you?"

"Yes, thank you". Lorraine stood there in front of her quietly seething, but knowing deep inside that it was pointless to pick an argument with this woman. She had known her intermittently for around three years now and was convinced that she was rather unhinged. It seemed to her that virtually every conversation would at some stage get back to her wonderful life and equally wonderful husband. For Lorraine that was rather difficult to listen to as she was still in the midst of a heavy split and impending divorce from Chris.

"It's just that you never called to say you wouldn't be there, and they looked so lost when you hadn't turned up. I felt awful for them and…"

"…but you were there so why should I worry Lorraine?"

"…because what if I hadn't been there?"

"…but you were! Honestly what on earth do you expect me to say to you? You have brought them home and I am very grateful, but how many times do I have to say thank you?". Caroline was bristling now and stared hard at this ugly woman stood in front of her. How dare she bring all of this into her wonderful cottage and start to question her. "…and of course it's not as if you have a wonderful husband who depends on you like I do. Do you understand how much of the day is taken by thinking of how to make him happy, how to keep him content? What to make for his evening meal, what clothes to put aside for tomorrow, what special treat to give him each night? Do you realise how difficult that is? No of course you don't, because you no longer have a husband to take care of, so why on earth are you going on about a simple little favour that you have done for me?", she almost cried the last few words as her face began to flush in anger. "So Miss unpretty I would suggest you take your moans and complaints elsewhere and don't come anywhere near my children, husband or indeed my house again!". She exuded anger and stared directly into Lorraine's blue eyes, which had started to water. "Now you have made me angry, so I am not going to make you a coffee. Goodbye", and with that Caroline turned her back and folded her arms in an act of total defiance. Lorraine stood there rooted to the spot and the seconds it took her to turn around and walk quietly to the door seemed like hours. As she left she turned back to say something, but Caroline had her back to her and would not move until this woman was out of her life. "Goodbye I said". Lorraine could only silently mouth a whispery "Goodbye" and with that left the cottage never to return. Caroline heard her leave and close the door and then started to giggle to herself. "Stupid cow". She laughed out loud and then found herself so amused that the tears started to run down her cheeks leaving long black streaks of mascara. Soon she was in such fits of laughter that her stomach ached and she found it difficult to breathe. Upstairs Ben and Shelley heard their mother laughing loudly and both agreed that she was in a good mood and so soon forgot about the shock of her not turning up to pick them up from school again.

\*　　　　\*　　　　\*

Tom arrived home slightly later than usual, a fact not lost on Caroline. She was there waiting as usual, but her demeanour was that of distraction. She had calmed herself after the hysterical departure of Lorraine and had gone about the usual domestic duties with added vigour. The children had not misbehaved and had been fed and bathed in double quick time, Shelley falling asleep in her arms as she carried her upstairs to bed. The lamb casserole was quietly simmering and her preparations for the evening ahead had been as thorough as normal. There was something not quite right though, and as she looked up at the plaque glinting in the moonlight above the bed, she determined to find what it was. When Tom came through the front door she could almost immediately smell it. It was the smell of uncertainty, the smell of fear, and even the smell of dishonesty. She could not tell if the aura came from her husband, or if indeed it came from within her, but she knew it was there.

"Hello darling", she smiled her widest smile at the man who dominated her thoughts and being each and every waking second. "How was your day?".

"Fine". A single word answer and almost too much for him.

"Dinner is in the oven, and I am your desert". The familiar flirtatious manner was too predictable and now entirely unwelcome.

"Good, but I'm not really that hungry this evening. It has been a long day". Tom took off his coat, put down the briefcase and entered the kitchen, full of the sounds and aroma of the evening meal. George looked up briefly, accepted the pat on the head with grudging kindness, and immediately went back to sleep. Going to the sink to grab a much-needed glass of water, he spied the nail pushed deep into the worktop and what seemed to be a length of string attached to it. He pulled it out and ran his finger over the hole it had left. "Have the kids been playing in here?"

"What?". The question came from deep inside the living room and was partially drowned by the emerging sounds of The Carpenters singing 'Yesterday Once More'. Again for the hundredth time he inwardly groaned as he prepared for the evening ahead. "I said", raising his voice a little, "have the kids been playing in the kitchen tonight?".

"Oh yes". Caroline had wafted towards him in a frenzy of perfume and intimate desire. "but I told them off and put them straight to bed". With that she flung her arms around her husband and kissed him passionately on the lips, a kiss that mixed lust and love together. "…and soon I will be putting you to bed too".

The rest of the evening was as the previous and the one before. A fine meal, only just palatable for Tom, and then the usual frenzy of love-making before he was allowed to crawl into bed and rest his body. His body could rest, but his mind could not. Throughout the whole evening he had allowed himself to wander down the road to infidelity. He had thought of Janet each time and this had helped in his excitement. Caroline could never know what was flashing through his mind and in a way that became even more attractive. It seemed to him the perfect solution. What he could never know though was that Caroline could know and did know. She had looked deep into her husband's eyes at the right moment and then had entered even deeper into his mind and soul and had seen something that she had not liked. It had disturbed her and had made her realise that her mission was even more important now than ever. Later, when Tom gently snored, she returned to the kitchen and stared out at the moonlit sky. Her eyes bore deep into the blackness and saw the void that needed to be filled. From the heart of the forest a crow, awakened by the unusual presence, flicked its beak and focussed on the image directly in front. It stared as hard as the eyes that were focussed on the heavens and saw the demon dancing before it. The crow turned away, unable to understand the workings of such a moment, and flew away. It flew far away, never to return to that place.

\*　　　　　\*　　　　　\*

That night Janet returned to her flat and thought of her life. Did she see something today, or was it her over vivid imagination? Should she continue this charade or just come right out and tell him? She could not tell whether his melancholy was to do with his wife, or if it were something even more serious. How she longed for him to share his secrets, his thoughts, loves, ambitions, and yes his life with her. She wanted him so badly at times it almost hurt with the aching deep inside. As she climbed into her bed she dreamt of his arms enfolding hers as they both drifted into a loving embrace followed by deep sleep. She allowed the thoughts to fly around her mind, the fantasies becoming more and more real, before finally succumbing to the tiredness of the day. Maybe tomorrow will be the day she whispered to herself before drifting away. As she entered the first moments of her twilight hours, the distant rumblings of a thunderstorm grew ever louder and the slow persistent drops of rain became heavier ready to unleash their torrent.

# CHAPTER EIGHT

"Come on Ben, we're going to miss it". Mary and Ben were running across the road to the bus station. His mother a few feet ahead with a large and battered brown suitcase in one hand and an outstretched arm toward him as he attempted to keep up. The bus, number 73 to Eadlethorpe, was waiting and ready to depart. The station was a heaving mass of double and single decker buses with passengers embarking and disgorging in a mass of seething humanity. Amongst them were the usual inhabitants of these places, aimlessly wandering with neither purpose nor destination, choking up the place with their presence. A concrete maze of activity and inactivity. It was this place that Mary and Ben were rushing too. Mary to say goodbye to her beloved son, Ben to say hello to a new life away from the hell of the inner city world that he had been brought up into.

Following the visit from PC Henrose, both Mary and Chippy, but especially Mary had decided that the only way to ensure Ben's future would be to get him away from everything he had known and was likely to know if he continued his life on the Charley estate. Dale could follow in time, but for the time being they had to concentrate on Ben's future. It was an astonishing act of parental care that had previously been missing from their lives, but they both realised that although their lives had become a wasteland of drug addiction, they had a duty to ensure that their children avoided such a thing. For that reason Mary had contacted her mother, Prudence, and asked her for help. Prudence, long despairing of her daughter's life, readily agreed and arranged to convert her spare bedroom and would be there to meet little Ben off the bus. For Ben it was a heart-wrenching moment when he realised he was to leave his family and little Dale, but his inner being told him, even at that early age, that this is what would be his salvation. Sadly he never had the opportunity to say goodbye to his only friend at school, Mr Adams, but it was a minor worry, and so it was now that he and his Mother were rushing across the road avoiding the raindrops so as to catch the bus that would take him to a cleaner and happier life.

"Remember to call and write as often as you can". Mary hugged her elder son with an intensity that she hadn't shown for so long. It was only a two hour journey into the countryside, but to say goodbye to her firstborn it may as been on the other side of the World. Deep down she also knew that this was effectively a way of saying goodbye, and also a realisation that she had failed as a mother. Any parent who is forced to let her child live with another, even if in this case it was her own mother, has to admit to themselves that they have failed. It was a harsh and hurtful lesson, and she tried so hard not to allow the churning of her stomach and the knife in her heart become visible as she hugged Ben in a wave of tears. "Your nan will take care of you and we will visit as often as we can". Ben stood speechless and looked hard at his mother's face, once so beautiful, now so drawn and haggard, so unrecognisable. "I will write Mum. Don't worry"

"I know my darling. Your dad will get us a car and we can come and see you. Nana is sorting out a new school and soon you'll be able to see Dale. He'll be okay, we'll look after him." She gave him another huge kiss and hug and pushed him towards the bus which was soon to leave. "Ben…". Ben turned and looked at his Mum. "I…we love you. Bye". Ben smiled and waved weakly, handed his suitcase to the driver who in turn put it into the hold, climbed the steps and disappeared into the bus. Mary stood and cried silently to herself. Goodbye Ben.

As the bus left the station, Ben, sat at the very back looked out to where his Mum was when he left her. She was nowhere to be seen.

He looked hard as the images started to recede as the bus pulled away and down the main road out of the town. He stared until his eyes hurt from the effort, looking toward where she had been and where she would be if she was walking back home. There was no sign at all and after a while, as the station disappeared from view, he turned away and looked ahead of him, a small tear in his left eye as he wondered whether he would ever see his Mum, or his Dad or even Dale ever again. The pain of missing was already digging deep into his soul and the thought of the new life, although a lot better then the one he was leaving, suddenly filled him with a silent despair. He was not to know that Mary had broken down in spasms of tears the moment Ben had got onto the bus. She had been helped by a kindly old woman as she broke down and had been almost carried to the nearest bench, just out of eyeshot from her son. She watched as the bus pulled away and waved silently as it left the station. Her tears came and the grief already started to hit her in waves. The old lady sat with her until she regained her composure, whilst the numerous passers-by, passengers, pedestrians and the rest of humanity walked by without a second glance. She was just someone in the corner who would quickly get over whatever it was that was upsetting her.

On the bus, midway down, was a large, noisy and boisterous family. They had boarded in a flurry of mock expletives, melodramatic actions and a propensity to let the rest of the small world they had just inhabited, know exactly what they were doing. The mother, a large and physically unpleasant woman, carrying a grubby and loud young child, made a huge moment of finding her seat and then proceeded to shout rather loudly to her entourage to tell them of her good fortune. "It's alright, the seat's large enough for me arse". With that she laughed loudly as the rest of the passengers prayed silently that she was not staying for the full journey. Trailing behind her were two similarly proportioned women, slightly younger but just as large and ungainly. They both carried the same looking child, indistinguishable from boy or girl. As well as the human baggage came the practical baggage too. Three pushchairs, at least a dozen bags of separate sizes and a healthy contingent of carrier bags, full to bursting with nappies, bottles, cans of coke and crisps. They had resolutely refused to allow any of it to be stored in the hold, so the three seats they should have taken soon became six. Thankfully for them the bus was only half full. As one of the fat girls eased herself down into her seat, plonking her child alongside, she caught Ben's eye. "Hello love, on yer own?". Ben tried to smile but his face was still a figure of anguish and all he could do was to look straight back at her without mouthing a word. "Miserable bleeder", she said with ill disguised contempt. "Got a real miserable sod at the back", she said to no-one in particular, but loud enough so that everyone could hear. The rest of the passengers pretended they couldn't hear, busying themselves with reading books or turning up the volume on their personal stereos another notch. She continued, "All I said was you on yer own and he just looks at me. What a miserable little sod he is. Not surprised he's on his own eh?". The older woman laughed too loudly.

"Shut up Muriel and sit down…leave the little bugger alone"

"Alright, but just not nice is it? Won't speak to him again. Wonder where his ma and pa are…probably abandoned him for being too noisy!". With that all three laughed and immediately upset their three children who in turn cried and sobbed in unison. The bus continued on its way with the passengers speeding up every mile as the family from hell continued their non-stop talking. For poor Ben he felt more alone than he had ever felt in his entire life and he would have given the whole world to be back home with his family, even if his mum and dad were in the front room smoking, it was better than this.

After only half an hour one of the girls, Sally, got up and clumsily made her way to the front of the bus to talk to the driver. He was not at all pleased with this interruption and harsh words were spoken, but eventually he was forced to back down and agree to her request. She was desperate for the toilet, and as the coach didn't have one she insisted that he stop at the next service station. It was unscheduled but he had little choice. As she returned to her seat with a look of triumph on her face, she turned to the older woman and said with more than a glint of glee "Told him, sodding know it all!". Ben stared ahead of him and wondered when they would get to Eadlethorpe. He soon realised that he too was becoming in need of the toilet and not knowing about the conversation between the driver and the girl, he wondered what to do. At first he tried to ignore it, but each bump in the road made the need more insistent and it was soon pressing. There seemed to be no way the bus was going to stop, so he felt he had no choice but to ask the driver if he would be willing to stop. It seemed quiet easy, especially as he had just seen one of the women go up and talk to the driver. He got up tentatively and tried to make his way slowly to the front. As he approached halfway, where the family were spread out on three bench seats, with bags blocking the aisle, the bus hit a bump hard which sent him sprawling across the carrier bags that were spread on the floor. As he crashed downwards he felt something break beneath him and realised it was one of the baby's bottles. Cold milk started to ooze from the plastic bag all over his shirt. Muriel turned and screamed at him. "You little bastard, look what you've done. Look mam, he's broken Danny's bottle the little shit."

"I'm sorry, I fell". The words stumbled out of his mouth with fear and shock, but Muriel was in no mood to be charitable. "Get off it you sod. Look what you've done, and that's a new bottle as well". Ben got up and tried to edge away whilst the other passengers, alerted to the mayhem, tried to get a better view, peering over their shoulders or standing in their seats. No-one offered to help.

"I'm sorry, I just wanted to see the driver".

"I'll give you see the driver....."

"I need the toilet and was just going to ask him if he would stop"

"You horrible little prick. You're going to pay for this!".

The driver decided enough was enough and had pulled over to the hard shoulder with alarming haste and was now scurrying down the aisle. "What on earth is going on?", he demanded. Ben faced with the anger of the three women and now the driver started to panic and burst into tears. He turned to run away but only the back of the bus faced him. Nonetheless he ran back with the words of the family, the driver and assorted irritated passengers ringing in his ears. In his blind panic he pushed at the emergency door at the rear and amazingly it opened first time. A gust of wind caught him full as the cars on the motorway sped by. It didn't perturb him as he jumped clear and scrambled up the embankment, leaping over the wire fence and ran full pelt into the adjoining field, leaving behind the amazed family and a now stunned driver. Their words were lost in the wind and it was only when he had run the full length of the field that he felt safe and free from the brief vision of hell that he had experienced. He'd stumbled twice in his haste and had scraped his knee against a protruding rock, but had carried on, his legs hurting and feeling like jelly. Once settling down and after relieving himself against a stone wall which made him feel better, he caught his breath and looked at his surroundings. He was in an open field, the grey skies above ready to open once more, and not a house in sight. The motorway was far away, and even if he changed his mind and made his way back, the bus would be far gone by now. It was at this point that Ben felt alone. Totally alone. There was no-one around, and no-one to turn to. He sat down next to the stone wall and began to cry again. He cried heavily for a long, long time, the tears cascading down his face, his body convulsed in spasms, and wished he could see his mum and Dale again.

# CHAPTER NINE

For Frank Bolton it could not have gone any better. They had toasted their new agreement with a few glasses of expensive red wine and he had watched Sara become more animated as the alcohol had loosened her tongue. She had tried to keep her icy-cold veneer intact, but after the third glass had started to giggle uncontrollably at one of her own jokes. They had laughed at anything and everything and by the time she and Verity had left to go back to their flat upstairs, Sara was sufficiently relaxed enough to receive a gentle kiss on the cheek. It had given him a frisson of excitement as he felt her soft skin against his lips and the faint smell of red wine on her breath, but he had promised her, and indeed himself, that he would honour their agreement. It was a long term plan and one that would reap the rewards in the future. His only concern was that of little Verity. She had been sulky and sullen for the most part of the day and had amused herself by turning the television on and watching cartoons. He had tried to engage her in conversation, but soon gave up, far too old to understand the special type of talk that was needed to amuse a three year old child. It was going to be a difficult journey with her, but it was one he felt confident of finishing. It would just have to wait until a later date, that was all.

The next day Sara had woken with a huge hangover but a steely determination to make this agreement work. It was not for her but for little Verity. She remembered the days when she had entertained men so as to make sure that her daughter would have a happy life, and in a way this was no different. If Verity didn't like Mr Bolton then it would have to be something they would have to deal with. She would be grateful in the future, of that there was no doubt. On that first day of their new life, she had attacked it with vigour. After dressing the two of them and dampening the thunder in her head from the wine with at least three cups of very black coffee, she had gone back downstairs and immediately dragged Frank shopping. It was not something he was expecting, but as they had trundled from one department store to the next, he had started to enjoy himself. The sense of pride he felt at having a young lady and her daughter with him was palpable. He wondered what the other shoppers and shop-assistants thought as the new 'family' chose curtains, table covers, new cutlery and matching dishes. Did they think he was their father, or maybe an older lover? It excited him in a way and for the first time he felt as if he belonged. His new 'girlfriend' as she had described herself yesterday, was certainly playing the part. As well as seemingly ready to completely refit his apartment, she was ready to change his image too and was determined to restock his wardrobe.

"A blue shirt and yellow tie would look just right with the suit. Let's have a look for some", much to the delight of the old sales assistant who had spent most of the morning re-arranging the suit section just for something to do. Suddenly in had wafted this rather unusual family and had started to spend their money as if there was no tomorrow. He had shown the older man a variety of suits, and the young girl with him, presumably his daughter, had insisted that he had bought all three. Now they were looking at matching shirts, and all the time he had kept a mental mathematical check of how much commission he would get.

"Sir, this is a very fine make and if I may say so, would look splendidly with the grey two-piece"

"We'll take three in different shades" was the instant reply from the young girl, before the older man had a chance to open his mouth. "What about boxer shorts?". The man had been rather taken aback by the forwardness of the question and was immediately convinced that she in fact wasn't his daughter at all. No matter, he had supplied everything she had asked for and had gladly taken a swipe of the man's credit card, and as he had watched them leave his shop saw that the older man seemed happy with his lot. Lucky sod, he thought.

"Now what about me and Verity?", Sara turned to Frank, already overwhelmed with a bundle of bags. "You've got new things for your apartment, and new clothes, we should have some too."

"Okay, only seems fair". He had watched with delighted amusement as his girlfriend had gone on this mad spending-spree and really hadn't minded at all. It wasn't as if he couldn't afford it, "but let's stop for lunch first". Lunch had quickly become a three course dinner washed down with a bottle of rather special claret and a huge fizzy drink for Verity. She had been given a colouring book and crayons by the pleasant waitress and was now beginning to enjoy herself whilst her mummy and this man giggled together. The lunch lasted for over an hour and thankfully once they came out into the crisp, fresh autumnal air, the effects of the alcohol had taken their effect on Sara and she began to feel a bit drowsy and in no mood for more shopping. They would finish it tomorrow, she had announced, and with that they had caught the first available taxi back home. It had already been an expensive day for Frank, and when he had added up the expenditure on his credit cards, it had come to the region of around a thousand pounds, and with the promise of more tomorrow, but he actually could not have been more content with his life. Sara had actually kissed him on the cheek once they had returned to his apartment and said that she would be back in the morning, and to make sure he was ready. He had smiled willingly and put on his favourite jazz CD and sat quietly and contemplatively for the rest of the evening. Life had suddenly taken a turn and certainly for the better.

The next day was just the same. A mad cocktail of spend, spend, spend, all of it on Sara and Verity. For little Verity there were new frocks, shoes and toys, including a huge dolls house with all of the model furniture exquisitely made, but which cost a fortune. It made her happy though and for the first time she looked up at Frank and said "thank-you". It was prompted by her mother, but it was a start and it made him feel good. For Sara there were new blouses, a selection of skirts, both long and short, designer shoes and at least three pairs of denim jeans that she spent an age trying on. She also treated herself to some new sexy underwear, not lost on Frank as he stood outside the shop peering in. It gave a hint of the future, and it was a future that he was very much looking forward too. Again there was an expensive lunch and again his credit card was given a serious investigation, but again he didn't mind. He was happy with his new life and didn't matter how much it cost him.

In fact that was the way each and every day became for the three of them. Sara would announce that they would go out for the day, and almost inevitably they would end up shopping and spending far too much money. At no time did she show any conscience about the amount she spent, and at no time did Frank show any concern at his rapidly-dwindling finances. He was a rich man and he was enjoying spending it on his new family. Even Verity seemed to be gradually, albeit slowly, warming to him. Each day would always end the same way with Sara retreating from his apartment back upstairs, but each day with a renewed sense of optimism he looked at her and looked forward to the end of the three month trial period.

*         *         *

At the end of the day Sara stood at her window and stared down to the street below. The sun had faded fast and Verity was long asleep, exhausted by another round of shopping and exploring the new toys that were bestowed on her on a daily basis. She was still unsure of her uncle Frank, but Sara could see she was warming fast to him. That made her a little more content. For Sara these were unsure days. Standing at the window she cradled her glass of red wine and thought of her life. She remembered the horrors and cruelty of Elio and gave an involuntary shudder. Her hatred for that man was now almost beyond her grief for him. She took another sip and allowed the alcohol to slip down her throat and warm her mind. A rain-drop hit the window pane and gently began to drift downwards leaving behind a snake-like trail. It was followed by another and then another. Down below the last-minute shoppers and stressed office workers were quickly making their way home. Cars and buses competed for space in a perpetual line of horns and expletives. She thought of the men who had since used and abused her and felt a shiver of revulsion. She thought of the future and Frank downstairs. How had it come to this? She had no feelings for him in the days he had been one of the many who had paid for her private entertainment, but his kindness, especially financial, had shown him in a new light. She wondered whether she could continue. Each time she thought of him though, the image was replaced by her Italian lover. It was one that she tried so hard not to allow, but the visits were becoming increasingly more and more regular. When you try to stop yourself from thinking of something, it's a little like having an elephant sat next to you and you try not to look at it. Almost impossible. Closing her eyes he came again. His presence, his smell, his feel. Gently she swayed with the memories with what was and would never be again. Another gulp of wine and the numbness replaced the pain of grief and longing. In the distance she heard the faint sounds of a woman's cries, somewhere outside, or then maybe in the apartment block. She was unsure and it was too unimportant for her to think of. The rain hit the window pane with a new vigour and slowly the light of the day receded to be replaced by the gloom of an early evening. She shivered slightly and instinctively pulled her woollen cardigan closer to her shoulders. The central heating was on full, a luxury she no longer needed to worry about nowadays, but the coldness was permeating through the walls of the building. With her eyes closed she returned to the early days and the way it was. It comforted her, but saddened her too. She could never see a time like that ever again.

Her moment was shattered by an earth-shattering explosion. It reverberated through the building from outside and made the walls shudder. It was so loud and so unexpected that people on the streets below almost instantly, and as one, threw themselves to the floor in a fear of attack and in a moment of self preservation. Cars screamed to a halt as drivers momentarily lost control, half in belief that they had been involved in a terrible crash. The clouds above, at first fluffy and white, very quickly, almost too quickly, turned to a deathly grey and then a deep, deep black. They covered the skies and in a haste that had never been seen before, they unleashed onto the world below. The soaking was intense and nothing and no-one could escape their anger. In the bedroom beyond Verity had woken and had cried out in fear. Sara turned to comfort her, but before she could she saw the terrifying fork of thunder that for a split second lit up the sky before yet another explosion of sound. The walls shook again and the cries of the woman in the distance had become a scream of panic. Below the people scurried to and fro in what had become almost complete blackness, the street lights not ready to be switched on at such an early time of the day. The headlights of the vehicles hardly penetrated the dark and the world appeared to have slowed to a crawl. Sara quickly ran to her sobbing daughter and wondered why these things were happening so often now. The weathermen had said it was a result of global warming as records had never shown these kinds of events before. It could not be explained any other way they said. Whatever it was all there was to do for Sara and Verity was to climb into bed and close their eyes to the carnage outside. There were some things that just could not be explained, and Sara had too many other things running around her battered mind to worry about it.

*         *         *

The woodlark knew what was happening. It had nothing to do with a cold western front or global warming or indeed any other kind of worldly explanation that had been given. The woodlark had seen it before and did not want to be a part of it again. It could see deep into the soul of the world and knew that the only thing it could do to protect itself would be to flee as far away as possible. It had already flown from its home in the forest, and now it was time to fly further away. This stopping-off point was a mistake, but if it could leave soon, it would not be a fatal mistake. These were not good days at all.

# CHAPTER TEN

St. Mary's Preparatory School
Wood Lane, Little Hanwick, Dorset, LH2 DO1

Monday 17th June 2003

Dear Mrs. Bolton,

It has recently been brought to our attention that you have not made sufficient preparations for the collection of both Adam and Shelley at the end of the schooling day, and that on more than one occasion they have been collected and taken home by another parent. This has caused unnecessary anguish for your children and inconvenience for the parent involved. Whilst attempting to keep an eye on all children when they are in the school grounds, we are powerless once they have left and therefore we rely heavily on the presence of a parent or guardian to escort them home in the evening. Unfortunately this has not been the case quite recently and we must urge you to take more care and provide a safe means of escorting your children once they have finished their daily studies. It is regrettable that we have had to resort to writing to you regarding this matter, but numerous telephone calls have not been answered or actioned upon.

If there are recurring problems concerning this then please contact me or the teacher involved at the number below and we will endeavour to find a reasonable solution. It may also be helpful to have an informal talk where we could discuss the progress, or otherwise, of Adam with his studies. I am pleased to say that Shelley continues to enjoy nursery school and is a delight to all of her teachers. May I also remind you that the fees for the transport of Shelley from nursery to St Mary's each day are once again due quite soon.

Yours sincerely
Miss Pamela Hepburn
Head Teacher, St Mary's school.

# CHAPTER ELEVEN

PETERSON MIDDLE SCHOOL,
Leeds Fairground Road, Charley, LE1 1ED
Monday 24th June 2003

To the parents or guardians of Ben Fuller,

We are writing in relation to the recent absences from school of Ben and would appreciate a letter by reply, or better still a telephone call to explain Ben's non attendance. As you can appreciate, any regular non-attendance by a pupil causes concern and is eventually passed on to the local education authority who will then act as they see fit. Please would you contact us without further delay with a date for Ben's re-appearance at school, and I trust we will not find ourselves in a position where we have to contact you again over this matter. If you have any queries please do not hesitate to contact me on the number below.

Yours sincerely
Peter Whitehead
Headmaster

# CHAPTER TWELVE

MOUNT ELIZABETH FIRST SCHOOL
Rectory Road, Old Windmill, Scarborough. SC1 1YB

Friday 20th June 2003
Dear Miss Palazzo,

I am delighted to confirm that your daughter has been accepted as a pupil at Mount Elizabeth School as from the start of the next term, subject to the usual payment of fees. I am sure Verity will enjoy her schooling days with us and will go on to benefit from a first-class education in the extremely pleasant surroundings that Mount Elizabeth affords. I feel confident that you will not regret your decision to entrust your child's educational needs with us and we look forward to meeting you and Verity on our Open day on the 1st July.

Please accept my best wishes and if there are any questions or queries concerning any of the above, then please do not hesitate to get in touch with me during school hours.

Yours sincerely
Miss Anne Smythe. Head of teaching studies.

# Chapter Thirteen

Caroline had received the letter and immediately consigned it to the rubbish bin, only half read. She had no time whatsoever for the petty problems that these people tried to impose on her. As far as she was concerned both Adam and Shelley were quite adequately taken care of, and in fact the more she thought of it, the more annoyed she became. How dare this woman have the audacity to write to her about her children! She'll certainly be taking this matter a little further, and by the time she had finished with Miss 'high-and-mighty' Hepburn, she would be sorry she'd ever crossed her. Anyway, there were far more important things to bother with. Firstly she had to go to that irritating woman Lorraine and make her peace with her. It wasn't that she had felt any guilt about their argument yesterday, but more to do with the fact that she knew Lorraine was of help to her, especially where the children were concerned. It was a tedious business, but one that she had to endure.

She put on her summer jacket and made her way to Lorraine's cottage. It wasn't far so she could walk amongst the trees and bracken and breathe in the fresh, crisp summer air. Along the way, she stopped to pick a handful of ragwort from the side of the road and carefully arranged it into a pleasing posy as a present for her old friend. It wasn't the prettiest of flowers and had been rumoured to have caused unknown distress to grazing horses, but she certainly wasn't going to waste newly-bloomed daffodils on this woman. Lorraine wouldn't really be able to tell the difference anyway. As she crossed the lane

64

she spotted in the distance two roe deer playfully skipping amongst the heath, oblivious to any other presence. She stopped and looked. The beauty of the scene filled her with pleasure and she felt an almost irresistible urge to run headlong into it and embrace. Standing and staring, she watched their playful, nervous movements, delighting in the innocence of the scene, but presently she became bored and decided to move on. They sensed her presence and immediately darted away as quick as they had appeared back deep into the undergrowth. These were the moments that Caroline lived for.

Lorraine's cottage was like her own, set some way from the main road of the hamlet. It gave her seclusion, but, according to Caroline, gave her also the excuse not to take care of it properly. It was similar to her own, white-walled with a thatched roof, but in Caroline's eyes, that was where the similarities ended. The garden, if it could be called that, was badly overgrown and had not been tended to for a long time. Weeds and nettle bushes had replaced the array of blooms that appeared every spring-time. The wooden fence that surrounded the property had been in need of repair for months and had in parts fallen away completely leaving gaping holes that gave an unsightly appearance. There were rose bushes climbing the side of the front of the building, which once upon a time had given it a picturesque quality, but now they had died and the withered stems and stalks gave an air of decay. Caroline didn't like approaching this place as she could still feel the beauty but the neglect had strangled the life out of it. Lorraine had recently had a particularly difficult time with the split from her husband, but that was no excuse to allow such a place to fall into disrepair. It was criminal. She really must talk to her about it and make her realise the error of her ways. That would wait though, she thought as she uncertainly picked her way through the growing weeds on the garden path leading to the cottage. Firstly she must make amends for yesterday.

Lorraine opened the door and was immediately taken aback by Caroline's presence. "Oh, hello. I didn't expect to see you"

"Hello Lorraine. I'm sorry I didn't call in advance but was passing by and thought I would come and say hello" Lorraine was pretty sure that no-one just passed by her place anymore, especially since she'd been left alone by David. "It is such a beautiful day, and I feel so bad about the way I spoke to you yesterday, what with all of your problems and suchlike, that I thought I would try and say I'm sorry and see if we can be friends again". With that she proffered the posy of ragwort, which Lorraine accepted, not really sure what to do with what she thought were a bunch of weeds.

"Well that is nice of you I suppose. You had better come in." She stood to one side and allowed Carline to enter into the hallway. She felt very drab stood alongside her, in her old cotton t-shirt and a rough and worn pair of denims that she had retrieved from the washing basket that morning as she had no other pair that were clean. Caroline of course looked and smelled stunning. She was wearing a flowing patterned skirt and a brilliant white cheesecloth blouse. Slightly old, but she seemed to be one of those women who could wear clothes that had come and gone out of fashion, yet still create the desired effect. She was also wearing a very expensive perfume, which Lorraine had no idea what it was called and was sure it something that she would now never be able to afford. The aroma as Caroline wafted past her toward the kitchen was almost over-powering but pleasant nonetheless. "I'm sorry, but the place is such a mess." It was an unnecessary apology as Caroline was hardly a regular visitor, but one she felt she had to make. "I just don't seem to get the time to do anything nowadays". That made Caroline smile to herself, as she really couldn't see what it was that Lorraine did have to do, now that she didn't have a husband to look after. Yes she had Peter, her six year old son, but he no longer lived with her, so how difficult was that? A quick look at the dirty dishes piled up in the kitchen sink confirmed her suspicions that this woman had let herself go.

"Well I can understand how difficult it is for you", she lied. "..and I suppose my unreasonableness hasn't really helped has it?". She turned to look at Lorraine, who was quickly trying to tidy away the pile of clothes on the wooden dining table so as to make room. "I thought as a way of saying sorry and thank you I would come round and give you a hand. Is that okay?"

"Would you like a coffee?"

"I will make it, don't worry"

"Oh ok. The cups and everything are in the top cupboard. Coffee is only instant. Sorry" Lorraine had never been comfortable in the presence of this woman, and certainly wasn't feeling that way now. Right from the beginning when they had first met after Caroline and her family had moved into the cottage at the end of the track, there had been a feeling of unease in her presence. At first she believed it was because of her stunning beauty, something which David had commented on on more than one occasion leaving Lorraine to start to feel irrationally jealous, but after a time when she had convinced herself that David had no interest in his attractive neighbour, the feeling of unease continued, and she had never understood why. Maybe, she reasoned as she watched Caroline busy herself making two cups of steaming instant coffee, it was because she just looked so gorgeous.

"Sugar?"

"No, thank you. I need to watch my weight. David said I was beginning to look a little fat and I needed to lose at least a stone..." she caught herself, realising that already she had started to talk about David, "....sorry".

"It's okay, I know it was such a bad experience for you. There, a strong cup of coffee. Nothing like it to get you going eh?". They sat at the kitchen table, across from each other, and Lorraine couldn't help but notice that the top three buttons on Caroline's blouse were unfastened, leaving a little too much cleavage. It struck her as being rather odd and something that she herself would never do .

"So Lorraine, what you need is to get out. Get away from this place and start to enjoy yourself again. You really don't look that well. The problem is when you have a traumatic experience like yours is that you start to neglect yourself. You are an extremely attractive woman and it's a shame when that is allowed to be ignored. I was thinking that yesterday as we were talking, and if I may say so…" Caroline's eyes burned into Lorraine's, "…that hairstyle doesn't do you any favours at all".

"Oh". There was nothing else she could say to that. In fact there was nothing else she could say to anything. She just sat there staring at this woman who had invaded her house with her strong smelling perfume and stunning beauty, not to mention that air of unpleasantness that came with it too.

"I am going to help you get your life back again. I really am. I just think you need to sort yourself out, and let's be honest Lorraine….," Caroline then gestured to the kitchen sink and then to the dirty washing piled on the floor, "….I think you need a bit of help" Lorraine didn't know what to say so just sat there and sipped her coffee. The unexpected arrival of this woman, who she had never expected to see, was disturbing and something that she hadn't expected. It had impacted on her daily routine, although with the tediousness of her life at the moment, it should have been something she welcomed. She sat there and listened to her new found 'friend' as she went through a list of things that she was going to do make her life better than it was now. Firstly she was going to help her around the house starting with washing the dishes. Then the two of them were going to tackle the dirty washing, followed by a good clean both up and downstairs and make the place a little more homely. The garden would take a little more time but she knew the name of someone who would be very cheap and was an expert at transforming the mess that it had become. It would take some time for the flowers to bloom again, but oh it would be so worth it. The final act of this new forced upon friendship would be to book an appointment with Caroline's own hairdresser and "try and repair that mess". It was all a bit too much for Lorraine and she really didn't know what to do or say, but for the afternoon they got down to the task of cleaning her cottage. It was not at all pleasant having an almost complete stranger rummaging amongst her private life, but Caroline seemed to revel in it. Even the basics like emptying the washing basket of her dirty clothes, underwear included, hardly seemed to faze her. It was all sorted and thrown into the washing machine, whilst the clothes that had been sitting in there from yesterday were hung out to dry and aired in the afternoon sun. Each bedroom was giving a thorough clean, including the washing of the bed linen. The bathroom was scrubbed until it sparkled, including the toilet, something which mortified Lorraine having someone else polish the toilet bowl. The upstairs landing was vacuumed and dusted and all of the windows throughout the cottage were polished until they were so transparent that it was almost as if they weren't there. Lorraine could hardly keep up. All the time Caroline talked and talked and talked. About nothing in particular, but it was constant. Every now and then Lorraine would catch Caroline looking at her intently and she found herself quickly turning away, uncomfortable as she felt her eyes burning into her.

"This is very nice of you, but honestly Caroline there must be other things that you would rather be doing", as she busied herself with dusting the sideboard in the living room.

"Nonsense. What are friends for?...," and with that she touched Lorraine's arm and smiled sweetly, ".....and you are my friend". Lorraine felt herself blush.

"Thank-you". The touch was held for a moment longer than she felt was expected and she instinctively pulled away slightly so as not to give offence. Caroline did not seem to notice.

"We will do a lot together you and I. I feel we are going to become the best of friends", and with that she emerged herself in the job of sweeping the floor and shaking out the rugs that had not been cleaned for months. Eventually the whirlwind had subsided and the two of them, all cleaning duties completed, sat down at the table again with another cup of coffee. Lorraine was exhausted, both physically and mentally, while Caroline just seemed elated. The effort of the work had left its mark though and there were beads of perspiration above her eyes making her forehead glisten slightly. It gave her natural beauty an extra edge, something which Lorraine almost found intriguing. Despite the harshness of the words, she knew that Caroline knew a thing or two about looking good, and if nothing else she could do worse than take her up on the offer of a new hairstyle. They sat there silently, occasionally exchanging a silent smile. It was too unreal and Lorraine couldn't wait for her to leave so that she could at least get the rest of the day to herself. Caroline looked at her new found friend and imagined the things that she had in mind. It gave her a warm glow inside and a desperate need to go home where she could experience it in solitude.

"Going now. Got to go and get Tom's dinner. I'll pop round tomorrow and we'll sort out the hairdresser. See you" With that Caroline got up and left the cottage almost as quickly as she had arrived, leaving Lorraine trailing in her wake with just the aroma of the expensive perfume to remind her that she'd been there at all. "Bye"

"Goodbye…and thank you" she muttered as she watched her disappear down the path. "See you tomorrow then…"

Caroline walked home with a spring in her step and light heart. It had been a good day so far and she intended to make it even better once Tom returned this evening. She wouldn't bother going to the school to pick up Adam and Shelley as there really wasn't any time now, and besides Lorraine would do it. After all it was the least she could do after everything she had done for her today. Everything was looking good, but then she saw something that made her stop and give a cry. Lying on the road, some half a mile from where she had saw it earlier, was one of the roe deer. It was dead, obviously knocked down by a passing car, and its head had been crushed. There was blood seeping from the open wound and she was sure she saw it give a spasm as its body breathed out the last goodbye. It had only just happened and Caroline wanted to find the person who had committed such an act and teach them a very painful lesson. This was beauty transgressed in the worst possible way. It hurt her badly and she so wanted to pick up its tender body and carry it home. Instead she sobbed all the way back with tears of frustration that her beautiful day had been ruined by the callousness of another.

*                *                *

Tom and Janet sat across from each other over the table in the busy restaurant and were for a while lost for words. The invitation to lunch had come as much out-of-the-blue from Tom than both of them could have imagined. In the three years that they had worked together, there had never been a time when they had socialised, apart from the one weekend in Scarborough, but this morning he had woken with a feeling, an urge, a desire. It had nothing to do with Caroline but had everything to do with Janet. It was almost a revelation and so when he had suggested that they go for a spot of lunch at the rather trendy pasta restaurant next door, she had been taken completely by surprise. It was unexpected, but it was pleasant. "How do you feel today?". It was more than a general question. "You seemed,....how can I put it, rather sad and distracted yesterday". She looked deep into his eyes as she spoke and saw her reflection. "I feel a lot better today thanks. Sorry if I wasn't much company yesterday, I've just not been myself recently"

"I know, a woman can tell when there is something wrong, ...I can tell". She picked up the cloth napkin and started to wrap it around her fingers as she spoke. "Tom...if there is something wrong...", she subconsciously moved herself a little closer over the table toward him, "...I would love to be of help. We've known each other a long time and I see you as more of a friend than a boss." She wasn't sure what else to say or whether she should say anymore but felt her eyes moisten as she looked into his. "No matter what it is, I would like to be here for you".

"That is very sweet of you." He leant over and touched her hand gently and kept it there. She didn't pull away. "I have started to realise that my feelings for my wife are not what they were....", He didn't

71

mean to blurt it out, but once started there was no stopping, "…it's not that she has done anything wrong, or that she has changed, it's just me. She is loving and caring and so very beautiful, but I'm just not sure if I love her anymore. I have found myself thinking more and more of someone else recently and I just don't know what to do….". He almost whispered the last few words and let his eyes drop away from hers and looked hard at the empty plate in front of him. Janet felt her heart beat faster and she was sure the sound could be heard above the noise of the packed restaurant. She so wanted the someone else to be her. Please, please, please let it be her.

"It's okay, I understand". She tried to sound composed but wasn't sure she was succeeding. "These things happen. I've never been married, but I've had enough relationships to fill a lifetime and I know how it's so easy to become distracted…." She was struggling to find the right words but she placed her free hand on top of his and squeezed. "….could you tell me who this someone else is?". He looked up and into her glistening eyes and just smiled. He did not need to say anything. She realised, squeezed his hand tighter and smiled back. Deep within, her stomach was jumping somersaults and her heart was almost ready to burst. She slowly leant over the table and planted a slow and lingering kiss on his lips, oblivious to the other diners who may have thought it slightly unusual. He returned it, delighting in the softness and sensuality. This was not like the mad, lustful desire that his wife showed him each and every night, this was so much nicer. This was perfect. This was right.

That afternoon they returned to Janet's one bedroom flat and made love. It was passionate and urgent. It lasted briefly and then it started again. They explored each other as if all of the frustrations of the last three years were being let out at once and afterwards they lay in each other's arms and slept. Their colleagues noticed their absence but didn't comment. One or two may have thought there was something amiss, but most knew of his love for Caroline and her stunning beauty, so very few would have thought that Tom Patrick and his pleasant secretary Janet would be embarking on a passionate love affair. If they had voiced their mischievous thoughts then they would have been immediately dismissed as foolhardy. It would be just a little too unbelievable.

Back at the cottage Caroline sobbed quietly to herself. The sight of the deer had struck at her heart and upset her deeply, but now the pain was being dredged up from deep within her soul and she felt the loss more than even she expected. She felt a void open up with nothing to fill it and she wondered at what it was that made her feel so empty and without hope. The sobbing increased in its intensity until it became a heaving of uncontrollable spasms and the tears ran down her cheeks and soaked into the collar of her pretty blouse. She clung onto the kitchen table for support as she felt her legs buckle beneath her, her fingers turning white with the pressure. Her heart was about to break and she felt her throat tighten until she could hardly breathe. She gave a gasp as she felt herself suffocate and then she fell in a heap on the floor, curling into a foetus position. For the next hour she lay there and cried. She cried like she had never cried before in uncontrollable burst. This was not for the deer, but for something far more important. She felt the loss of something far more beautiful and it tore her apart, inch by inch. Every fibre of her being was now crying out for the loss and the grief she felt was beginning to wash over her until it all-consumed her. Something had left her and there was nothing she felt she could do about it.

# Chapter Fourteen

Ben woke up as dawn was breaking. He was shivering, hungry and very, very confused. The barn was dry and the hay quite comfortable to sleep on, but the cold of the night had entered his bones and he needed to move around to increase the circulation in his body. Outside it had been raining heavily in the night and the ground was glistening with the dampness of the downpour. He got up and took in his surroundings remembering last night. He had found the barn after walking for what seemed miles in no particular direction at all, stumbling across fields and climbing hedges as he tried to get as far away from the motorway as he possibly could. It became dark very quickly and as there were no roads to follow he realised the best he could do would be to find shelter and make a decision in the morning as to where he should go. There was a farmhouse in the distance, with lights on, but he didn't feel he could approach it as they may have known of the trouble on the coach and the last thing he wanted was to have the police track him down there, so he decided to bed down for the evening. The barn was quiet, warm and dark and within minutes he was fast asleep leaving behind the unpleasantness of the day. His sleep was fitful and his dreams disturbing, and by the morning the reality had returned to him. The memories from yesterday came flooding back from the morning when he said goodbye to his mum to the late evening when he stumbled across the barn. His mum...it was only a day ago yet it seemed forever. The thought of spending time at his old flat again seemed an impossibility. He wondered whether his mum had been told that he hadn't arrived at nana Prudence's house, and if she had what would she be doing now? Would she have called the police and they were now attempting to search for him? He'd seen that kind of thing before on the television when kids his age had runaway from home and the parents had spoken to the reporters with tears in their eyes, begging for their children to come home. Mostly they did, but occasionally you would then hear of the child's body being found somewhere and the police then starting a murder investigation. It made him shudder and the tears welled up, pricking his eyes as he thought of mum, dad and Dale. He wished he could return, but his dad would just scold him and his mum would then put him on the bus to nana Prudence again. Life was unfair and he couldn't understand what he had to do to make it better. Firstly though he had to eat as his stomach was aching due to the lack of food. He hadn't eaten anything since breakfast yesterday and that was nearly a whole day ago.

The farmhouse was his best bet. He could maybe sneak into the kitchen and steal some bread and milk if there was no-one there, or he could maybe try and find some eggs but he wouldn't know what to do with them if he found any. Maybe he could just go to the front door unannounced and ask for food. Maybe the people there would take pity on him and feed him, but then they may go and call the police and he didn't want to have them involved anymore.

He crept up towards the building. It was about half a mile from the barn and the way was muddy. There was a grey stonewall that surrounded the house with a wooden gate that had an overgrown path leading to the front door. It had the appearance of being rather ramshackle, but to Ben that hadn't even registered. All he could think of was his empty stomach. He knelt down behind the wall and peeked his head above, careful not to be seen by anyone, if there was anyone there at all. The house was larger than he had thought last night and in the dark mist he hadn't noticed that it was part of a larger group of buildings that seemed to be deserted. There was little sound but he could every now and then hear the sound of a horse shuffling in one of the nearby buildings. To his right was a faded red tractor that didn't look like it had been used for a long time, and a huge contraption that looked like it was once used for cutting hay. He only knew that because he'd seen old films at school when he was being taught history. The front door, huge and wooden with a large horseshoe handle, seemed firmly closed, and there seemed to be nothing from within that suggested anyone was at home. He crept around the outside of the wall to the right of the house until he came to a gap in the wall where the stones had fallen away and not been repaired. He could now see to the back of the building and into the windows that seemed to be in the kitchen. One of the windows was slightly open and that was just what Ben wanted. He quickly, so quickly that no-one could possibly have spotted him, ran to the window and within an instant was climbing through the small gap in the window and falling gently to the floor in the darkened room. It was, as he guessed, the kitchen. It was dark, still but wonderfully warm and there was the fresh smell of bread coming from the large oven that was on the far side. It was almost overpowering and his stomach groaned as the thought of it. He stopped and listened for a sound, but there was none. His eyes soon got used to the gloominess of his surroundings and he saw that it was a small kitchen with a sink to his right with another window looking out to the empty fields beyond, a large table that dominated the centre of the room, the large black oven on the wall opposite, lots of shelving filled with jars and tins of food, plates, glasses and cups and saucers, and just to his left there was a large wicker chair faced towards an open fire that was smouldering slightly giving off a slight warmth that had taken the crispness off the morning air. There seemed to be a bundle of clothes lying across the arms of the chair, and Ben thought he may help himself to them after he'd got something to eat as his own were now wet and dirty.

Creeping slowly toward the oven he tried to avoid the creaking of the wooden floor, but as the whole house seemed to be in silence, he could only assume that whoever lived there was out and had left the place unattended. The oven door was hot and he nearly burnt his hands as he took hold of the handle and opened it slowly. The aroma of fresh bread filled his nostrils and he eagerly grabbed hold of a huge piece of it before taking a large mouthful. It was hot, almost too hot, but it tasted so good, almost melting in his mouth. He took another and then another, devouring it as fast as he could.

"What do you want?"

He spun in terror toward where the voice came from. It was from the wicker chair and what he had thought were the bundle of clothes. Staring directly at him were two large and watery eyes that dominated the grey and wrinkled face of an old woman. On her head was a large white shawl that fell below her shoulders, covering what looked like an old and tattered nightdress. What Ben noticed more than all of that though was what the old woman was holding. It was a large and very menacing shotgun and it was aimed straight at him. "I asked you what do you want?". The voice was firmer and more threatening and any thoughts he had of making a dash for the window were forgotten as he found himself staring down at the barrel. For a moment he didn't know what to say or do. He was struck with terror and felt his knees start to tremble. Swallowing the last mouthful of still warm bread he tried to utter something in reply, but the words wouldn't come. They were lost in the terror and refused to appear.

"If you don't answer then I can only do one thing. I will call the police. It's up to you".

He swallowed hard and somehow overcome his fear and muttered a few words. "I was lost and just wanted to eat something. I'm sorry, I don't mean any harm"

"No-one gets lost around here. Where you from?" the figure in the chair shifted slightly to get a better look at Ben, still with the shotgun aimed directly at him. As the old woman moved a glimpse of daylight from the window caught her face and Ben could see that she was extremely old. She was so old that he thought she wouldn't be able to move that quickly, if at all. If it weren't for the shotgun then she would have not been able to do anything at all. "I'm from

Leeds, but I got lost on my way to me nans. I slept in the barn and just wanted to get summat to eat before I carried on. I'm sorry but I thought there was no-one here".

"You thought there was no-one here so that was okay to come in and steal my bread. I suppose then you would have taken my money as well. I know all about kids like you. How old are you?"

"Thirteen"

"I was thirteen once, but too long ago for me to remember. I'm eighty-five now you know". The woman shifted in her chair once again and lowered the gun ever so slightly. "Come closer and let me get a good look at you".

Ben moved slowly toward the old woman, his legs still shaking. "Why you're only a slip of a thing. Your folks not feed you then?"

"My mum and dad live in Leeds with Dale and they had sent me to stay at nana Prudence for a while cos I keep getting into trouble and the policeman thinks I need to get away. I was on my way on the bus but a horrible woman got me into trouble and so I had to run away. I slept in your barn last night". He hadn't meant to blurt it all out but as he spoke he saw the woman smile. "I was really hungry and I came here to get something and then I saw the window and then the smell of the bread......I'm sorry".

"Oh dear, you really have got yourself in a mess haven't you?"

"I could leave and I won't bother you again, I promise"

"..and where would you go then?"

"I don't know. I could go back to the road and see if I could hitch a lift. I've done that before you know..."

"I'm sure you have young man". The old lady lowered the gun to the floor and with a great effort she lifted herself from the chair. She was a slight figure, almost skeletal with thin and bony arms and legs. As she spoke she wheezed as if out of breath, and it was obvious even to Ben that every movement and action would be an effort. He could run away and she would never catch him. He could, but he didn't. "You can't go anywhere though without a good meal inside you. Don't want you fainting by the roadside do we?"

"No", he whispered, looking at the old woman as she walked unsteadily to the far wall where she pulled down a jar of strawberry jam. "Get the bread out young man, we may as enjoy it whilst it's hot. What's your name?"

"Ben"

"Alright Ben, let's have some bread and jam. Put the kettle on and we'll have a nice cup of tea as well eh?"

Ben did as he was told, not sure what to expect and not sure what this woman had in mind for him. He was so hungry though so any thoughts of leaving in a hurry would certainly wait until he had eaten. He filled the large black kettle with water from the tap and placed it on the hob ready to boil. The old woman busied herself with slicing the newly-baked bread and smothering it with thick butter and jam. "Nothing like newly-baked bread eh? Arthur says it's his best ever meal. We had better save some for him, he'll be back in a mo. He's just gone to look at the sheep, one of them was fretting last night and making a terrible sound. Have you heard the noise sheep make when they are unhappy?" She didn't bother to look at Ben or wait for a reply but just continued her ramblings.

"Such a noise. Kept us both awake half the night. Told Arthur he should go and see it. He wanted to take the gun but I said no. Can't go round killing a poor sheep just because it kept us awake. I told him I would keep the gun here safe and well until he gets back. Good job I did eh?". She glanced an amused look at Ben, who didn't say a word. He stood there motionless not knowing what to do or say. His mind was overwhelmed by the idea of the bread and jam so that he couldn't think of anything else. The old woman finally finished preparing a couple of huge slices and handed them to Ben who eagerly started to devour them. There hadn't been a meal that had tasted this good before. "My you really are hungry aren't you?". The old woman handed him a large cup of milky tea, which Ben took a sip of and then continued to eat without a word.

"So I know what you are called, would you like to know my name?" Ben just nodded. He wasn't sure what he wanted except some more of the delicious bread and jam. "Well I will tell you. My name is Hannah and my husband's name is Arthur." She made her way back to the old wicker chair and sat down with tired and uneasy movements. "We've been here for nearly forty years, just the two of us. Never had children, couldn't. Doctor said it was me. Arthur wasn't that bothered. Never complained, never worried. We just got on with our lives together, just the two of us. We looked after this place all this time. Used to get visitors but they don't come the way they used to. You're the first for so long. Really nice to have someone else here. Arthur will be back soon.....". With that Arthur returned. The kitchen door opened and in he stepped. Ben swung round to look at him and was surprised at what he saw. Arthur wasn't frail like Hannah. He was about six feet tall, quite slim and with greying temples that were at odds with his full head of mousey hair. He wore a huge black overcoat with large brown Wellington boots and carried a heavy rucksack over his left shoulder. Ben, who was never very good at these kinds of things, guessed he must have been at least ten or possibly fifteen years younger than the old lady.

"Hello Arthur. You seen the sheep?"

Arthur didn't reply but mouthed a grunt in her direction, hardly bothering to notice Ben who had finished his bread and jam and wasn't quite sure what to do now. "We got a visitor. His name is Ben and he's run away from his home so he's come to stay with us for a while". Ben wasn't sure what to say. He looked at Arthur who gave him a quick glance and then continued to ignore him, relieving himself of his heavy bag and overcoat before taking off his wellingtons and throwing them in a heap in the corner. "There's some bread and jam on the side and the kettle just boiled. Me and Ben are going into the living room and talk some more. Join us when you want to", and with that Hannah heaved herself up from the chair and took Ben gently by the arm and led him into the room next door, a dark and cold room that hadn't seen or felt any warmth seemingly for years. "Don't worry about Arthur. You'll like him. He's just a little shy with strangers. Always has been that way, especially with young uns like you. Never had to deal with anyone your age you see". Ben shivered involuntarily and looked around him. He couldn't tell whether it was due to the cold or the discomfort of his situation. He felt bad and wished he could escape but he was now deeper into the farmhouse and didn't have any idea as to what to do or where to go. He sat on the old and scruffy sofa and listened to the old lady as she started to recite her life to him.

*      *      *

*"Police are still searching the surrounding areas for missing schoolboy Ben Fuller. The thirteen year old was last seen yesterday afternoon running away from the motorway after an argument with other passengers on a bus taking him to Eadlethorpe. The driver of the bus, Andrew Forsythe, confirmed that Ben had absconded when questioned over the incident during the journey from Leeds and had disappeared into nearby fields before the driver or other passengers could stop him. Police say they are not unduly worried as of yet, and are hopeful that Ben will make contact with them or his parents. His mother, Mary, has appealed to Ben to get in touch as soon as possible. Ben was travelling to stay with his grandmother for a while before the incident took place. Peter Askins, BBC Radio Leeds"*

# CHAPTER FIFTEEN

The day that Verity started her new school would be one that would live in Sara's mind for the rest of her life. Dressed in her blue and grey singlet with tunic and matching wide-brimmed hat, she looked so cute that it almost reduced her mother to tears. It was a day that she thought she might never see, but with the single-mind ness that she had shown since the encounter with Frank, and his financial kindness, her precious little daughter could now start to enjoy the life that Sara had always wished for. The first day was an emotional one as she waved goodbye to Verity at the school entrance, and then watched as one by one the other new pupils were led into the building by a kind and matronly teacher. At first the older boys and girls just ignored the new batch, but like all children their natural behaviour got the better of them and new friendships were made. Sara hoped that Verity would become a popular pupil and make lots of friends in this new life. For Sara the first day was the longest. She'd missed Verity from the moment she had returned to the apartment and had counted down the seconds before she could return in the late-afternoon and take her home with her. As each day went by the anxiety receded, especially when at the end of the first week she went to see the form tutor for an interim report on how her child had taken to a new school.

"She is just lovely. You must be very proud of her Mrs Palazzo"

"I am", Sara smiled broadly, not wanting to spoil the moment by correcting her marital status. That probably wouldn't have been such a good idea anyway, especially in a school like this where single parents are not always as accepted as might be elsewhere.

"She seems keen to join in with all the other boys and girls, has a naturally pleasant disposition and an eagerness to learn. She will be just fine". The lady, wearing a rather heavy tweed skirt with a high-necked blouse that showed her grey-hair almost alarmingly, smiled sweetly. *Verity would be just fine.......*

For Frank it had been just one whirlwind since that first day when he had put the suggestion to Sara. She was now so much part of his life that he couldn't, or preferred not to remember a time before he had this new family. She and little Verity had completely taken over his way of living and each and every day was a new one to be savoured and cherished. He had spent lavishly on them both, and if he had shown any worry or resentment over the financial state of the relationship, he had carefully hidden it. He was aware that his bank balance was beginning to dwindle, but all he could do was to look to the time, not too far away now, when Sara would again give herself to him without the usual financial payment. The fact that in effect he would still be paying for whatever pleasures he would receive in the future cheerfully eluded him. He had a girlfriend in his life and he was happy beyond measure.

"I need to go down to London next week and was wondering whether you would like to come with me?". The two of them were sat alone in the living room of Sara's apartment; just an hour after Verity had drifted into a sleep. The atmosphere was relaxed with Miles Davis playing in the background and the usual glasses of red wine to accompany him. "There's a new property that I'm acquiring and as well as seeing my accountant, I thought I might go and see a new insurance broker. They contacted me last week with a more than generous offer, and it makes sense for me to nip into their offices in Hammersmith so I can kill two birds with one stone so to speak". This was all news to Sara but it wasn't particularly interesting to her either. She really couldn't concern herself with Frank's business dealings, and as far as she was concerned, as long as Frank stood by his side of the deal, she would continue to play out the part of his loving girlfriend.

"That would be nice. Verity is on a half term holiday, so we could make a few days of it. Take in a show, do some shopping and look at the sights. Have to get a central hotel though as London is such a large place that it would make sense for us to be in the middle so we can explore everything properly. Let's get on the internet and book somewhere really nice eh?.."

Frank smiled and looked at her. It felt like he was falling in love.

# Chapter Sixteen

Caroline crept so quietly along the half-hidden path toward the clearing in the woods where the bridleway had left a soft and grassy glade. She had walked this far into the forest before and so knew it well, but she still went cautiously so as not to disturb any of the creatures that lived there. She carried with her a small rucksack that had all that she needed to complete her task today. A large net, about four foot square tied with elasticated string, a bag of pecan nuts and assorted household rags that she had collected over the years when clearing out wardrobes and drawers etc. soon she found the perfect place, just on the edge of the glade, and knelt down onto the still damp forest floor. The sunlight hadn't managed to break through the canopy of the wood yet, so she gave out a shiver, despite the thick black fleece that she wore. She then went to work. Firstly she took out the net and opened it to its full size and then gently tied the elasticated strings to two separate roots from one of the main spruce trees leaving the front open. At the doorway, as it looked, she sprinkled the pecan nuts in a haphazard fashion and then so that the remainder lay within the netting. Then finally she packed the back of the newly-laid trap with the soft rags. It meant that any badger or squirrel that had been tempted by the nuts would eventually enter the netting and the pressure would then automatically close the opening with the elasticated strings. The rags were there so that the poor creature would at least have a comfortable bedding should it be some time before Caroline had the chance to return. She stood up and looked at her handiwork and felt an immense sense of pride in herself. The trap was ingenious and once it began to take effect she could then surround her home with the beauty of the woods instead of constantly having to traipse into the forest to experience it herself. A very clever idea.

Her next task was one that she had thought of with relish and had excited her from the moment she had crawled out of bed this morning. Even during the morning's usual breakfast preparations, and even as she had kissed Tom goodbye it had constantly been there. She knew exactly how she was going to do it and so scampered quickly back to the cottage to prepare herself. Deep down she felt a tingle of excitement as she ran through the woods, and at any other time she would have stopped alone to enjoy the moment, but today was different. Today it would be Lorraine's turn

\*             \*             \*

"Hello, I was wondering when you were arriving". Lorraine swung the door open with a huge welcoming smile as she saw Caroline approach on the now newly-tidied pathway. "I've just put the kettle on".

"Lovely, but I've brought something a little stronger today so we can sit together and have a girlie afternoon". Caroline was holding a bottle of red wine and Lorraine's heart jumped as she saw her friend and the way she looked. She couldn't quite believe how she had changed toward Caroline since that unpleasant day in the cottage, and in a way it almost felt like she wasn't in control of herself, but the moment the two of them were parted nowadays, Lorraine immediately missed Caroline. She had thought of her constantly, even replacing the insistent memories of David, which although odd she had subconsciously refused to admit. All she knew was that Caroline had brought something fresh and exciting into her previously drab existence and the two of them always seem to have fun together. She had helped her out of a terrible crisis and whenever she had tried to repay the favours, Caroline had said no and the inevitable "..what are friends for?". This was a deep friendship and one that made her very happy.

Caroline swept past her into the gleaming cottage and again Lorraine received a whiff of expensive perfume which almost left her feeling quite dizzy. Caroline looked a dream, with a loose white top and a pair of figure hugging jeans, but didn't she always?.Although Lorraine had now made more of an effort, this time trying on her pretty floral-patterned skirt and a beige jumper, she still felt very much second best. They soon went about uncorking the wine and then with a couple of glasses in their hands they retreated to the living room where the warmth of the sun cascading through the large bay window gave the place an inviting air. Caroline immediately settled herself down on the white fluffy rug by the empty fireplace, while Lorraine sat on the chair opposite, curling her legs beneath her body, now totally at ease in the presence of her new found friend, something which seemed unthinkable just a couple of weeks ago. Lorraine found herself unwittingly admiring the beauty of Caroline, and on too many occasions to be comfortable, she had found her eyes wandering to the unbuttoned blouse and the glimpse of Caroline's breast seemingly bursting against the fabric of her brilliant white bra. The conversation began innocently enough, talk of the garden, the children and how well behaved they were at school, and of such ordinary things as the new window lay-out at the greengrocers. "Well putting fresh fruit and veg in the window is hardly going to do it any good, especially with the sunlight shining on it. Turn it all yellow and start to wither".

Caroline agreed. " I bought some broccoli there last Thursday and by the weekend it had all gone off. Terrible smell". It was just two old friends catching up on the kind of gossip that an onlooker would find mind-numbingly boring. As the wine flowed though and the conversation became looser, Lorraine started to lose all inhibitions. "David was good, but he only wanted to do it in one way, and for me...well you know, it never quite worked...", as the talk got on to the topic of sex. "I used to have to excuse myself afterwards and disappear into the bathroom for a couple of minutes..". They both giggled at the thought, " I bet you don't have those problems with Tom do you?". Her speech started to become a little more slurred as she took another generous gulp of wine, emptying the glass.

"No, we have no problems in that department", replied Caroline as she lent forward to replenish Lorraine's glass, her blouse falling loose as she bent down. Lorraine hoped that she hadn't made it too obvious as she made a point of looking, but Caroline was completely aware and lingered in that position for just long enough to be necessary. "…in fact, without trying to blow my own trumpet, I would say that I am very good when it comes to giving pleasure." She moved away slightly and stared deep into Lorraine's eyes, making her blush ever so slightly. The inference was clear, but to Lorraine it was uncertain. She took another gulp of the red wine and felt it warm her as it soothingly slipped down.

"Really?..." her voice was a little shaky and she felt herself start to become nervous.

"Yes, really. In fact I would say that it is my best feature, an ability to make the person I am with enjoy the moment completely." Caroline took a gentle sip of her wine, and without any noticeable gesture or movement, somehow made her blouse open even further, now exposing a large part of her left breast as it strained against the constraint of the bra. Lorraine couldn't help but give a silent gasp as she wondered whether the frantic beating of her heart could be heard. She felt a tingle deep inside her and suddenly the curiosity she at first felt was now being replaced by desire, something she hadn't felt for a long, long time. Since David there had been no-one, but she had often fantasised about the one time before she met him, with the girl at the party when they had both got rather drunk and had somehow ended on the bed together, almost as a joke. It had come to nothing due to the embarrassment they both felt, but she often wondered what it would have been like…

Caroline was totally aware of the effect she was having on her 'friend' and was inwardly loving every minute of it. Every action, every word spoken, every accidental moment had been meticulously planned and so far it was all going exactly the way she wanted it to. As each second passed she could feel Lorraine's presence coming deeper and deeper into her power. A furtive lick of her lips and a demure smile made Lorraine visibly gasp, and Caroline realised that this was actually going to be a little easier than she thought. That mean she could have even more fun. As she took another sip from her glass, she apparently absent-mindedly started to gently caress her inner bosom with her left hand, whilst all the time saying nothing and staring deeply into Lorraine's eyes. The effect was totally hypnotic and for a moment Lorraine watched as this stunning beauty played out this sensual act just for her. She wasn't sure if at first she had mistaken what she had seen and quickly turned away to look at the fireplace, but just as quickly she had looked again, and there was no mistake. Caroline was slowly, almost without realising it, caressing herself. Her heart pounded so strongly and she felt her hands shake with a mixture of excitement and apprehension. Another large gulp of red wine, and the two of them stared deeply into each other's eyes. "I want to watch you..." whispered Lorraine, her voice quivering with excitement. She couldn't believe what she had just said. "Don't stop..".

Caroline did as she was asked, totally in control of the situation and knowing exactly what she was doing. She allowed her hand to gradually move over her breast and then started to caress her nipple through the fabric. Lorraine was completely transfixed and she felt the desire become an extraordinary feeling of lust and want. She re-arranged herself on the chair to make herself more comfortable, privately aware that if she had continued to sit that way, she may have given way to the pleasure on her own before Caroline could even touch her. She watched as Caroline slowly unbuttoned her blouse and let it slip from her shoulders, and then gently lay herself on her back. Slowly her hands moved further downwards over her bare stomach and then teasingly started to unbutton her jeans. In a moment she had removed them and was now gently caressing the top of her white panties. Lorraine didn't move, but every fibre of her being wanted her. "Carry on....let me watch you." Caroline did. She put her hand inside and then probed deep down into herself, slowly feeling the excitement rise as her fingers expertly manipulated herself. Lorraine could feel her own excitement rise. She had fantasised about moments like these, but this was better than anything she had ever thought of in her private moments. She so wanted to make love to Caroline now, but also wanted to enjoy what she was witnessing. Soon Caroline herself started to give in to the probing and caressing of her own fingers and she started to feel herself approach orgasm. It was too quick though, she needed to have self-discipline if she was to enjoy this afternoon, so she pulled back and reached out for Lorraine. In an instance she was lying on top of her and Caroline expertly probed her tongue deeply into Lorraine's welcoming mouth. Soon they became more insistence and desire took over any inhibitions Lorraine had. The top and skirt were almost ripped off in their urgency, teeth clashing against each other as she rammed her tongue into Lorraine's mouth. Lorraine was shocked by the roughness of it, not quite what she had expected, but her sexual desire was at such a high that there was no resistance. Belying her build, Caroline had enormous strength, and physically pulled Lorraine over her and then pushed her to the ground, pinning her down. She could feel herself on the verge of coming again, and now wanted more than just her own fingers for the pleasure. Lorraine didn't resist. She wanted whatever Caroline was about to do to her as she tried to move to grasp a breast in her mouth. She succeeded briefly and felt the hardness of the nipple brush against her lips, so wanting to kiss and caress, but Caroline was now at a more intense stage. As the two now naked bodies writhed against each other, Caroline manouvered herself upwards until her thighs straddled her lovers face. Gently lowering herself, she felt the softness of Lorraine's tongue enter her. "Go on...do it".

No prompting was needed as she pushed her tongue deep inside as Caroline started to moan and move frantically over her. At the same time Lorraine reached down with her right hand and started to touch herself. Caroline looked behind and saw this, making her excitement rise even further, and now thrashing and cursing, she rubbed herself furiously over Lorraine's face, the tongue trying desperately to keep up.

For Caroline the pretence was now gone, she had succeeded in her plan, and now she was going to take the pleasure. "Come on you bitch...lick me...come on". She grabbed hold of Lorraine's head and held it firm, so that she found it almost impossible to breathe. "Come on...you want me". It was rougher than Lorraine had expected and a flash of discomfort took hold as she felt the strong thighs cradle her neck and wetness begin to suffocate. She tried to loosen the grip, but found she wasn't strong enough and started to panic. The desire she felt seconds ago was being replaced by a feeling of concern. This woman was becoming like an animal, and she stopped touching herself and tried to remove Caroline's thighs from crushing her, but nothing could stop her. She started to squirm with discomfort, but the more she struggled, the more Caroline responded with curses. All she could feel was the suffocating wetness as Caroline rubbed herself into a frenzy against her, until she finally came in a huge and shattering moan. Her orgasm was so intense that she held Lorraine's head between her thighs for nearly thirty seconds as she came and then collapsed on top of her in a heap. Somehow Lorraine extricated herself and broke free, her desire now replaced by fear. This wasn't what she expected, and she wanted to be away from her quickly, but Caroline had other ideas. She looked at Lorraine in a way that scared her, her face flushed with excitement. "We haven't finished yet......"

"I'm sorry Caroline, but it's not what I want. I thought I did, but I'm sorry...can we just forget it". Lorraine tried to get up quickly but was stopped instantly.

The stinging of the hand across her cheek not only stunned her, but hurt so badly that tears immediately came to her eyes. She rocked back and lost her footing, falling to the ground, a huge red whelp immediately appearing on her face. In an instant Caroline jumped on her and pinned her down once more. "You wanted me" she said and then slapped her face hard again, "Now you've got me…." There then followed two more hard slaps as Lorraine sobbed tears of pain and fear. "Now lie there, and enjoy yourself."

# CHAPTER SEVENTEEN

There had never been any question that Ben wouldn't stay at the farmhouse. Hannah had found a new friend to take care of, while Arthur didn't seem to care one way or another. In fact he hardly ever spoke a word to either Hannah, or indeed to Ben himself. He rose every morning at dawn and disappeared into he fields with a rucksack slung over his shoulders, only to return at meal times and last thing at night. It seemed a lonely existence for Hannah but one that she had come to terms with. For Ben, he very quickly realised that life there would be far more preferable to anything outside the farmhouse, especially when on that first night he had been shown to the spare room. It looked as if it had been made ready for his arrival with a huge bed covered with a large flowered duvet, oak chests that spread along one side of the bedroom, and an old fashioned chamber pot that was there for 'emergencies' as Hannah put it. The room was so very warm and inviting, a level of comfort that little Ben had not had the fortune to enjoy in his life. He'd slept so soundly that night and had woken up well after mid morning to the sound of birds singing and the countryside living. It was such a difference to the sounds of the old block of flats with the screaming and shouting over the noise of babies crying and the regular sounds of sirens. For the first time he woke feeling totally refreshed and despite the aching pain he felt whenever he thought of home and his mum and dad, there was a more insistent feeling deep within himself, that of pure contentment. He felt he could be quite happy there.

"Come on young un, it'll get cold unless you get stuck in". Hannah had made him a huge fry-up for breakfast. Three eggs, two slices of bacon, a couple of large sausages, fried tomatoes, beans and toast, plus a huge pot of tea. It had been the first time he had ever had such a sumptuous meal first thing in the morning, and he quickly devoured every morsel. "My you really do like your food don't you? Arthur reckons you need feeding up a little. Says your under-nourished and has told me to look after you." Ben found that a little confusing as all of the night before he had hardly seen Arthur after the initial meeting and certainly wasn't aware of any talk between him and Hannah, but it wasn't important and all Ben could do was to enjoy the attention he was receiving. In fact it soon fell into a regular routine and a comfortable way of living for young Ben. Over the next few days Ben found himself becoming more and more at ease with the two of them and at times even tried to engage Hannah in conversation. It wasn't easy as she did tend to ramble on at times about nothing in particular, but as she was insistent in taking care of him, it made no odds to him. He tried once to talk to Arthur, but received such a disdainful look that he chose never to try again. As long as he kept out of his way, then he felt that life at the farmhouse would be a breeze. After a while he even stopped the constant missing of his mum and dad and Dale, although occasionally at night, before he went to sleep, he thought of them and wondered how they were, and whether they were missing him. He wondered too whether the police had begun searching, or had they just assumed that he had disappeared? With no television in the building, and radio always tuned into an old station that played nothing but ballads from the war, he hardly ever got the opportunity of finding out. After a while though, it stopped bothering him. His days were planned and he was happy with his life. Each morning after the huge breakfast he was begin his daily chores, sweeping out the fire grate and then replacing the old wood and coal with new. Checking on the hens that ran amock in the garden. Occasionally brushing down the large and rather temperamental shire horse in the stables and generally helping

Hannah around the kitchen. It was a simple life but one that Ben fell into with ease. He started to enjoy himself and even began to look forward to the daily game of 'scrabble' in the afternoon whilst devouring more jam and bread with the familiar huge pot of tea. He couldn't be happier....

*        *        *

"I understand how difficult this is Mrs Fuller, but we do need to ask you some more questions". Sergeant West looked sympathetically at the poor woman sobbing in front of her. She had only ever attended one other missing-child interview before when she was a rookie cop many years ago and had always dreaded having to go to one again, but her partner had specifically asked for her attendance, so there was no choice.

"I just want him back. Please will you find him!" Mary was slumped on the floor of the scruffy flat, a picture of despair, whilst her partner was stood at the window staring out at nothing in particular. They had both taken Ben's disappearance badly, proving that no matter what the circumstances, a parent's love of their children is still as strong as any emotion. For Mary it had been a private hell and torture as she had over and again relived the moment she had rushed Ben on to the bus and waved him goodbye. She was a poor mother and now she had been punished for her lack of care by having her first born disappear into nowhere. There had been no sightings since the poor boy had runaway from the bus. The police had issued a country-wide alert and had posted his picture on as many outlets as possible, including a brief slot on the local 'crime-busting' TV programme. The family who had encountered Ben had been interviewed by all of the media, all of them seemingly enjoying their short-lasted moment of fame. Yes they had spoken to the boy, but no they denied shouting at him. In fact didn't they ask him if he wanted a drink as they felt sorry for him travelling all that way on a bus alone? Shame on the mother for letting him go all that distance without any company. What kind of parent would do such a thing? They were certainly NOT to blame and they would do anything at all if they could turn the clock back and stop him from running away. They were so concerned that they had promised to pay at least a small percentage of their exclusive fee that had been paid by the local newspaper to any charity to look after such unfortunate children as that Ben. Unfortunately they hadn't come across such a charity. So what could they do?

This only added to Mary's overwhelming feeling of shame and guilt. She had abandoned her child and had been pilloried by all of society for it. Well all of the local community, who belying the belief that the poor all stick together in moments of crisis, had all without exception roundly turned on the family. Names were called, stones thrown at the windows and poor Dale had been kept away from school as the other children had taunted him about his older brother being washed up on the beach with a knife in his back. The only one who seemed to be unaffected outwardly was Chippy. He had kept calm and had stood by his wife, but deep down he was a mental wreck and had convinced himself very early on that poor Ben had come to a bad end. He watched with a feeling of helplessness as Mary, the true love of his life, had very quickly fallen to pieces. She didn't have the strength, either mentally or physically, to cope with such a crisis and had completely dissolved. There was nothing he felt he could do to save her.

"Mrs Fuller? Is there anyone else who you may think Ben could have contacted? Anyone, like a relative or possibly a friend?"

"There's no-one". The words were hardly audible as Mary whispered in between sobs. She had cried constantly for three days and now had no energy to even speak. "No-one that I know of."

The two officers looked at each other. PC Henrose had expected such a thing all those weeks ago, but it was never a comfortable experience being proved right in moments like this. "I don't think there is a great deal else we can do here". Angela West agreed with a silent nod of her head and crouched down to the slumped figure of Mary.

"Mary…", the first name felt more appropriate at this time. "…we are doing everything we can. I promise you that most of the time these things have a happy ending. As soon as we come across any snippet of information, then you will be the first to hear." She reached out and touched Mary's arm in a gentle and caring gesture. Mary looked straight into her eyes, her face a picture of utter despair. Eyes blotchy with a lack of sleep and constant crying. "She focussed on the lady in the uniform looking down at her. "Just find him… please. That is all I ask…please just find him".

Angela West got up and turned away, but not before she shot Chippy a quick concerned glance. He looked down at his wife, then stared at the two officers in turn before turning his back once more, lost in his thoughts as he stared straight ahead out of the window at the gloomy skies above. Days like these……

"What do you think then?", Angela West asked her colleague immediately they were out of the building and out of earshot.

"About the boy, or about the parents?" It was an open question and one that didn't really have an answer.

"Both"

"My feeling is that the parents are genuine. I've been coming here on and off for the past five years or so, and although they don't look or act like middle-class surburbia, they care for their kids." He noticed PC West throw him a questioning look. "In the only way they know how. It may not be from the perfect-parent handbook, but I've never known them ever to hurt either Ben or Dale"

"And Ben?"

"To be honest," he thought briefly before going on, aware that he could be accused of an unprofessional snap judgement. "I think he's gone"

"Really?" His colleague stopped and turned to look at him as they reached their squad car. "Why, it's not been that long and here may not be any leads but you know these things clear themselves up more often than not"

"I don't know Angela" It was unusual for him to use his partner's first name whilst on duty. "I just sense something. I just sense that he's gone".

PC West looked deep into Jim's eyes. "I think you're wrong." She hesitated a little. "No, I hope you're wrong".

Jim Henrose opened the door and heaved his large frame behind the steering wheel and waited for Angela West to join him in the passenger seat. He turned and looked at her, only now noticing the heavy blue eyes that his working partner had. She looked concerned, more than she had shown when in the flat. "So do I".

# Chapter Eighteen

"So you see Mister Patrick, it really is a quite impressive package we can offer you." Tom Bolton beamed brightly at his client sat opposite him. He felt that his pitch had gone well, and that Frank Patrick, an older man who was probably a little brighter than he looked, was quite keen. Certainly his partner seemed interested and if there was going to be a debate he could imagine that she would be the one who would make the final decision. "With the initial five per cent reduction and the three year guarantee, plus the fixed interest rate, you would find it difficult to match this policy anywhere in the capital, although you are of course free to try". He smiled at both of them in turn. Frank continued to read the sheet of paper in his hand, trying to understand every minute detail, whilst Sara had seemingly made up her own mind. "I think it looks good Frank. Why don't we sign and then it's sorted."

Frank grunted and continued to read, his eyes not wavering from the sheet for a second.

"I think your husband will see that it is a very generous offer". Sara looked at Tom with a look that suggested he had over-stepped the mark. He decided not to say anymore for fear of losing the sale, a very lucrative deal that could earn his normal monthly commission in just a day. "Let me get you both another cup of coffee whilst you talk between yourselves." He got up and left the two of them alone.

"This is a little boring Frank you know. Isn't it just straightforward?"

"These things take time. You can't just rush into any old insurance policy. Especially with the number of places I'm looking after." He tried to hide his slight irritation. He had readily fallen in love with Sara, but her child-like nature had at times become rather tiresome. For not the first time today, he'd wondered at the wisdom of bringing her to the meeting. Maybe he should just have allowed her to go shopping as she had initially suggested, especially as there wasn't the added burden of looking after Verity who was with the new au-pair that Sara had hired last week. That was the problem though, he was finding all of this additional expense concerning and had spent most of the previous evening studying his rapidly dwindling bank balance. The deal that had been struck all those weeks ago had at first seemed entirely satisfactory, but he now had serious doubts as to whether it was all worth it. After all, there appeared to be little chance of actually getting Sara into bed again in the near future, and so in his own mind it was a far better situation when he called once a week for her to pay her rental arrears in the usual way. These things continued to bother him.

"I am so bored, I'm off to look at the shops"

"No!". The severity of the tone surprised her and made her sit upright, staring intently at him. "This won't take too long".

"Ok", she felt a little unnerved, "I'll wait".

Frank kept on studying the papers until Tom Bolton returned with two cups of coffee. "Any thoughts?"

"I'm not sure about a couple of the clauses in paragraph three. I think I would like to take them away and look at them in my own time." Inwardly Tom groaned, but like the good salesman he was, he didn't let his frustration show. "That's fine, keep these copies for as long as you need them. Look are you both in town this evening?" Frank looked at him quizzically. "Yes, in fact we're staying at the Savoy on the Strand. We were going to take in a show later, but haven't decided which one yet".

"Well I have an idea, if you are both agreeable". He looked from one to the other. "I know a charming little Italian restaurant just off

Leicester Square. I have to work late with my secretary this evening, and maybe we could all meet up at around eight for dinner? On the house of course.."

"That would be wonderful". It was Sara who answered of course. "What do you think Frank? It would save having to book tickets and then walking the streets looking for somewhere decent to eat". Frank just nodded. He wasn't overwhelmed with enthusiasm at the idea of spending the evening with Tom Bolton, but at least it would be free.

"Good, we'll do it then. I assume your secretary will be joining us? I'm sorry I don't even know her name"

"Yes of course, Janet, yes I will see to it that she comes along". Tom beamed at them both. "Shall we meet at the hotel at seven thirty?"

\*              \*              \*

It was perfect, thought Tom. He could now call Caroline and tell her, truthfully, that he would be engaged with a very important client and wouldn't be able to get home this evening. She wouldn't be happy, but if he put on his sincere, apologetic tone and promised to make it up to her at a later date, what could she do? Then he and Janet can have a lovely meal, hopefully win a new client, and then go back to her flat and make love all night. He felt very pleased with himself as he walked back to his office after showing Mr and Mrs Patrick to the reception area. It was obvious that she had suspected something when he had mentioned Janet, but what the hell. They were hardly the most matched couple were they?

Later when he told Janet, she radiated with happiness. The idea of spending the whole night together made her dance like a butterfly inwardly, although she did try to show a certain amount of reserve when discussing the plans later. "Maybe you should start leaving some of your clothes and things at my place…just in case you need to stay again", she said whilst snuggling up to him in a quiet part of the office, unseen by anyone else. " Maybe I should. You never know when these kinds of emergencies are likely to happen again". They both giggled at the absurdity of it all.

Of course the conversation with Caroline wasn't anywhere near as easy. "But you can't just not come home. You never stay out after work". She sounded like a petulant child, which made Tom dislike her even more than he had over these past few weeks. Since getting together with Janet, he had seen his once-glorious wife in a completely different light. In fact, he had mused, if it weren't for the children, then who knows what would happen. "It is only for one day and I'll be back tomorrow night. The cottage is safe and it will be nice for you to spend some time alone tonight."

"But I don't want to spend time alone. I want you with me, my husband. What is wrong with that?"

"Don't be melodramatic darling", he tried to hide his irritation in his voice. "Promise I will make it up to you tomorrow".

"What is so important about this client then that he has to get special treatment?"

"It's not that he is special, it's just that he is only in London for another day and I'm really keen on getting his signature. It's a very big commission and could help toward our holiday costs. I'm only doing it for us darling...promise".

The phone went quiet for a while and he could just about hear Caroline breathing. Eventually she spoke. "Ok then, but only for tonight."

"I promise"

"I'll miss you"

"I'll miss you too darling". With that he put the down. His hands were clammy and rather shaky. He hadn't really lied to his wife before and it wasn't something that came easily or naturally to him. Whatever though, he could now concentrate on a lovely evening ahead. It was only a few minutes afterwards that he realised that he hadn't mentioned the children and he felt briefly guilty. It didn't last and he made a mental promise to himself to buy them both a present tomorrow to make up for his absence.

Meanwhile Caroline had put the phone down and stormed into the kitchen. There she stood at the window and stared deep into the dark forest. She could feel her anger rising, her blood boiling as she imagined the worst case scenario. She knew he was lying. She knew he was with someone else, and she knew she wouldn't let him, or her, get away with it. As she grasped the stainless steel rim of the sink so hard that her fingertips bruised, she formulated another plan.

In the forest, the fallow deer again looked toward the cottage. It had done this too many times recently and had become more and more aware of the presence therein. It was a place to be avoided. Above the sky darkened once more and the birds stopped their singing. Days like these were about to happen again......

*       *       *

At seven-thirty prompt Tom and Janet appeared in the foyer of the Savoy arm in arm like two people hopelessly in love, which they had both found themselves falling despite their best intentions. They had hurriedly changed after a passionate early evening at Janet's flat and were now looking forward to a relaxed night with the Patricks'. Janet had worn her favourite dress, a black off the shoulder satin combination with high heels that gave her a sensual look that belied her every-day appearance. Tom had chosen the rather predictable dark grey suit, but with an open top blue shirt that made him look a lot younger than he actually was. They went to the bar and ordered drinks and waited for the arrival of Mr and Mrs Patrick. Presently they arrived, he looking the now sophisticated gent that he had been transformed into, all tweed and cravat, while she looked like a million pounds had been spent on her. Swingingly fashionable with a low cut, full length flowered dress that had obviously come from the most expensive department store, complimented by an array of expensive jewellery bedecked around her neck, wrists and ankles. It was a stunning effect and one which almost immediately made Janet feel under-dressed. This was 'new-money' gone to bad, was her initial inner reaction, perfectly confirmed when Sara started to speak. It wasn't the accent or what she said, but how she said it. This was a woman who had found herself a good thing, namely Frank Patrick, and wasn't prepared to let go of it.

Pleasantries were exchanged and after a swift drink they were soon in a black cab and heading toward the "charming little Italian restaurant" just a mile away. Both Janet and Sara, aware of each other like only two women can be, attempted to start up a conversation knowing that their men had business to deal with for the evening.

"You have children Sara?"

"Only one, but she's back home with the au-pair". It was said in an almost condescending way, something which Janet was aware of but actually keen to ignore. "You have none?". It wasn't a question, but a statement that was unwelcome in its honesty and one that only served to pry rather than enquire naturally. "No, I don't".

Sara responded with a faint smile and said nothing more. In the darkness of the taxi Janet couldn't tell whether Sara was smirking or not, as she only caught a momentarily glimpse as a streetlamp briefly lit up her face. It was obvious to her that they were not destined to become friends.

The restaurant was everything it had promised to be, especially charming. They were seated in an alcove near the frosted-glass window that looked out onto the bustle of Leicester Square, Tom and Sara facing each other with Frank opposite Janet as courtesy dictates. This gave Tom the chance of attempting to charm Mrs Patrick, knowing that in most marriages it was the wife who controlled the purse strings. It also gave Janet the chance to talk to Mr Patrick, a two pronged attack almost which would hopefully reap the rewards later.

They ordered, all starting with soup to be followed by the main course of pasta and seafood, complimented by two bottles of very expensive chianti. They initially sat in silence preferring to enjoy the coriander soup, only occasionally interrupted by a complimentary remark concerning the general relaxed ambience of their surroundings. Sara especially felt slightly uncomfortable and was always a few seconds behind the others as she surreptiscously checked before picking up the correct spoon. She found herself secretly quite impressed at the way Frank had fallen into the other's company and had shown no signs of ill-ease. Even the way he ate his soup, with the plate angled away from him, was a sign that he'd had a better upbringing than most, something which secretly she had begun to admire about him.

The evening was naturally being paid for by Tom's expense account, and he was quite keen to impress his clients. He had began small-talk with Mrs Bolton and had noticed how little she seemed to know about her husband. Nothing too important but certainly enough to give him the distinct impression that all wasn't as seemed

initially. At one stage he'd started to feel slightly uneasy about the whole affair, especially as the two of them also seemed so mis-matched.

"So Sara, do you get involved in the business at all?"., as he expertly spooned the pasta. "Oh no", she replied dismissively, "it has nothing to do with me. Isn't that right Frank?"

"That's right. My business and no-one elses" It was clear by the tone of the answer that this was a point of conversation that was not to be followed. Tom smiled weakly at Frank and concentrated on his meal. Yes there was something unusual about their relationship, something which Janet had also become aware of, but as far as Tom was concerned he should let it lie and not get too involved. As long as the contract for insurance cover was agreed and signed, then that was all that really mattered, but maybe this was going to be a lot harder than he expected.

Outside a lone figure stood in the doorway opposite, hiding from the unpredictable rain and the possibility of being seen. Caroline stood and stared intently at the brightly-lit restaurant, and through the frosted glass she could make out the unmistakeable figure of her husband sat opposite a young lady, clearly engrossed by everything she had to say. His body language gave away the fact that he was enjoying every moment of her company, and at one point she saw him lean forward in his seat and pour from a bottle of what she assumed was wine into her glass. She stood there transfixed with a mixture of horror and despair. She felt her body stiffen with anger and her throat tighten as she saw the two of them together. It had been what she had expected, but the confirmation just made it worse and her whole being cried out with anguish. She felt herself shrink deeper into the doorway, the darkness almost suffocating her. At one point a group of young men, on the final leg of a very drunken evening, saw her as they staggered by and offered a variety of verbal suggestions, none of which were particularly complimentary. They didn't linger long though after Caroline had pierced them with an icy stare. A very quick departure and leave her alone, was the order of the day. She looked like bad news and certainly not worth pursuing.

For Caroline, the sense of betrayal was immense. The love of her life, the only person who had ever meant anything to her, her husband, the father of her two children, the man she had invested so much emotion into, was now with another. It was too much, and the temptation to march into the restaurant was almost too great, but there was an inner sense of discipline that stopped her. It cried out to her in dark moments, telling her that there was a greater purpose and that her time would come soon. She knew what she had to do. The mind's photograph of the woman would stay with her, so much so that she would recognise her at any time and at any place. This woman would not continue like this. Caroline had a plan, one that would have a devastating effect on the woman who shared the table with her husband. Time would prove her right and soon her beloved husband would come running back to her. The woman in the window laughed loudly, not that Caroline could hear it, but she could tell. She was laughing at a joke told by her husband, a moment of brevity shared by the two. A moment that should have been shared by her and Tom. The anger pulsed deep within her. She felt more than betrayal, she felt humiliated. This woman, from what she could see through the less than transparent window, was not as attractive as she. There was nothing she could offer Tom that she couldn't. There would be nothing she would ever be able to offer again.

Caroline stood and watched for over an hour and gradually the anger and resentment was replaced by the clinical intensity that she harboured deep within her mind. As she stood and stared, never taking her eyes away for a moment, she acted out her plan in her mind's eye. It wouldn't take long. This woman would be of no concern soon, especially to her husband. He'll see, she thought, he'll see.........

With that, she walked away and to her car parked on a double yellow line. The parking ticket on the windscreen was ripped away and cast to the ground, as she got in and raced away in a trail of wheel-spin. With a bit of luck she would be home before either of the children had woken up.

# CHAPTER NINETEEN

Lorraine stared at the mirror and tears that hadn't stopped falling, welled up once more. The face that looked back at her was now unrecognisable. The right eye was now partially closed and had turned completely red, with heavy bruising around the eyelid and traces of blood. Her upper lip was swollen and the bite mark on her left cheek was raw and open. Her earlier groomed hair now hung down in clumps and was tender where parts of it had been torn out at the roots. As she slowly and gently removed her tattered jumper, she winced with the pain. There were bite marks all around her breasts. Her chest ached with the thudding pain where she had been repeatedly thumped and her stomach felt as if a knife was slowly turning around inside. None of that was like the intense pain she felt further down. What had happened to her was unlike anything she had heard of before. She had screamed for mercy but had been ignored, and each time she had begged it had made the punishment even worse, almost as if it had been some perverted sexual game. How could she do it? How could one woman do this to another, and why did she allow herself to be betrayed like this? She felt utterly worthless. The humiliation she had endured would stay with her forever and she felt she would never be able to show her face ever again. There was no anger, just utter revulsion. The demons that drove the woman on were too much for her to bear. There was nothing she could now do. She couldn't go to the police. The embarrassment would be too much, followed by the disbelief and then the sniggering remarks which would inevitably follow about lesbian-lovers. Once the newspapers got hold of the story she would become a freak show. It was never meant to be this way, and after she had really believed, even if only for a moment, that Caroline had become her friend. She wished she could turn the clock back just a few hours before she opened the door and let her inside. As she had left she had turned to Lorraine and sneered "Hope you enjoyed that, because I did. If you are lucky I might come back again. That would be nice wouldn't it?". Lorraine wanted to scream at her, but her mouth was too full of blood and she could only feel like heaving with her own vomit. For hours afterwards she lay on the living room floor unable to move due to the pain, until it became too cold. Only then when she looked in the mirror did she fully comprehend what had happened........

The tablets would work soon. She knew if she took enough they would have an effect. She lay down on the bed and for the first time the pain eased. Closing her eyes she allowed herself to drift away. Thoughts and memories came flooding back. Her mother smiling as they walked through the field to the market hand in hand. The first day at school and the welcome the headmistress gave them all in assembly. Her first kiss with Jason, all wet and sticky. The first time she lay with David. The night they sat on the beach and discussed the future, the sand between their toes and the sea-air lightening their senses. All these thoughts and dreams invaded her once more. The tablets will work soon, she thought. They did, and soon there was nothing but blackness.

# CHAPTER TWENTY

*"There's something strange about that relationship don't you think?"*

*"......and there's nothing odd about ours then?" Janet threw him a mischievous glance. They were back in her flat, the lights out and the room only lit by the moonlight, casting deepening shadows across the floor. Tom lay on the bed, naked except for his boxer shorts, while Janet slowly undressed. "Well, yes you're probably right...but even so, they were odd".*

"Does it matter?", she climbed onto the bed and top of him relishing the strong arms encircling and wrapping themselves around her. "You got what you wanted. They signed the contract which makes for a pretty good night's work eh?". He smiled and pulled her towards him, kissing her deeply and passionately. When they pulled apart he looked at her glowing face and caressed it. "I couldn't have done it without you". She closed her eyes and felt the strong fingers trace her eyes, cheek and finally lips. She leant down and kissed his neck..."and don't you ever forget it".

*           *           *

"I know there was someone watching. Each time I looked out of the window I could see them. I think it was a woman, but just couldn't tell. What do you think, a spurned lover, or maybe even his wife? They didn't look married did they? Far too much in love with each other to be married".

Frank just carried on staring out of the window and took another slug of the very expensive brandy whilst Sara continued her talking and readying herself for bed. He felt tired, not a physical tiredness but mentally and emotionally. The past few weeks had been wearing, not least on his bank balance, and he was now becoming a little sick of the lifestyle that his 'partner' had effectively forced on him. All this money and so far little to show for it. He was better when he used to go to her flat and let off her rent. It was easier that way. It may not be the end of the agreement in terms of time, but as far as he was concerned, it was most definitely the end of the contract. Tonight he had been distracted and had agreed to take on the insurance cover more out of necessity than anything else. He just wanted to get away from that awful restaurant and the awful Tom and his bit-of-stuff Janet. Of course they weren't married, anyone could see that, now all he could hear was Sara chattering on about it. He turned and watched her as she stepped out of her dress, revealing matching underwear, the kind that always appealed to him. Skimpy black knickers that showed more than they hid, and black bra that held every curve. As he looked he felt the familiar stirring and yearning and decided, almost subconsciously, that tonight he would demand payback. He got up and walked towards her as she turned and sat down to remove the make-up from her face. She saw him in the mirror approach and knew instantly what was about to happen. Closing her eyes she refused to allow the revulsion build, feeling the hand lay itself on her shoulder. It was payback time.

\*            \*            \*

She couldn't remember how she had got back so quickly, but in no time at all Caroline was approaching the cottage, the headlights catching a glimpse of the front door and briefly lighting the downstairs window as she turned the corner into the drive. The journey had been a blur and at one time she was convinced she had almost doubled the speed limit on the motorway. Even if a patrol car had spotted her, he would have had a difficult time catching her. On the way she had played the scene over and over again in her mind, bristling with every repeat image of Tom and that woman laughing and joking together. She imagined what they had got up to afterwards and where they were. Was he caressing her the way he used to with me? What was she doing to him, the slut? She would pay for every touch and kiss and pout and smile that she gave him. Tenfold, a thousand fold, even more. The only thing that stopped her from following them from the restaurant were the children on their own, and if one woke up and found the place was empty, all hell would break loose. The police would be called, social services would get involved, oh and it would be so difficult to explain where she was. So damn frustrating. Even Lorraine couldn't help her anymore. Bloody woman sobbing and snivelling on the floor this afternoon. What was wrong with her? On the way back she had passed her cottage and it was in darkness. Shame because she quite fancied going back and showing her that it was only a game. They both would have enjoyed that and then Lorraine could have been the friend again and looked after the children, but no it wasn't to be. She'd obviously gone out and was enjoying herself. At least Caroline had brought her out of herself. She never used to go out before they had become friends. I bet she's out now and telling everyone what a wonderful afternoon she'd had. Bloody woman.

The cottage was quiet. The kids were still asleep. She had got away with it. Sitting down in the darkness of the sitting-room she opened a bottle of brandy and poured a huge glass, downing half of it in one. It burnt her throat and she allowed it to slide harshly down into her stomach and then she filled the glass to the brim and sat and thought and thought. The plan was becoming clearer and was taking a form of its own. No-one would take her husband away from her, especially a made-up little tart like that. She closed her eyes and saw her in her mind's eye and then she allowed herself to fantasise about the punishment she would exact. It stirred her and she smiled. Outside an owl screeched as it swooped down toward a field mouse, out in the open far too late and far too vulnerable. The mouse struggled for its life but in vain as the owl flew majestically into the night. A collective shudder swept through the forest as the creatures all felt the surge that had overcome them. Many had seen and felt it before. The newcomers shrank back in terror, and not a one of them dare approach the cottage. Days like these were happening again......

# CHAPTER TWENTY-ONE

"So just take your time. Say what you have to say and then I'll look at it and if it needs changing, the words like, then I can do it for you". Hannah opened up the red-leather bound writing pad and placed it on the dresser adding a fine gold ink-cartridge pen next to it. She looked at Ben's face, a picture of anguish and confusion. "You know you will have to contact them, and this is the only way really"

"But I don't know what to say. They may get angry"

"They're your parents. They'll understand". Her tone was warm, soft and comforting and put him at ease. She turned on the cabinet lamp, which cast shadows over the room and patted his shoulder. "Take as long as you need. I'll be downstairs making bread. I'll bring some up later for you and you can show me what you have written."

Ben smiled and turned to look at the blank piece of paper in front of him and thought. As Hannah left the room he closed his eyes and visualised his mum and dad and little Dale. Tears welled briefly and an overwhelming sense of guilt surged within him. That was the cue for him to put pen to paper.

*Dear mum, dad and dale,*
*I know I should have been in touch a long time ago, but I was scared about the bus and the horrible family. I didn't want to get in trouble with the police and Hannah said that if they came then they would take me away and put me in care. Anyway how are you all. Hope dale is good and not missing me and mum you haven't been crying a lot. I am ok*

*here in the farm and really enjoying myself. I miss you all a lot at times and sometimes cry at night when I go to bed, but I think you would be pleased if you saw where I was living. My room is huge and really comfy and Hannah and Arthur are really nice, especially Hannah. Tell dale that I will come and see him again soon and if all the others are beating him at school then I will come and sort them and they wont bother him again.*

*Miss you mum. Miss you dad. Miss you dale. Bye for now*

*Ben x*

When Hannah returned around three hours later she found Ben asleep on the bed gently snoring. Quietly she put down the plate of hot bread and jam and a newly-brewed cup of tea and then picked up the letter that Ben had spent so long working on. She quickly read it and allowed herself a little chuckle. Folding up the paper she put it into her apron pocket and quietly left the room and returned downstairs to the kitchen.

# CHAPTER TWENTY-TWO

Sara woke the next morning with a warm and insistent glow deep inside. Stretching her arms and body she luxuriated in the warmth of the comforting duvet. The morning light was breaking through the chink in the curtains, illuminating the room in soft and welcoming shadow. Lying there, staring at the ceiling, her mind wandered back to the night before and the passion that she had embraced completely. Her intensity had surprised even herself, and was totally unexpected, not least to Frank. She smiled as she thought of him and the caring and gentle way he had made love to her. So unlike those days when it had been an act of necessity and had been as passionless and cold as any she had experienced with the hundreds of men who had paid for her favours. There was something that he had touched within her, something that had become more than just a physical need, but something that had caressed her inner being. Was it possible she could actually love this man? For so long she had looked upon him as a means to an end, a pay day that would continue for as long as she continued to play the game. He had taken care of her and Verity. He had pandered to her every need and had never complained, and yet all of the time she had taken him for granted, knowing that she always had the upper hand. Now she felt a deep longing for this man and a belief that maybe he could be the man she had hoped that Elio would be, or the father that Elio should have been. It made her heart jump a little when she thought of the future and what could be. One night of deep and intense love-making had made her realise how deeply she felt for him, and as she crawled out of the warmth of the bed she promised herself that she would share those thoughts and feelings with him when he returned from his early-morning stroll. She smiled to herself when she remembered the way he leant down and kissed her cheek gently as he silently got out of the bed and left the room. He had always been an early riser and had every day since she had known him, got up and taken a stroll as the morning began. She had almost reached out to him as he left, but had stopped herself instinctively. Now she wished she had. Walking toward the bathroom she skipped gently like any other woman who had fallen in love. Her mind filled with a thousand thoughts all at the same time. She thought of Verity and herself, and Verity and Frank, and Verity, herself and Frank. The three of them and everything that they could do together. The future they could have. She determined that she would no longer depend on him entirely and would maybe get herself a part-time job, but not something that would take up too much of her time. She had Verity to look after still, but also now she had to think of Frank. He was another part of her life now and she was willing to embrace it entirely. It made her happy, so wonderfully happy that she almost felt tears well in her eyes, and she had a yearning to open the window and shout at the top of her voice, telling the whole world how happy she was. It made her giggle, and as she allowed the memories of last night to re-invade her mind, it made her want him to return quickly.

The knock on the door abruptly interrupted her thoughts. "Hang on", she shouted to no-one in particular. "Just putting on my dressing-gown". A voice replied from the other side, but she couldn't distinguish the tone or the gender as the door was very sturdy and heavy like most in top-class hotels. As she returned to the bed and wrapped herself in the silk gown that Frank had bought her she had a fleeting feeling that maybe this was the porter bearing a gift of flowers for her from her lover Frank. "Coming…", as she almost ran to open the door, "…sorry, but I've only just got out of bed", as she pulled the door open allowing a gust of wind to enter the suite from the cold and uninviting corridor.

The first slash caught her across the right side of her neck. At first there was no feeling, just horror as the glint of the blade temporarily blinded her. Then she felt the pain sear deep inside and the warm trickle of blood seep down onto her silk dressing gown. As Sara staggered back she saw the machete rise again and in an instant cut deep into her neck once more. She couldn't scream, she couldn't stop it. She looked at the face behind the steel blade and didn't recognise the crazed features. The voice that screamed the foul words and expletives that followed the third cut was not known to her. She fell with a thud onto the bedroom floor, her blood quickly staining the cream matted carpet that covered the whole room. For a brief and almost incomprehensible moment she worried about the mess she was making as she felt the blood rush from her wounds, but as the machete ripped into her skin once more, the thoughts were quickly replaced by the sadness she felt for Verity. There was nothing she could do to stop the attack now, as the machete was wielded again and again on her fragile and unprotected body. As each cut opened a new wound she felt herself slip away and with it the life she had always imagined, watching her daughter grow up into the girl and then woman that each and every parent wished for their offspring. The arms that had at first instinctively tried to protect herself, were now flailing as each nerve was cut with each slash of the razor sharp blade. The pain was now being replaced by a numbness as she felt herself drift away. The machete kept on coming, the voice kept on shouting and she wondered how on earth all of this commotion could not be heard by anyone else in the hotel. Soon those thoughts disappeared, and in fact all thoughts disappeared from her mind as she fell deeply into the abyss. At some time the frenzied attack came to an end, but by that point Sara was no longer aware. It was over as quickly as it had begun, and for Sara there was nothing left.

At the end of the long corridor, Pamela Martin was pushing her mountain of clean towels and sheets very slowly on the unwieldy trolley that had been the irritation of her entire working life. As she tried to manoeuvre it into a straight line she heard a shout from the distance. A woman's voice raised in anger clearly upset with someone. At first she took notice. Too many guests treated this hotel badly nowadays. They seem to think that because they pay a lot of money to stay here, they can just behave in any way they want. There was no longer any respect left and Pamela had been witness to it too many times for it to bother her anymore. This was different though. The woman was shouting the most obscene things, filthy words that made her cringe. It just wasn't right. Looking down the corridor from where the noise came from, she could see a silhouetted figure against the sunlight making a pointing motion as if they were telling off a small child. This was no child she was talking to though. No-one could talk to a child like that and in that tone. "Do you mind please", shouted Pamela to the figure. It worked as the person turned to look back to where Pamela stood and then immediately fled down the opposite way. Honestly, she thought, these people are just awful. She left her wayward trolley and walked to the open door to see who was the victim of the foul abuse. As she approached she saw the blood stained machete lying abandoned on the floor and a cold sweat crept over her whole being. For a moment she stopped and stared at the red and silver blade, not daring to go any further. When she finally built up enough courage to look into the open doorway she wished deep down that she hadn't. The image would stay with her for the rest of her life, not that she was thinking anything like that at that moment. It was all she could do to stop herself from vomiting. For a while she succeeded, but it only lasted a few seconds. She was physically sick there and then on the corridor floor as the blood stained body of Sara Palazzo lay motionless against the cream matted carpet.

*          *          *

Tom manouvered his Jaguar around the two police cars slowly, trying not to obviously stare beyond the cordon that stretched around the cottage. A lone uniformed officer stood at the side of the road and gestured for him to drive on. His face was stern and suggested

119

that whatever was inside the cottage, it wasn't pleasant. Tom wanted to stop and get out and ask the officer what had happened, but a look at the number of reporters and television crews assembled nearby meant that he wouldn't have to wait long to find out. As he accelerated gently away he tried to remember who lived there. A young woman on her own if he recollected correctly. Not sure of her name but thought that she was an acquaintance of Caroline. From the school maybe? He hoped nothing had happened to her, but that seemed unlikely judging from the number of police cars there that still had there blue lights flashing despite being stationary. Down the path, just a few hundred yards from the commotion, he spotted George Pullen, the landlord of the 'Pig and Whistle'. A portly man, not unsurprising bearing in mind the obvious temptations in being a pub landlord, and again with that demeanour of a man who wonders how on earth he is going to afford to feed another child as Mrs Pullen was expecting for the fourth time. This time his body language had an extra air of despair and worry. Tom pulled up alongside him. "Hi George, what on earth has happened?". Although he wasn't a regular at the pub, he did feel that he could be on first name terms with him. At first George didn't respond, almost as if he hadn't seen or heard Tom, but then turned and looked at him with tears in his eyes.

"It's Lorraine. She's dead. Police reckon it could be suicide. Found with a bottle of pills next to her. Always knew she was unhappy you know, ever since David left her. Didn't think it was this bad though"

"Oh, that's awful". He looked back toward the cottage down the lane, and saw in the distant the flashing light of an ambulance as it pulled up outside. Suddenly he felt very sad. He's hardly spoken to her and yet she only lived a mile or so away. That poor, poor woman. "Did you know her well?" he asked George, who was also staring at the ambulance, his hands pushed deep down into the pockets of his corduroy trousers. "Not really, but it's a sad day when one of our own can lay down and say goodbye to the world, and not a one of us knows anything about it, don't you think?"

"You're right George. It's a sad day". With that he pressed the electronic window button and drove away to his own cottage just around the corner. Now was the time to be kind and considerate to Caroline. She'd lost a friend and needed his understanding and sympathy. The news he was going to break to her could wait for another day.

\*       \*       \*

That night she'd cried herself to sleep wrapped around his body. There had been no love making for once, just a deep need to hold him. She'd been like a vulnerable child and as he stroked her hair and spoke softly, he felt an enormous sense of love for her. A feeling he'd lost some time ago, but had now re-appeared in the strangest of circumstances. For the first time since it had begun, he felt shame over his affair with Janet. Imagining her lying alone in the flat in London, there was pity and sadness, but for the time being he felt the overwhelming urge to love and protect his wife, the woman he had promised to cherish all those years ago. It was a dilemma and one which didn't have an easy answer to.

"You would never leave me would you Tom?". The question was soft but insistent. He didn't answer at first but continued to stroke her hair. In the darkness of the night, lying together in their bed, neither could see the expression of the other. He stared at the ceiling and a myriad of confused images danced before him, heightened by the glimpse of moonlight that pierced the gloom. "No darling", he turned and cupped her face in his hands and leant down to kiss her, "No, I would never leave you". Her face was damp and he realised she had been crying. "You're too special to me". Wiping a tear away from her cheek in the dark he felt her sigh and in a moment her breathing changed. Soon she was asleep in his arms. He closed his eyes in the hope of joining her, but the images of his recent life continued to haunt him. He was in for a restless night.

# CHAPTER TWENTY-THREE

The money looked too tempting. It was just sitting there, so how could he ignore it? Ben had never stolen in his life, even all those days ago when he used to be the lookout for the older boys, but this was too easy. He'd seen it there before but had tried to ignore it. Each Tuesday Hannah left the pile of notes on the sideboard dresser for Arthur to put away and had nearly always immediately forgotten about it. Ben had seen it one day when he was sweeping the living room carpet and had quietly walked toward it, mentally trying to count how much was there. As soon as he had got close though, Arthur had come in and disturbed him, putting the money in his waistcoat pocket and leaving quickly. Ben had no idea what the money was for, but he always felt that it was something that had nothing to do with him, and it would be better if he wasn't to find out. Not that Arthur was likely to tell him anyway, as in the seven weeks or so that Ben had lived with the couple, he still had hardly spoken a word to him. Arthur was as much of a mystery to him now as he ever was.

Yes, the money looked tempting. Hannah was in the bathroom and Arthur was out in the fields and he was alone in the room with the money lying on the dressing room table. Even at his tender age, Ben knew the value of money. He knew what he could do with that amount. He thought of his mum and dad and Dale and how he missed them so much. With that kind of money he could somehow get back to see them, even if he still didn't know exactly where he was at the moment. Yes, Hannah had been good to him and taken care of him, bought him new clothes, fed him well and even tried to teach him things as if he was at school, but Hannah wasn't his mum, and he missed her so much. At night he had often cried as he remembered the flat he shared with them all, and wondered why they hadn't come looking for him. Maybe they had moved somewhere else and forgotten him? It made Ben deeply upset when he thought such things, and although Hannah tried to calm him with soothing words, she couldn't take away the longing he felt for his own family. She would understand wouldn't she? Maybe he could write her a note saying sorry and how one day he would return and pay her back? The more he thought about it, the more tempting it became. Life was getting boring at the farm too. He never went anywhere and everyday was the same. He had to get up far too early, sometimes when it was still dark. Then he had to go through his usual routine of washing the breakfast dishes, sweeping the floors and polishing the windows, and that was before he was allowed to go outside and collect the eggs from the chicken pens. That was his favourite because he could be all alone there and wasn't bothered as that was the time that Hannah always had her afternoon sleep. After that though there was the next round of duties, like stoking the fire, cleaning out the grate afterwards and washing yet more dishes from the evening meal. He did this all alone, as Hannah was nearly always tired, and Arthur was never there apart from at meal times. The money looked very tempting. He stared at it for what seemed an eternity. The farmhouse was quiet. All he could hear, apart from the ticking of the grandfather clock in the hallway and the wind whistling through the trees outside, was his own breathing, and it was becoming faster. He could do it. He could just pocket the money and run away. They would never know. In fact it would be the morning before Hannah would even notice he had gone, and by then he would be far, far away into the night. Where would he go though? It was cold outside and upstairs he had his comfortable and warm bed ready to welcome him. He thought of that and he thought of the money, and he just couldn't decide. Soon it would be too late and Hannah would return from the bathroom and he would be forced to stay a little longer. He looked at the pile of notes once more and wondered......

Out in the fields, Arthur slung his bag over his right shoulder and made his way through the woods back toward the farmhouse. The day was darkening and with the cover of the trees, his movements could never be detected. It was thankful that he knew every square inch of the forest and that he could trace his steps blindfolded if needed be. He was careful to follow his well-worn path so that not even a twig would be disturbed as he carefully tread back toward the clearing and the dim lights of the farm in the distance. The bag was heavy this evening, but the heavier the better as far as he was concerned. It meant it would be worth more maybe even two hundred this time? Catching badgers was not an easy way of making money, but it was certainly lucrative, as had been proved over the last few months. He was aware that he would have to look for another place to set the traps soon, before he was caught out. Even Hannah had implored him to be more careful, not that she knew too much about what he did. Silly woman, he thought to himself, what does she know anyway? It would only be a few more months and he would have enough saved for himself and then he could be off, away from her, the farm and the succession of boys who somehow seem to find themselves living there. How many has it been now? He mentally counted as he left the gloom of the forest into the moonlit open fields, carefully keeping to the hedgerow so as not be spotted by any innocent passer-by. There was Sam back in 78. He disappeared quickly. A sickly boy who spent most of his time crying and snivelling. Then there was that boy a few years ago. Malik his name, or something like that. He was older than the rest, but still a bit stupid for his liking. Took him on one of his badger baits one night, but he obviously didn't appreciate it and spent the next week or so complaining about how cruel it all was. He really was stupid, thought Arthur.

Suddenly he disturbed from his musings as he heard a rustling in the hedgerow a few yards ahead of him. Instinctively Arthur threw himself to the ground and crawled under the hedge, hiding his body as best he could, his dark jacket and trousers helping his camouflage. In an instant he felt the rush of air as a lone figure ran past him, splashing Arthur's face with muddy water from a nearby puddle in their haste to get away. Presently Arthur got up and looked all around him. The figure he didn't recognise and had all but disappeared into the gloom of the night, and as far as he could tell there was no-one in pursuit. Brushing himself down with his hand and wiping the mud off his face with his clean handkerchief, he determined that he would now definitely have to find another place. This was a warning, and as of tomorrow he would start to explore further afield before he was caught. He was a little confused by the figure and where they were heading at this time of night, but no matter, it was best not to worry about it too much.

It was only when he got back to the farmhouse that he realised who it was running through the night and why they were in such a hurry. A quick glance at the sideboard dresser and the emptiness where the money should have been confirmed it. That stupid woman had again left it there unattended and this time it had gone. It didn't take a genius to work out who had taken it too. "HANNAH", he shouted at the top of his voice, "WHERE ARE YOU?". There was no reply, but he heard a rustling upstairs and knew where she was. Well this time she wasn't going to get away with it. He placed the bag down on the kitchen floor and went to the cupboard in the corner. There he took out the walking stick that he needed occasionally when his back played him up on the cold mornings. He'd had it for nearly ten years now and it had always been dependable. Made from sturdy beech wood and carved with his initials at its tip, it felt comfortable in his hand. Over the years it had also had its other uses, like now. Climbing the stairs he heard Hannah start to whimper in the bedroom above. " No use crying. That won't save you tonight you stupid woman." He opened the bedroom door and saw his wife cowering in the far corner, between the bed and the wall. Her face was full of fear. "I'm sorry Arthur. I didn't mean it. I thought he was a good un. I'm sorry Arthur". Her pleading fell on deaf ears as Arthur took his revenge and the blows rained down on Hannah's poor defensive body. She won't ever do this again, thought Arthur.

Ben ran for his life. He hadn't run this quickly since escaping from the bus all those weeks ago, or was it months? He really no longer knew. His life had changed over that time, so much so that he didn't know what day it was, or what month, or was even sure as to what year. The other problem was that he didn't know where he was either. In all the time he had been living at the farmhouse, he had not once left it or its immediate surroundings. He was as much in the dark now as he was when he first arrived. It no longer mattered though, as he ran until his lungs felt like bursting, through wet and damp fields, dark and foreboding forests and up steep and slippy hills. In his back pocket of his jeans he felt the bulge of the notes. He hadn't had time to count them, but he was guessing there must be at least a hundred pounds there, maybe even more. It would be enough to buy a ticket on a bus back to his mum and dad and Dale, if he could find his way away from this living nightmare. All he could do now was to run and run before Hannah and Arthur found out he had gone, and more importantly, had taken their money.

*          *           *          *

As soon as Frank returned to the hotel he knew. It was a sense within that told him that something was wrong, something terribly wrong. Outside there were maybe a dozen police cars and a single ambulance surrounded by a slowly increasing crowd, and as he pushed his way through the enquiring throng and made his way through the foyer, his sense of foreboding grew. Inside porters and chambermaids were either scurrying around aimlessly, not knowing where to go or what to say, or some were just sat in stunned silence, gently being consoled by a comforting hand on the shoulder and offers of sweet, milky tea. In the corner of the vast entrance hall there was one chambermaid, the one he had smiled pleasantly to only yesterday as he walked down the corridor. Today she was slumped on the ground and had been sobbing incessantly, her eyes bloodshot and her face a mask of running black eye shadow. He noticed a slash of red on her white pinafore and it looked like her right hand was covered in blood as if she had cut it quite badly. She was accompanied by a female police officer who was holding her in her arms and whispering quietly. As Frank walked past he caught her eye and the look of horror and distress made his heart sink. He knew something had happened to Sara. At the lift he was stopped by a burly police officer, who quietly but firmly had told him that it was out of bounds due to an 'incident'. When he told him who he was and where he was heading, the police officer had then looked rather shaken, and had immediately looked for a colleague for assistance. Seeing his sergeant a few yards away he had called him over and told him that this was the gentleman who was staying in room 101 with Sara Palazzo. The sergeant had eyed him silently and then had gently led him away to a quiet corner of the foyer along with a female officer who had clearly not been prepared for such a task and looked like she was at any moment ready to burst into tears. He was motioned to sit down and was offered a glass of water but had declined. Moments later he wished he's accepted as he felt the bile rising in his throat. Within seconds he had succumbed to it and had been sick all over the plush carpet, splashes of which had hit the female officer on her legs and covered her left shoe. She didn't mind as the reaction was understandable. Frank had just been told of Sara's death. He sat there struggling to breathe as two more officers, both young females, came over to offer their help. One of them asked if he was alright and was anything they could get for him, while another said she would try and find someone who could make him a strong cup of coffee. Just for an instant Frank saw the irony of it. Weren't they in one of the most expensive hotels in London and she was trying to find him a cup of coffee? The moment passed as the realisation sunk in very quickly. Sara had been murdered in their room. Someone had come up to the floor and murdered her whilst he was out walking the streets no more than a mile away. They had come and murdered Sara, not the man in the room next door, not the old woman who was staying in the room opposite who he had waved to last night, not any of the other five hundred or so guests who were in this hotel, ones who may have been higher up the list for potential murders, businessmen, politicians, sheiks, financiers, criminals. No not them, but his own Sara. His loving and vivacious Sara, the woman who had come into his life and transformed it. It was Sara who had suffered.

He wanted to go up and see her, but they wouldn't let him. He wanted to run out of the hotel and pretend it hadn't happened, but they wouldn't let him. He wanted to know how she had died, but they wouldn't say much except that it hadn't been pleasant and that Mrs Martin, the chambermaid, had made the discovery, and although they realised how dreadfully upset he was, they would have to soon take him down to the police station to ask some routine questions. As he sat and stared blankly ahead with the soft and soothing arms of one of the female officers around him, he saw a bag being wheeled away on a hospital trolley from the elevator. He knew it was Sara and had tried to get up and go to her, but had been firmly stopped and told that it wouldn't do any good, and he wouldn't want to see her in the state she was in, but he would be expected to go to the mortuary later in the day to officially identify the body.

If it was a dream, it was a particularly bad one. A cup of coffee was offered and he took a sip without tasting. It was hot and ran down his throat, but he didn't notice. He kept thinking that something was not right. Surely he'd only walked out of this lobby two hours ago after gently kissing Sara goodbye, telling her he would be back soon. She hadn't replied as she was still sleeping, but he had patted her hair and smoothed back a few strays that were over her eyes and then had quietly crept out. That was only two hours ago and now these people are telling him that she had gone, murdered, and in such a way that he couldn't even see her face as she was being loaded into the ambulance. *This was not happening, he had to wake up.* He didn't wake up though and it had happened. He sat there for what seemed hours, but in fact was only around fifteen minutes and then was told that he would soon be heading to the police station, and that he would have to change his clothes. At first he couldn't understand why, but gradually realised that the police would need to check his clothing for signs of blood and other things that might suggest he'd had a hand in her death. As if he could ever hurt her. He wanted to shout and scream that he would never hurt a hair on her lovely head, but it wouldn't come. He sat in total silence. Only then did he remember Verity. Dear little Verity. What was he to do now? How could he tell her that her mummy was dead? Who would look after her? At that moment he broke down and cried. He cried like he had never cried before. His whole body heaved with the exertion of it all as he sobbed tears of despair. The female police officer caught him as he slumped to the floor and held him close to her body and whispered gently to him. She stroked his head and gestured with her eyes to her colleague to leave them alone for a while, and for the next half an hour Frank let out his whole emotional being as he imagined life without Sara.

# CHAPTER TWENTY-FOUR

The next morning Caroline felt alive. Jumping from her bed as Tom slept peacefully; she said the words out loud as she looked at the plaque glinting in the sunlight above the bed. "Beauty is beautiful when it is looked at in the right way", and with that she leant down and placed a wet kiss on his cheek, not caring if it woke him or not. She skipped down the stairs, knocking on the children's bedroom door as she went to wake them and then gave George a huge kiss on the nose and nuzzled him closely before opening the kitchen door and letting in the morning sunlight. George went bounding out into the garden and gave chase to a couple of rabbits who were quietly munching on the grass and minding their business. Breathing in the cool fresh air, she made a mental note to write something in her diary. She'd felt that today was a special day and one that needed to be remembered. Her handsome and strong husband had made her so very happy. He had told her that he would never hurt her and that was worth so much to her. She couldn't let the day pass without it being marked, and so she composed her ideas in her mind and couldn't wait to have the moment alone when she could write it all down.

The morning was a flurry of the usual excitement and activity with the breakfast making and getting the children ready for school. Adam and Shelley loved it when their mummy was in a good mood like this and laughed and joked and giggled all morning. Tom was also aware of his wife's startling mood change, but he was too engrossed in his own thoughts of guilt and concern to let it concern him. "You will be back at the normal time tonight?". Caroline hugged him as he was about to leave the cottage, feeling his strong body against hers and sensing a glimmer of excitement as she did.

"I shall try", he smiled down at her though not really sure what his feelings were at that moment. "I'll call if anything comes up".

"Be sure you do, otherwise something might not come up later, if you see what I mean", and with that she playfully grabbed him down below making him wince in surprise. She leant up at him with loving and desirous eyes and kissed him full on the lips. "Bye darling".

Her mood stayed that way for most of the morning. She'd taken the children to school and had sung songs to them on the way, waving vigorously as they went in through the gates, and then had returned to the cottage to shower and change. Standing under the hot and incessant spray she'd had erotic thoughts about Tom, but had resisted any temptation and had promised herself she would save any desire until she saw him later on, but first she needed to take a long and strenuous walk through the forest. It was what was needed to cleanse herself.

The forest floor was still damp from the morning dew and the trees gave a darkness that the sun couldn't illuminate at that time of day. Although there were bluebells appearing, the chill of the air gave a wintry hint and meant that spots of ice still clung on to the leaves and blades of grass. The fallow deer were leaping from one spot to another, nervously looking around them for fear of intruders, while the rabbits dashed about, constantly on the move. The woodlark that woke the village each and every morning had now long gone, and at this time in the morning the barn owl was safely seconded in a deep sleep. There was nothing to disturb Caroline and her thoughts. She sat down against a huge maple tree and pulled out of her shoulder bag her diary, briefly taking in the delights of the wild violet that was growing and thriving in the dappled shade of the wood. Out of the corner of her eye she espied a stoat meandering across the grassy ride in the distance, and then enjoyed the sheer majesty and beauty of an orange-tip butterfly that was busy busying itself amongst the scented primrose. None of this mattered any more to her though as she began to write..

Wednesday 26<sup>th</sup> June


*"Could it be that Tom was with someone? If he was then it would never, ever last. His life is mine, and mine is his. He knows that and nothing can change that destiny. The woman I saw him with is no more a challenge than any of the others. She will be, or maybe I should say, has been, dealt with. He will see her no more, of that it is certain. Who could come between such a perfect love as this? Who would want to destroy a passion and desire that is so all-consuming? Who would dare?*

*As I sit here against the old and welcoming tree and its warm and comforting embrace, as I have done so many times down the years, I feel a sense of belonging. I belong to everything around me, so totally and completely, it almost hurts. People like Lorraine could never understand that, silly woman.. ....oh there, goes another of those strange butterflies......"*She got up and in a instance had captured it between the leaves of the book, its fragile wings fluttering in a last act of painful defiance, before flickering to a stop. Caroline wiped away the residue of the crushed insect off the clean, white page and continued writing " *..back again now. I caught it and it is now going to be pressed on this page as a reminder of the moment. Bless it."* ....with that she closed the book firmly, crushing the once beautiful creature between the unforgiving sheets of paper, and got up and made her way back toward the cottage.

Later that day she took the car into town. There was no real reason to go there, except that after driving past Lorraine's cottage and seeing it surrounded still by the police and their wary ways, she felt the need to be in the company of others. For a brief moment she felt a pang of guilt, a feeling of conscience, but it didn't last. It never did. Tom wouldn't be home for hours, and she could make sure she would be back in time to pick up the children, especially as now her 'friend' had deserted her. Parking in the centre, Caroline took a walk along the main High street and made her way to her favourite antiques shop. It was the kind of place that could be found in a thousand towns, the customer welcomed by the familiar musty smell of old furniture and copious amounts of beeswax. The owner, a kindly old man who went by the name of Mr Robinson, had been there for over forty years. He always wore the same tweed jacket, and had down the years had a selection of corduroy trousers that had either been repaired as they had worn, or had been replaced by a pair looking exactly the same. On his nose he wore a pair of reading spectacles, that hadn't changed for about the same amount of time. Mr Robinson's temperament was placid and the type of person who had time for anyone, but as he saw Caroline enter in a haze of expensive jewellery and aromatic perfume, his normal demeanour left him. This was one person he just didn't like. Couldn't understand why, but the sight of this woman was guaranteed to put him on edge.

"Hello", Caroline beamed across to him as she helped the old door close on its hinges. Mr Robinson pretended to be extra busy with some paperwork that had been lying on his oak desk for a number of weeks. His courtesy and politeness hadn't left him completely and he nodded in her direction, a cursory smile falling across his lips. From now on he would watch her like a hawk. "Thought I'd come again and see if there's anything that might take my fancy….".

"You know where everything is….". Mr Robinson, Arthur to his friends, of which she was definitely not one of them, sat himself down in the large wicker chair and adjusting his glasses began to pour over the mounds of paper in front of him. None of it was urgent, except for a moment like this. Caroline, meanwhile, got on with the task of inspecting every item of furniture, and every piece of ornament the shop had. She'd seen nearly all of it before, but there was something she was desperate to find. She had seen it before, but had not gone with her instinct and bought it. Now the desire for it was too overwhelming. The only customer in the shop, it meant she had the opportunity of spending a much time as she wanted there, without any fear of being interrupted. Even the silly old sod who owned the place wouldn't stop her from spending the whole day there should she choose to. At the far end of the shop there was a staircase leading to the basement where some of the older furniture had been stored for years, the kind that people would look at and admire, but would probably never consider buying. Caroline made her way down the stairs, the musty odour becoming quite overpowering. It smelt of years of accumulated dust and un-swept floors, but had a pleasant effect. There was a bright un-shaded light bulb illuminating the room, casting long and dark shadows toward the far corners. Along one side there were a variety of large furniture pieces, chest of drawers, oak-panelled tables, huge mirrors that had been mottled with time and an assortment of the unusual. A table that seem to stand on four elephants that made up the wooden legs. A chess set that must have been a couple of hundred years old, but unfortunately was missing at least a third of its pieces, and bear-skin rug that looked as if it hadn't been swept or cleaned since it was taken off the poor animal in question. Caroline gave them all a cursory glance, as she did the large bookshelf on the opposite wall, packed with hardback novels boasting the names of authors long gone. Most of them hadn't been taken down from the shelves in years, never mind opened to be read. They were all uniform in shape and colour, a darkish blue that had faded with time, with gold braided titles just about visible on the sleeve. If anyone had the time, or the inclination, to take an interest in them, they would surely find a treasure or two, and maybe even a financial windfall from one of the original editions that had been slowly fading away in the unnatural light of the downstairs basement. None of that mattered to Caroline. She was only interested in one artefact, and as her eyes focussed on it, her heart leapt a little. This time she would definitely have it.

\*             \*             \*

"Dead?", her voice trembled slightly as she uttered the horrible word.

"I'm afraid so Mrs Bolton. We can't say for definite until the coroner looks at the body, but we believe it was an overdose of some kind". The young police officer tried to show authority in his voice as he completed the words, but it was a situation he found too hard to deal with, something his years in the academy had never really prepared him for. Standing at the doorway to Caroline's neat and pleasant cottage, he took out his notebook and tried to compose himself. "I know you were a friend of the deceased and I was just wondering if you were at all aware of any problems she may have had recently, something she may have shared with you?". He looked into Caroline's eyes and for a moment he felt like he was floating. They were extraordinarily beautiful, and in fact they mirrored her perfectly, as he found her physical beauty almost too stunning. It was the first thing he had noticed when she had answered the door, a radiance that immediately lit up the dullness of the morning.

"No, I'm not aware of anything really." There was a slight tremor as she spoke and for a moment he noticed her blue eyes watering ever so slightly. "We weren't the best of friends, but she did help with the children. I didn't really see that much of her".

PC Weston shuffled his feet slightly as he took notes. "Your neighbour from the Galloway Cottage said she saw you go to her cottage just three days ago. She said she saw you visit a couple of times. I was just wondering if there was anything then that may have given you the idea that Miss Hempton was upset or saddened about anything? Just a routine question Miss, that's all".

Caroline smiled weakly, *"Bloody nosey cow"*, she thought. *"I will remember her!"*.

"No, there was nothing at all. She seemed fine, and yes you are right, I did visit on a couple of occasions. She was struggling a little, you know after her husband David had left her. I just went and helped her tidy the place up a little. I think she was grateful for my help". She looked directly at him, her face serene and calm. Inside she was shaking with anger. *"Bloody woman, bloody, bloody woman."*

"Well it seems you were the last person to have seen her alive, as she was pronounced to have died less than 76 hours ago. She would have still been there undiscovered if it wasn't for the milkman calling to collect his money. Seemed she owed quite a lot and he was getting a little concerned.", he pretended to make notes in his book, but found himself captured by the radiance of the woman stood before him. "It could be that her money worries were starting to get the better of her".

Caroline said nothing but looked directly at him. Her face and demeanour didn't change. "Obviously we know little at the moment, but we will need to talk to you again Mrs Bolton. There really isn't anything to worry about, but until the exact cause of death is established, we need to keep a completely open mind."

"Of course officer", She smiled. "Would you like to come in for a cup of tea or something?"

"That would be nice Mrs Bolton, but unfortunately I have quite a few calls to make, but thank you for your kind offer"

"Anytime". She reached out and squeezed his hand. "Lorraine was a lovely woman. I do feel desperately sorry for her. I hope everything works out in the end", and with that she turned away and closed the door, leaving PC Weston standing bemused and rather puzzled. He stood there for a few moments, not quite knowing what to do, and then slowly returned to his car and radioed the station. As he drove away from the cottage he took a quick glance into the living room window and saw Caroline Bolton staring directly back at him. There was a strange, almost disturbing look on her face. She hardly seemed to notice him, but was staring straight through him as if he wasn't there. She was certainly an odd one, and he felt he should keep his eye on her, for more than one reason.

In the peace and quiet of the living room, Caroline stared at the young police officer as he drove away and noticed the look he gave her. At that moment she knew that she had him. It was easy. As it always had been, it was far too easy. She knew that he would not cause any trouble the next time he came to visit, and in a way quite looked forward to the challenge, if challenge was the word. She then thought of Lorraine and an irritation came over her. Some friend she had turned out to be, especially after everything she had done for her! Just goes to show you can't rely on anyone anymore. There was also a sense of sadness too, not for Lorraine, but more for the fact that she had lost a playmate. *Damn, just have to find someone else now.* Now to pick up the children and the usual round of banal conversations she had to endure with all of the other mothers and sad and lonely fathers. It was the part of the day she absolutely hated, but at least she could play the part of the grieving friend should anyone ask about Lorraine. *Bloody Lorraine. Now she should have been doing this*, she thought as she put on her woollen coat and threw a pink scarf around her neck. *Damn, damn, damn.*

*        *        *

For all of his young and battered life, Ben Fuller had known misery, only occasionally interspersed by moments of happiness. The time in the farm had been a pleasurable oasis amongst the sheer despair of drought that his years in this world had given him. Now he was alone again, and on the run, with nowhere to go and no-one to care for him. At his tender age, when a boy dreams of his mother and her loving embrace, little Ben no longer remembered what it was like to have that feeling of warmth and security. All he knew now was that he had to find a way of maybe returning home, and with the money he had in his pocket, he would have a better chance than without. He had run from the farm in any direction, ignoring the plaintive screams and shouts behind him. He knew that what he had done was wrong, but there was no-one who would tell him that now. He knew that he just had to get away and that no matter how lovely Hannah had been to him, there was something in the farmhouse that was not to be and the sooner he rid himself of it, the better.

137

So he had run and run and run until his legs ached so badly that he could hardly stand without wincing. Resting against a hedgerow on the side of corn field he contemplated what he should do next. Somehow he had to get back to his family, but he had no idea where he was, never mind in which direction he should be heading. In all the time at the farm he had never found out exactly where he was, and each time he had broached the subject with Hannah, she had changed the conversation and talked about something else, almost as of she didn't want him to find his way home. The letters he had written back home had never been replied to, and that started to make him think that maybe they hadn't been sent in the first place. He couldn't understand why, but he knew that the farmhouse was no longer where he wanted to be. Sitting against the cold and harsh roots of the hedgerow, he contemplated his next move. He needed to find a main road where there would be cars and buses, and then he needed to stop one of them, the way he'd seen people do in the films on the tele. Maybe then one of them would give him a lift home, or maybe tell him which way to go. He had money in his pocket and knew he could use that. Thinking of his mum and dad there were now no more tears. They had all gone, and he felt like he had grown out of such silly behaviour. No, tears wouldn't help. What would help would be if he kept a cool head and a plan of action.

For a while he fell asleep, his mind and body totally exhausted by the exertion of the last few weeks and in particular the last few hours since fleeing the farmhouse. It was a fitful rest, brutally shattered by the sound of a flock of birds flying in unison away from the clump of trees nearby, disturbing the branches and leaves. At first Ben had no idea where he was, but quickly he remembered and got his bearings. A quick check to see if the money was still in his pocket and hadn't been spirited away whilst he was dozing, and then he made his way across the open field in the general direction of what he thought was a house in the far distance. It was difficult to see, but he guessed it must have been at least five miles away, so he continued heading toward it, traversing fields that had been cultivated, and others that were barren. He also had to leap across a bubbling stream, just about clearing it without getting his feet too wet, but continued to head toward the welcoming sight of a house and hopefully help. In time he got close, and only then did he question the wisdom of turning up at another strange house, not knowing what was in store. He so wanted to find the way back home, and was sure that someone there would at least tell him the right way to go, but after the farmhouse, he no longer felt comfortable knocking on the door of a complete stranger.

"Howdo..."

Ben turned round quickly in shock toward the voice. "Not seen you here before have I?". The man was probably in his late fifties, so Ben thought, and looked like he was a farmer. He was wearing a long grey coat that covered green corduroy trousers, and on his head he wore a flat grey cap. He was unshaven and looked like he hadn't had a wash in months. Ben just stood and stared, unable to utter anything in reply. He couldn't tell if this man was friendly or not.

"That's my farm there...", the man pointed to the house ahead. "Where are you going?"

The man was quite well-spoken and certainly didn't give the impression that he was a farmer, not that Ben at that moment really cared. Briefly they stood in silence just looking at each other. "Well..., cat got your tongue then?".

"No", Ben wasn't sure what to say but felt he should at least try to be friendly so as not to get himself into trouble. "Sorry, mister, but you scared me".

The man smiled at this, but it wasn't a sinister smile, but a warm and comforting smile that suggested he found Ben's appearance amusing. "Nothing to be scared of, young man. Where have you come from then?", looking around at the expanse of fields and meadows. "There isn't a house for miles".

"Oh, I live with Hannah and Arthur from over there". Ben pointed behind him, not knowing what else he could have said. The man looked in the direction that Ben was pointing and shrugged.

"Never knew there was anything there to be honest. You been walking long?".

"No, not really".

"How are you going to get back?"

"I'll probably walk, it's not that far really".

"Well", said the man, walking past Ben now and heading off toward the house, "I'm off in for my tea now. You're welcome to join us for a sandwich before you head off back if you want."

Ben so wanted to say yes as he was beginning to get hungry again and the thought of a sandwich and drink made his stomach rumble deep inside. "No thank you, as I've really got to get back. I promised I wouldn't be away for long and I think I've gone a bit too far. They will both be worried about me".

"That's ok, but make sure you get back safely won't you....I could drive you back if you want?"

"NO...no, thank you". All Ben could think of was the 'kindness' of Hannah and Arthur and he really couldn't trust anyone at the moment.

"Ok, ok, no problem," putting his arms up in mock surrender. "You take care of yourself"

"Thank you sir", and with that Ben turned to the direction he had just come and made his way away from the watchful eyes of the man. He wanted to run, but that would have attracted too much attention, so he walked slowly and deliberately, making sure he didn't look back. Only when he had crossed the second field did he dare to look around, and to his relief he saw that the man had long gone and all he could see now was the distant glimpse of the house and the dim light shining from the front window.

It was after the man had eaten his chicken sandwich and drank his second cup of sweet, milky tea that it had dawned on him. It had just flashed back into his mind in an instant. He'd remembered the newspaper and radio reports of a boy who had gone missing off the motorway about twenty miles away and the police had conducted a house to house search in the surrounding towns and villages.

He'd never been found, and although the search hadn't officially been called off, it had certainly been scaled down. There was the suggestion that the body may have been found in the estuary, but three deepwater searches had found nothing. He'd heard his distraught mother on the radio pleading for any information and had secretly cursed her for allowing such a young boy to travel so far on his own. Eventually the media had lost interest and nothing else had been heard…maybe until now. He'd been down in London on business when the police had called at his farm as part of their enquiries, but he had immediately contacted them when he got back and that had been it. Now he wondered whether this was the boy. His description was similar, although the boy he had just met had a mass of unkempt hair and certainly wasn't the fresh-faced youngster the police had described him as….but then if he'd been sleeping rough? He'd never heard of Hannah and Arthur, and was pretty sure there wasn't a house closer than at least five miles away. He suddenly felt rather foolish and guilty that he'd let the young boy disappear into the unknown. Anything could come of him? He quickly rushed to his kitchen telephone and dialled the number.

"Walsdown police station"

"Peter, it's Bob?"

"Hi Bob" came the answer down the phone, "what's wrong?"

"Remember that boy who went missing all those weeks ago?....."

*       *       *

By light the following morning, there were two police cars parked outside Bob Finlay's farmhouse, and inside questions were being asked and notes taken. It was soon established that the boy was almost certainly Ben Fuller following the description given, and in time small sections of the media were on hand to follow up the lead. The story of the missing teenager was no longer national news, but was still of some interest on a local level, and so both regional television, and the local radio stations were vying for the attentions of Bob Finlay, and indeed anyone else who may have any snippet of information that may heed the sighting of little Ben. The police meanwhile followed the interview of Mr Finlay by visiting the farmhouse of Arthur and Hannah Ramsbottom. It was established reasonably quickly that they had befriended little Ben, and it seemed they had treated him well. Hannah in particular was genuinely upset at the lad's departure, and both officers who attended, PC Khan and WPC Durham, were satisfied with the explanations given over his stay there. Their visit was frustrating in that there were no new leads on little Ben and where he may be now, but in a way the interview with the Ramsbottom's was not entirely fruitless. From the moment Jane Durham saw the tell-tale signs, the black eye and the visible shaking in her husband's presence, she knew that poor old Hannah was the victim of domestic violence. It didn't take long after some gentle probing to find that Arthur had regularly beaten the frail old woman, and with just a gentle arm and a reassuring word, it wasn't much longer before Hannah was telling all about Arthur's nefarious night-time activities in the woods. Poaching was very much illegal in this part of the country, and certainly frowned upon by the local populace. Arthur Ramsbottom was soon going to be in a great deal of trouble. For little Ben, naturally fleet of foot and driven by a sense of self-protection, he was far, far away. Far enough away for only the neighbouring police force to now have any real interest in the plight of the runaway.

# CHAPTER TWENTY-FIVE

"I've known her for so long, and I just think she suspects something". Tom was lying on the bed, fully clothed, staring at the ceiling. The flat was hot and clammy, so the bedroom window was fully open, letting in a welcome cool breeze, but also the irritating sounds of the traffic from below, and all the other noises accompanying city life. "But has she said anything?". Janet replied, folding her white blouse and placing it into the top drawer of her cabinet, followed by half a dozen pairs of knickers and an assortment of socks and tights that had been retrieved from the airing-cupboard in the hallway. Oh how easy it was to become domesticated with someone in such a short space of time, she thought.

"It's not a case of her saying anything, it's to do with the way she acts". There was a slight irritation in his voice, something which Janet had noticed from the moment he had arrived at the flat a couple of hours earlier.

"But you said that she is always a little odd".

"Odd maybe, but never suspicious"

"How can you tell then?"

"I just can"

"….and that is enough is it?"

"It is as far as I am concerned. It's not that I'm saying we should stop seeing each other", he turned onto his side so that he could look directly at her. She stopped the sorting of her underwear and stared back at him, "I just think we should be a little more careful"

Janet didn't say a word but returned to her underwear sorting. For a while Tom lay there and watched, before losing interest and returned to staring at the ceiling. For a while there was silence, and Tom wondered what he could say to break it, but then…"do you not love me?". Tom turned again and looked at Janet. She was sobbing quietly to herself, and in a moment he saw her vulnerability and her charm and her loveliness and in a moment he knew he did. "Yes, you know I do." She smiled the radiant smile that she reserved just for him and carried on packing away her clothes, her tears still silently falling down her cheeks. "…because you know I love you. I love you with all of my heart and all of my soul. You know I couldn't let you go, not now". He got up and held her tight, nuzzling his face against her neck, feeling the wetness of her tears streak his face. "I know, and you know that I wouldn't let you anyway. Don't worry about Caroline. I can deal with her". He held her for a few seconds more then released her and walked into the living room of the cramped flat. "Just putting on the news, no idea what's going on in the world nowadays you know".

"…and I suppose that's my fault eh?". The voice was more cheerful, but still strained. "Let me know if the Prime Minister has resigned, or the Queen's dead, or maybe your useless football team have won a match yet. Now that really would be a story. In fact if they win between now and the end of the month, I'll buy you lunch at Fredericks….now isn't that a good deal. Are you listening darling?". Walking into the living room she wiped away her tears with a tissue. "Darling, are you listening to me or what?"…but Tom was no longer listening. He was staring directly at the television screen totally motionless, his face a mask of horror, because he couldn't take in what he had just seen.

*　　　　*　　　　*

I just don't know what is happening. It's like the whole world has gone mad". Tom sat in his favourite armchair and stared into the bright and comforting flames of the open fire that Caroline had stoked in readiness for his return. She had always done that when the air had gone cold, and despite the warmth of the day, the nights had recently become uncomfortably cold. "First the woman from down the lane, and now this….", his voice trailed away, unable to finish the sentence.

"I know darling, but don't think of it too much". Caroline stroked his hair gently and blew gently into his ear. She was sat on the arm of the chair, one leg seductively positioned between his, her arms cradling him. "Let's forget about it this evening".

"I can't. The police spent all afternoon talking to me. They asked all kinds of questions. I felt like I was becoming a suspect".

"Now that's silly and you know it. They were just asking questions. They have to, to eliminate you from their enquiries."

"She was such a lovely woman too. Seemed a lot younger than her husband, but he clearly adored her. Had a little girl too. She kept talking about her all evening. Poor mite. Who's going to look after her now?".

"I know darling. It's just so cruel, but talking about it won't bring her back. You mustn't worry yourself." She nuzzled her face against his neck and kissed it softly but persistently. Tom sat there unable to respond, lost in his private grief for the woman he had only met once, and was never to see again. It had been an awful couple of days with the news of the death at the cottage down the lane, then the horrific slaying of Miss Palazzo, plus the added personal burden of trying to keep his relationship with Janet secret from Caroline. It felt as if the weight on his shoulders had become too much

, and he just wanted to escape somewhere alone, free from responsibilities and concerns. It wasn't to be though and he knew deep down that he had to keep up the pretence of his marriage to Caroline. Not that he found that difficult. Despite himself, he felt constantly sexually attracted to her and now was no exception. He was sure he was still in love, but the suffocation of her attentions was becoming oppressive. How could he ignore her though? As he felt her lips and tongue run along his neck up to his ear lobes, and her hand stroke the inside of his thigh, any resistance was inevitably likely to crumble. At least he felt grateful in the knowledge that she couldn't possibly suspect anything, not with her behaving this way toward him every evening. He turned his face toward her and kissed her, firstly softly and then with more urgency, his passion arising. She pulled away from him, a look of lust and desire in her face, a look he had seen so many times which she had reserved for him virtually every night of their married life. It was difficult to become tired of it. She pulled herself away from him and lay down on the white fluffy rug in front of the fire, her arms above her head, her body inviting him. "Forget her", she whispered softly, "take me now"......

# CHAPTER TWENTY-SIX

For the last few weeks since Ben's disappearance, each day had been the same for Mary and Chippy Fuller. Each day had melded into the next, with each one becoming more depressing and with less and less hope. At first they both believed that Ben would magically re-appear, sheepishly apologising to them both for being such a nuisance, and promising never to do it again. They both inwardly played out the conversations they would have with him, quietly scolding, but outwardly relieved. Then as each day of little or no news passed, the hope slowly began to fade away. Once the media had become bored with the story of a boy's disappearance, and had started to concentrate on other aspects of the case, such as why was such a young boy being sent away to his grandmother's, and why was he allowed to travel on his own? Once these questions had been asked, the Fullers started to lose the sympathy of their neighbours, and people being people started to ask uncomfortable questions. Poor Dale was the first victim. Not content with the grief he was feeling for the loss of his older and protective brother, but he also had to run the gauntlet of the teasing and name calling from his class-mates. He started to run away from school, and once this had been noticed by his teachers, it was decided it would be good for him to stay away for a while until Ben came home. Dale became withdrawn and would stay in his barely-furnished and less than comfortable room. Chippy found himself ostracised by his mates, and any odd jobs that he had been given in the past to help make ends meet, abruptly stopped.

What savings they had, and there were few, slowly diminished as they were wasted on the usual supply of drugs, but the added destruction of drink too. Each day began in a haze from the evening before and continued for the day.

For Mary the suffering was at its worst. She knew what people were not just thinking, but now outwardly saying to her face. How could a mother let her son go like that, and why was he allowed to travel on his own? What kind of mother was she? It pained her so badly, that she could now no longer function. Her closeness to Chippy, something she had always enjoyed, was gradually dying away, and her ability to mother Dale was now diminished. Instead of piling all of motherly instincts on to her younger son, she found it hard to acknowledge him. He was a reminder of Ben, and she was now finding it hard to know what to do. The social services were regular visitors, certainly more than when they were all a family living in the squalor of the flat, but they couldn't really be of help. The police were constant visitors too, especially PC Henrose, who had almost become something of a family friend, but he could bring no news. As he often said, the old cliché of no news is good news, but Mary couldn't find any solace in his words. Each day was becoming more and more desperate, and the each member of the grieving family was slowly disintegrating in their own painful way. Only once were they given any hope, and that was when they heard of the farmer who had stumbled across a young boy, but then no further news had returned them to their state of despair and longing. At least it should prove that Ben was still alive, but the sighting hadn't been conclusive, and so the uncertainty remained. Life had taken a serious turn for the worse, and as they faced each day separately now, they wondered if it would ever improve. The tears had stopped falling, the nights were continuously sleepless, the days were endless. All they wanted was for Ben to return. That was all. Then everything else would take care of itself.

It was one day, mid-afternoon, the wind outside was howling and the rain splattering against the window panes. Mary was alone.

Chippy was out somewhere, where she knew not, or at that time even cared. Dale was upstairs in his room, becoming more and more withdrawn from the outside world, something she was aware of, but was physically incapable of doing anything about. She'd been sat on the only comfortable chair in the house for what seemed like ages, her mind now no longer taking anything in, just an empty shell, as empty as she felt inside. The cold had entered the room, but Mary wasn't aware. She sat staring into nothingness, a numbness that had almost completely taken over her being. It was at that time, when all hope was virtually vanquished, when the overwhelming sense of loss ached at every fibre of her being, that she saw him. At first she didn't realise, her mind had ceased to function and she had just stared directly ahead, not seeing or hearing anything. He was just there. Stood in front of her, wearing the same clothes she had seen him in last. He didn't gesture, or come to her, but stood and stared. Mary looked back and gradually realised that her son, her long lost and abandoned son was stood just a few feet from her. She didn't move, she couldn't. She felt that every limb and sinew of her body had suddenly been tied down and had paralysed her completely. No words could escape her mouth, although she tried to call his name. There was no sound, and all she could do was to stare at her first born. Ben didn't move toward her, or make any attempt to talk to her. He just stared, a lost vacant look on his face. It accused in its nothingness and a thousand words could not have said any more to Mary. She sat there, totally transfixed as Ben slowly raised his right arm and extended his hand in a pleading gesture. He wanted her to come to him, but Mary couldn't move. Her body was rooted to the spot like she had been heavily drugged. She wanted to run to him and hold him in her arms, but no amount of effort could make her move. She tried to call his name, but found that she couldn't move her lips, and there was no sound to be heard either. All she could do was to look at him as the tears started to run down his cheeks. She wanted to hug him so badly, hold her son in her arms and tell him that no harm would ever come to him ever again. She felt his hurt and despair, but there was nothing she could do to help. She wanted to scream louder than she had ever done before, but she was completely paralysed, her whole body had become useless. She wanted to tell him how much she loved him, but it was impossible. She sat and watched as he stood there silently pleading, and then in an act of immense sadness, returned his arm and very slowly turned around, his back to her. *Please don't go,* she thought, but the words couldn't be spoken. She sat and watched in her private torment as Ben then slowly disappeared until he had faded away completely. The sadness pervaded every inch of her being as she watched her son disappear until there was nothing left. It was then, and only then when he had gone, that she felt herself released. She screamed. She screamed hard and long, a scream that came from deep within her soul. It cried out and reverberated, a scream that told of a mother's sheer and utter despair. Her whole body shook with the effort, her sobs making it hard to breathe. She had seen him and he had gone away again. She knew not whether it was a dream or a vision or a message, but there was one thing she did know amongst the overwhelming despair of his presence. One thing that only she could now know. She knew that Ben was alive. Of that she was sure. *Ben was alive!*

The next day she decided Ben's fate lay in her hands only. The police had failed to find any leads, never mind finding Ben himself. Successive media campaigns had failed to help and her poor son was still missing. Now was the time for her to take positive action and go looking for herself. Chippy wasn't so sure and pleaded with her to stay. It was bad enough losing his son, without his partner leaving too. It also meant that he would be left to look after Dale alone, something which he really didn't feel capable of doing.

"I just have to go...you must understand".

"If you had any idea as to where, then I would agree with you... but where you going to go eh?"

Mary had no idea. All she knew after 'seeing' Ben yesterday was that she knew he was still alive and she just had to find him.

Eventually Chippy relented and squeezed her as she put a few of her belongings into a tattered bag. He had tears in his eyes as they hugged. "Take care of yourself and come back in one piece."

"Of course I will. You know I have to do this?". She looked into his eyes and saw for the first time in a long time the love he felt for her. "I do…and promise me one thing".

"What is that?"

"Bring Ben back with you and then…", he pulled away and looked at their bleak surroundings, "…we'll find somewhere better than this. We'll get ourselves sorted out".

"Ok…I promise". With that she turned her back and walked out of the door, leaving Chippy alone staring at the void that had just engulfed him. "Come back soon", he whispered.

Mary knew the only way she would ever have any chance of finding Ben would be to do the things that her son would do. It meant getting into his mind and reacting to any situation the way her young boy would, in his frightened and confused state. She had to re-trace his steps, no matter that the police had done it a hundred times already, she now had to do it herself, alone and without the media circus that had accompanied her the last time. That meant returning to the bus station and catching the same bus at the same time as the one she last saw Ben as he waved goodbye. It was a less than comfortable experience as she sat herself down on the back seat, knowing that it could have been this very seat on this very bus that her son had been on that dreadful day. As it pulled out of the station, she turned to look out of the rear window at the bench where she had been sitting, and tried to imagine his feelings, the pangs of hurt and rejection as he waved goodbye to his Mum. It brought not just a lump to her throat, but tears that stung her cheeks and a vast sense of loss deep in her stomach. It also made her more determined that she would find him. He was alive, of that she had no doubt, but she had to make sure that she found him before any lasting harm was done to him.

As the bus rumbled its way out of the city, past the crumbling and oppressive tenement blocks that had scarred it, she transferred herself to Ben and what he was thinking. In her mind she became a 13 year old again, still looking at the world with a sense of wonderment and awe. Every new experience was to be embraced and treasured as the march of age started to gather apace. She watched the children with their rusty skateboards roll on the graffiti-strewn boards and wished she could be there with them. She smiled as the boys ran across the road, dodging in between the cars, and one of them then gave an obscene gesture to the driver who had pipped his horn. As the bus overtook a large family utility car, packed with children, she wondered what it would be like to pull out her tongue at the mother in the driving seat. In the seat two rows in front of her, there was a large woman who had an equally large hair style that culminated in a long black ponytail that had managed to hang over the seat back. Mary thought how easy it would be to cut the ends off with a small pair of sharp scissors and then lay them gently on the top of her head, so that when the lady combed her hair, a large chunk would fall to the ground. It made her smile and in a way took away the hurt of her missing son. Mary became a young teenager again, and if it helped her soul, then she would stay that way.

Soon the journey took them out of the large and now unwelcoming city and to the surrounding countryside, a haven and respite from the drab and grim surroundings that she had shared her life with for so long. The dull grey colours were soon replaced by the vibrant green of the lush meadows and woods that flashed by her window as the bus gradually increased its speed now that the shackles of the congested traffic had been loosed. As she stared at the changing scenery, she briefly returned to the reality of her, their, situation and wondered why it had been so long since they had shared anything like this. Why had they continued to live the existence of poverty and despair and had never tried to raise themselves above it. There was a whole world out there, and one that they had hardly touched. Maybe this was the moment when she and Chippy would re-evaluate their lives, and hopefully, please God, Ben would be with them.

Soon they got to the motorway where the coach had stopped and Ben, for whatever reason, had run away into the countryside. Mary knew exactly where the spot was and she knew she had to somehow get the coach driver to stop there. So she got up and made her way to the front to speak to the driver. He wasn't too pleased to be interrupted as he was attempting to manoeuvre around a large articulated lorry into the middle lane, but once she had explained herself to him, and he had looked twice at her face, there was no way he could refuse. "Ok love. It's not what I should be doing, and if the bosses find out then I'll be in real trouble, but I suppose...", he looked at her lost and listless eyes as he slowed the vehicle down, "...some things are more important." Mary smiled at him as he pulled over to the hard shoulder and came to a stop, releasing the door. "Thanks".

"It's ok...and good luck. I've got a son myself, about your boy's age. Don't know what I would do if he went missing". The driver sat and waited for Mary to climb down and then watched as she clambered over the fence and disappear into the adjoining field. He felt a tear of sadness well up and had to swallow hard to stop himself becoming emotional. Closing he door and setting off once more he then turned on the intercom and spoke to the other passengers. "Sorry about the delay ladies and gentlemen. Every now and then you get the opportunity of doing a good deed and making yourself feel better. That was mine. The rest of the journey will be un-interrupted.". With that he accelerated and left Mary to continue her lone search.

# CHAPTER TWENTY-SEVEN

PC Weston had driven away from the cottage deeply disturbed. It wasn't just the intense physical attraction he felt for the woman he had just been interviewing, but the fact that he knew deep inside that she had lied to him. He hadn't mentioned the cuts and bruises that had been found on the victim's body, especially as initial examinations had suggested they had occurred just before the overdose. That meant they would have been inflicted at about the same time that Caroline Bolton had last seen her, yet the injuries were too violent for them to have been caused by another woman. Unless there had been another intruder, and according to Mrs Hempton, who watched everyone and everything like a hawk, there had been no visitors to the cottage after Caroline had been there. Yes there could have been an intruder, but there were no signs of a break-in anywhere in the cottage and whoever had caused the violence could only have gone through the front door as the back had been closed for so long that the weeds in the back garden had actually grown halfway up its length. He needed to talk to Mrs Hempton again, that's for sure.

*             *             *

Caroline went to the bedroom after watching the policeman drive away, a smirk on her face. She just knew he would be back, and then next time she would be so ready for him. She felt the familiar tingling of anticipation, but today there was no time for such things. She went to the cupboard and pulled aside the dresses, skirts and blouses that were hanging haphazardly and reached deep down to the back where on the floor was a carrier bag that she had put there yesterday, so that Tom would never know. Pulling it out gently she then opened the bag and took out the artefact she had bought yesterday. It was magnificent. The cover was old and frayed, its oriental writing only just visible. The brash colours had faded away and so the bright reds were now just a dull brown, but it was what was inside that made it so attractive. She oh so slowly withdrew the gleaming foot of solid steel. Gripping the handle she saw it glint in the sunlight. A true 18$^{th}$ century sabre knife. Never been used, according to the idiot shop owner, but who cares she thought, swishing it around the room so that she could hear the wisp of wind as the razor sharp knife cut through the air, it will be used soon. Of that's for sure!

*      *      *

"Do you think people suspect?"

"I don't think so. Why, what makes you think that?"

Tom and Janet were together in the office. She had just brought him his first cup of coffee of the day, hot and black, the way he liked it, and she was sat opposite him staring at her new lover across the desk, the way they had done for so many years. Now of course it was different as there was a new meaning to their relationship, although there were times when she felt the obstacle of the desk was a barrier to their real love. There were still the family photos with Caroline's stunning features beaming out at Tom every time he looked at them. Janet couldn't help the jealousy, but knew there was little she could do to change that, although the thought of changing the bigger picture and taking Tom away from his family was one that had occupied her mind constantly these last few weeks.

"People smile in a strange way at me now, and I'm sure I saw Terry and Phillipa pointing toward us earlier".

155

"So what, let them think whatever. Just the usual office tittle-tattle. Ignore it."

"Glad you feel you can. Remember it's me who has everything to lose". Tom sat back and looked at Janet, feeling very uncomfortable.

"Can I remind you too Tom Bolton, that you also have everything to gain.". Janet had a steely look that suggested that she would not let go, no matter what the future might bring. Tom smiled a little and softened inside. "Yes I suppose you are right. I should stop worrying about things. After all I've got it made haven't I? A beautiful wife at home who can't keep her hands off me and a loving mistress at work who wants to marry me. What more could I want?". At that point he realised he had said something terribly wrong as he looked at Janet's face. She went ashen in despair and was just about to get up and leave. "I'm so sorry Janet. I really didn't mean it like that". His voice was soft and comforting. "I was just being sarcastic. Do you really think I would be with you if you were just a bit on the side? You mean more to me than that?"

"Do you still sleep with her?"

"You know I do. How can I not and her not suspect?"

"How often?"

"Janet....."

"How often?". The tone was demanding and shrill. Tom looked outside the office and thankfully no-one was aware of the conversation, or if they were they were pretending to ignore it.

"Virtually every night..." he whispered.

"Virtually?"

"Well the only time we don't is when I stay with you, but she has always been like that. Ever since we got married she has almost demanded it every evening. After a while I just got used to it. Surely you've heard the lads here laugh at me all the time?"

Janet didn't answer but just stared into space, her mind a million miles away from the conversation. She tried not to imagine, but the thoughts were there.

"If it means anything, I no longer enjoy it. All I can think about is you", he leaned over and held Janet's hand across the desk, oblivious to whether anyone could see from outside. She didn't pull away but looked at him, tears welling in her eyes. "I love you Janet". Gradually the smile appeared on her face and she whispered back. "I love you Tom", and for a moment it was all fine and there were no more reasons to speak. No more words were necessary, but both knew that this was to be a difficult time no matter what was to happen.

At lunchtime in her flat, after they had made love, she poured him a cup of coffee and sat on the sofa next to him. "Would you leave her?".

"Maybe I would, but the kids are so young. What would happen to them?"

"There is always a way you know. Anyway, I'm not saying leave her now. All I'm asking is, would you leave her?"

"I suppose I would...for the right woman." He turned to her and smiled. It was all she wanted and needed to hear and she squeezed his arm affectionately. "Good" she said, "now drink up otherwise we'll be late back and they'll all be talking again".

Later Janet made a promise to herself that she wouldn't think of him with her. During those long and lonely evenings, she would try and occupy herself with other distractions so as not to imagine in her mind's eye Tom and his beautiful wife in the throes of passion. It would be too painful, but one thing was for certain as far as she was concerned, it wouldn't last for long. Now that she had Tom after all these years of wishing and hoping, she was going to keep him forever, no matter what it took.

*          *          *

Caroline stood at the kitchen sink and closed her eyes. She concentrated hard, harder than ever before and imagined the images before her. It had become so much more difficult now that the woodlark had deserted her. She couldn't understand why as it had been there forever, but one morning it was gone and had never returned. Without her friend she'd had to conjure up the images from deep inside her alone and it had become an almost physical barrier. This time though it happened and the images were closer and more vivid. She saw the young policeman approach her cottage, his apprehensive steps and his hesitant manner. She heard the conversation they had as she pulled open the front door and followed him into the living room. She smelt his fear, but also smelt the unmistakeable aroma and scent of longing. She knew that at any time......Opening her eyes, she knew instantly again what she must do. Staring deep into the forest it grew in its darkness and foreboding. The trees, which were swaying gently in the autumnal breeze, began to rock violently back and forwards. The birds screeched as they fled and the piercing eyes of the wood creatures stared back directly at Caroline, trying once more to peer deep into her troubled soul. She resisted their probing and with a guttural laugh and a thin smile, she turned away and awaited the return of PC Weston.

\*        \*        \*

"Mrs Hempton is a typical village busybody. You know the type Sarg, knows everyone's movements. Where they've been, who with and at what time. She said that she could see right into Lorraine Masterton's cottage and knew exactly who went in there. She'd sit in her living room and watch the world go by, her world being the village."

"Go on", the sergeant listened intently. He was in his fifties now and had seen it all and done it all, but knew when there was something not quite right about a case, and this one was such. He sat down and gestured PC Weston to continue.

"You see, she is effectively housebound after she had a stroke a few years ago and so she can't do much more than just look out of the window, " Andrew Weston was warming to his theme now, " and so she knew every visitor to Mrs Masterton's cottage. In fact she told me virtually every visitor she'd had for the last three months as her living room window looked directly at the cottage and she could see all the people who would go up the path. Anyway admittedly there could have been another intruder after Caroline Bolton went to see her, but there were no signs of a break-in and there really isn't anyway anyone could get in via the back entrance as the garden is so overgrown. That means that Mrs Bolton was probably the only person to have seen her at the time of the overdose and at the time we think the injuries occurred".

Sergeant Tullett lowered his now ample frame onto the sofa chair of his functional office and sat silently for a while, looking out of the window at the municipal park. There were children playing on swings with their mothers in tow, while in the distance a rather chaotic football game was being played by young teenagers on the one remaining pitch that hadn't been sold to developers. It was a serene scene, the kind that is played throughout the country, yet not more than twelve miles from here, a woman had been badly beaten in her own home and had then seemingly committed suicide. No matter how many times he had had to deal with such matters, it never failed to sadden him that there was so much inhumanity in today's society.

"Ok", he finally replied after what had seemed an age."There's not much we can do at this early stage until the pathologists report, but we can keep an eye on this Caroline Bolton. I suggest you pay her another visit tomorrow. Be gentle but find out exactly what her movements have been for the last three weeks. We may be able to get some idea as to the real relationship between the two. Also talk to the local school and see if you can get a little more info from there, but remember to be discreet."

"Yes sarg.", and with that PC Weston left the room not knowing whether he was looking forward to the meeting with Caroline Bolton the next day or not.

Later that night he dreamt of demons. They were black and the size of bats with huge ears that flapped as they flew to within inches of him. As they came close they gave out a piercing scream that reverberated around his head, so loud that it became physically painful. They floated around his head scratching with their long fingernails as they swooshed around him. He tried to fight them off but there were too many of them. He put his hands up to his head to try and protect it, but one or more would break through his futile barrier and draw blood with the razor sharp finger nails until his head was a mass of blood and his mind throbbed with the pain. He screamed for them to stop, but they just carried on with their curdling screams and flashing cuts. When he woke up he was drenched in his own sweat and had to get out of bed and duck his head under the cold tap in the bathroom. His head throbbed with the pain of the dream and as he looked intro his own reflection in the bathroom mirror, he wondered what on earth he was facing later that day.

*Tuesday – July*
*Why does this happen? Why is everything disappearing? Where is the beauty anymore? If Tom goes my life is over. There will be no reason to continue. Adam and Shelley will need to find another mother because I can't do it alone. I WILL NOT LET HIM GO. Last night he showed no passion, no intimacy. It was just a moment for him. Whoever is threatening our happiness will pay, but firstly I have to deal with the policeman. Now how much fun will that be....?*

That morning, after she had kissed Tom goodbye and then dropped off the kids at school, Caroline prepared herself. She knew this was a minor distraction in her attempt to keep hold of the beauty she had surrounded herself in, but it was something that had to be dealt with. There was only way she could deal with a problem like this, in the same way she had dealt with similar problems down the years. Her natural beauty had been a help to her in times of crisis as she could use it to her own advantage with men and women alike, and had when it was called for. She felt no shame or guilt as everything she did was with one sole aim, and that was keep Tom in her life and make him as happy as could be. For that she would do absolutely anything....

She had bathed carefully and then put on the stocking and suspender set she had bought the week before. It had been for Tom, but she could easily get another pair for the weekend. She'd then put on her low cut white blouse, last worn when she had spent time with Lorraine. "Damn Lorraine. *She left me too! Why does everyone go?...*". She tried not to think too much, especially negative thoughts, as she pulled on her brilliant white skirt that showed a flash of thigh every time she moved. As she admired herself in front of the full length mirror in the bedroom she felt the familiar tingling of excitement at the anticipation of what was ahead. Reaching down she touched herself between her legs and briefly felt her sex. She then reached up and caressed herself on her neck, either side just below her earlobes. It would give out the aroma of passion and would work far better than any fancy perfume she could have bought from the most expensive department store. With that she looked at herself, smiled and returned downstairs and awaited the arrival of PC Weston.

He arrived at 10.15 precisely, as he had said when he had called that morning. As he got out of his patrol car, he immediately felt a bout of dizziness and had to briefly hold onto the car door to steady himself. It was a summer's day, but the trees around the cottage looked dark and foreboding, while the gentle breeze that had accompanied him as he drove to the village had quickly transformed itself into a howling gale. Looking toward the cottage he saw the front door open and Caroline Bolton stand there in expectation. If nothing else she's a confident woman, he thought. He began to wonder at the wisdom of coming here first when he could have visited the school or even the old woman down the lane, but all that would be doing would be putting off the inevitable. He needed to be strong and compose himself, and with that he shut the car door and walked down the pathway to the front door, Caroline standing there with a welcoming smile on her face. "Hello again" she smiled as he approached. " I was looking forward to seeing you again".

"Thank you Mrs Bolton". He tried to sound composed but her radiance left him feeling even more un-nerved. "Of course you know why I have returned".

"Of course I do. Now come in out of this terrible weather. It's awful isn't it?"

"Yes. Not exactly a summer's day", and with that he entered the cottage passed Caroline and briefly smelt an alluring aroma that he couldn't quite place. It was pleasant and had an immediate effect on him. "Come to the living room". Caroline briefly touched his arm and guided him through the wooden door to the left into the pleasantly furnished room. "Sit down on the sofa and I'll bring us some tea".

"Thank you Mrs Bolton, but this will not take too much time."

"Oh it's no bother", said Caroline smiling sweetly as she made her way to the kitchen. "A cup of tea will do you the world of good. You look a little peaky if you don't mind me saying. Oh and please call me Caroline".

"Thank you ...Caroline". It was against his professional principles but he just found it so difficult to behave in a normal manner. He sat down, took a deep breath and tried to compose himself once more, taking out his notebook and pen and placing it to his side on the settee. He took time to look around the room. It was well furnished in that typically English-cottage way of decorating. All chintz and flowery patterns. There were numerous family photographs above the large fireplace surrounding an Edwardian grandfather clock. A couple showing Mrs Bolton, her husband and two fine looking children, but far more showing just her and her husband. Pictures of them at the beach arms around each other, or sat at a picnic table in the woods, or one very intimate portrait of the two of them lying together almost naked on a bed in an intimate embrace. It was an unusual photograph to display publicly and it also got him wondering who had taken it too.

"Here we are then, hot and steaming". Caroline's presence surprised him as he hadn't heard her return from the kitchen. He was also a little taken aback by her physical presence as she leant down in front of him to put the tray of teapot and cups on the table in front of him. It wasn't that she was particularly close to him or that she was invading his natural space, but he sensed her being far more strongly than anyone else. Also as she leant down he couldn't help but notice her blouse fall forward giving a glimpse of her fulsome breasts straining against her frilly bra. It was a moment of discomfort, especially as she lingered just a little longer than was absolutely necessary.

"Thank you". He tried not to watch as she leant back and then poured out the tea and milk into seemingly very expensive cups and saucers. All the time her blouse flapped loose and the aroma wafted over him again. It was quite intoxicating. "One lump or two?" It almost seemed a ridiculously smutty question, but it was said with sensuality. She bent down in front of him and as she did he then got an eyeful of a stockinged clad thigh as her skirt rode up her legs. "No, I'm fine thank you". Clearing his throat he picked up the cup and saucer and took a long gulp to steady himself as Caroline retreated to the chair opposite. She appeared to smile at him as she sat down, or maybe that was just his now vivid imagination.

"Now Mrs Bolton…"

"No, call me Caroline please"

"….Caroline. There are one or two questions I need to ask you concerning the death of Mrs Canon and the last time you saw her. You say that when you last visited the deceased she was in high spirits".

"Yes of course she was. We'd just spent the day together, drinking wine and giggling. It was so nice and so much fun. I do miss her you know". Caroline looked at PC Weston deeply, so that for a moment the dizziness he had experienced as he got out of the car returned. "She was so much fun"

"I thought you said that after her husband had left her she became very depressed?" He tried to stop his voice from shaking but he couldn't compose himself properly. Again Caroline looked at him and a smile returned to her lips. "Yes, but then I spent time with her and she started to feel better about herself".

Adam Weston sat there and looked at the beauty sat opposite him and began to wonder how someone as stunning as this could have possibly caused anyone any harm. It seemed inconceivable that Caroline Bolton would hurt anyone or anything. She radiated sexuality and goodness. "What did you do to make her feel better about herself?" he heard himself say. It wasn't a familiar line of questioning and really played no part in his line of enquiry. Putting down his now empty tea cup and saucer he looked at Caroline and began to imagine what it would be like...

"I did all kinds of things for her", came the now husky reply. "She needed to know that she could be cared for by another human being, and I played the part for her".

"In what way?". Adam leaned forward and again sensed the unusual scent that made his head spin in a not too unpleasant way. Against all of his instincts he was now becoming attracted to this woman sat opposite him. He knew how terribly wrong all of this was and how totally unprofessional this was, but the dizziness he was experienced, brought on by the scent of the woman, made his head fuzzy and unclear. He wasn't sure now but he swore to himself that he saw Caroline reach up and touch her breast as she spoke. "I did this" was what sounded like she said, but he now couldn't be sure.

"I don't feel very well. I'm sorry but I think I need to lie down briefly". Adam started to feel very dizzy indeed and found himself unable to focus properly. All the time he tried to look at Caroline but his sight was becoming more and more fuzzy and his hearing duller. He could see that she was now sat back in her chair and had pulled her legs up to her chest so that the her stockings were now visible, but it was like he was drunk and couldn't focus. She carried on talking in a husky tone that oozed sexuality but he couldn't make out what was being said. He thought he saw her touch herself and thought he heard a groan, but now his head was pounding and felt like he was going to explode. He tried to get up but his dizziness became worse and he immediately slumped back into his chair, his body now sweating hot and cold and a feeling of heaviness in his chest so that he found it difficult to breathe. In this state he didn't see or sense Caroline approach him, and certainly wasn't aware when she leant down and unbuttoned his trousers and slowly lowered herself onto him. In fact the next few minutes were nothing more than a dream, and a bad one at that. There was no sensation in his body except a numbness that stopped him from moving a limb or a muscle. He could sense the heavy breathing of Caroline as she sat on him, but he felt no pleasure. It was at that moment that he passed out as if in a drunken stupor, much to the amusement of Caroline who continued her movements until she felt herself reach an incredible orgasm. As she did she felt for PC Weston's neck and squeezed it so hard that he couldn't breathe, and it was only the fact that she came with such intensity and force that stopped her from squeezing the life out him. She then collapsed against him slowly recovering her composure and waiting for her breathing to return to normal. Then, after a few moments, she got up and re-arranged herself and the poor policeman who lay slumped on the settee and went into the kitchen to make herself another cup of tea.

When Adam Weston woke up he was firstly in a state of total confusion. Looking around him he didn't recognise where he was or what time or even day it was. His head pounded like he had been hit hard by a large object and as he moved the pain seared through his whole body. Gradually his senses returned and he remembered. He got up quickly, but the dizziness immediately returned and so had to slump back onto the sofa once more. From the kitchen he could hear movement and a voice gently humming to herself and he remembered it was Caroline Bolton. He then also remembered what had happened earlier, when he didn't know what was happening. In fact he wasn't sure if it had all been a terrible dream. "Mrs Bolton" he called weakly. There was no response so he tried again. "Mrs Bolton, could I talk to you?" With that Caroline walked back into the room with a big smile on her face and he knew that it hadn't been a dream and he hadn't imagined it. "So how are you now then?" she asked almost in a condescending way. "I have to say that I'm a little bit offended you know. I've never had a man pass out on me before, certainly not during anyway".

He felt horrified and tried to stutter a reply but she carried on talking. "The thing is PC Weston, you really shouldn't come to a woman's house under the pretence of questioning when all you wanted to do was ravage me. If that is what you wanted then you should have said and we could have avoided all the silliness at the beginning couldn't we?"

"Mrs Bolton…I really don't know what to say…it wasn't what I wanted" The words stumbled out of his mouth as he tried to compose himself once more, battling against the pain in his head and his aching limbs. Thankfully the dizziness was receding, but he still felt unable to move properly.

"Well" said Caroline standing above him in mock astonishment, "you really gave a good impression of someone who wanted me. You couldn't keep your eyes off my breasts and you kept looking at my legs so don't tell me you didn't want me. In fact I'm pretty sure that your sergeant at the police station would probably be quite interested in what I have to say if you deny that you came here for just one thing. I'll tell you what…" she bent down and leant toward him so that he sensed the aroma again "…if you go away and don't bother me again with your silly questions about that bloody woman, then I won't say a word. How about that then?" She put her lips close to his and brushed them gently against him. "Is that a deal?"

He got up, as steadily as he could, almost physically pushing her out of the way. He was too weak though which made her laugh as he grabbed hold of the furniture trying to inch himself away from this terrible situation. "Now run along young man and let's just have our memories shall we?". Her tome was mocking and she stood and watched as he somehow, painfully, made his way to the front door and left the cottage. As he breathed in the fresh air outside he felt his strength return slowly so that he could gradually walk to his patrol car unaided. As he picked his way unsteadily along the pathway he felt Caroline's eyes burn into him from the living room window. He didn't look back but he could hear her laugh. A cruel laugh that appeared to exude an evil that he hadn't experienced before. The wind was blowing harder than before and it took him a little time to get into the car and compose himself. *"Don't look back at her. Whatever you do, don't look back at her"*. He kept on repeating that to himself. He wasn't sure but he felt looking at her would weaken him, and all he knew was that he had to get away from the cottage as quickly as possible. He pulled the car away and drove slowly down the lane to the main road that exited the village, resisting the temptation to look back at the cottage or even think of Caroline Bolton. As he approached the junction he felt his energy re-enter his body and he suddenly felt stronger. He couldn't understand what had just happened to him, but he realised that he couldn't tell anyone, especially anyone at the police station. He would have to think of a story to cover up his last moments, but firstly he needed to get away from the village and take some time out to compose himself. As he pulled out left onto the main road, he was suddenly startled by his car radio crackling into life. He didn't actually hear what was being said. In fact at that point he didn't hear anything at all, especially the lorry that had come tearing round the corner at a speed just a little too quickly to be safe. As it careered into the police car that had just pulled onto the road at a speed that seemed a little too slow, PC Weston felt himself disappear into a black void. His mind became empty and for a brief and exhilarating moment he found himself fully alive once more with a vitality that invaded all of his senses. It lasted for a moment though as his car was forcibly rolled over by the weight and the speed of the lorry that had crashed into it. Within a few seconds it had rolled twice and into a ditch, and then almost immediately had burst into flames as the petrol tank splintered and ignited. For PC Weston there were no more feelings of pain or confusion as his mind went blank in an instant.

\*        \*        \*

    Back in the cottage Caroline had watched the police car pull away steadily and she had stood there with her eyes fixed on its rear bumper until it had disappeared from view. She didn't move but closed her eyes and waited. Then the sound of the crash, the terrible sound of skidding tyres and screeching metal against metal before silence. It was over. Far quicker than she envisaged, but it was over. She smiled to herself and returned to her kitchen to prepare the evening meal for Tom and the kids. Outside she heard the wind howl with an urgency and the trees sway so badly that it looked as if they may break loose from their roots at any moment. She felt the eyes burn into her soul once more, but this time she just felt impatience. Who are these creatures that judged her everyday? How dare they look into her and criticise her way of life? She decided that she would no longer let them dictate to her anymore, and with that she pulled down the kitchen window roller blinds, turned on the light and continued her chores. Outside she heard the wailing and the screaming that emanated from the forest, but this time she took no notice apart from one moment when she stopped and stood still. "LEAVE ME BE" she shouted at the top of her voice, and with that all went silent and calm once more.

# CHAPTER TWENTY-EIGHT

Mary ran and ran and ran. Where she was going she didn't know, but all she could do was put herself into her son's mind and try to imagine what he had done. She knew that he had ended up at a farmhouse and stayed for a few weeks, but that hadn't happened until the second night, so she needed to know where he had been the first evening after he had run from the coach. Across fields and through unbroken woods and glades she kept on wandering. It was cold, unusually for this time of year, and she kept wondering how poor Ben had kept himself warm if the weather had been the same. After what had seemed like miles and hours, she eventually came across a barn, deserted and abandoned. It was stood alone with the exception of a farmhouse a few miles in the distance, and she knew instinctively that this was where Ben had spent his first night. It was nothing more than a mother's belief concerning her child, but she knew this was where he had been.

Entering the building it was dark and dank and smelt of dampness and must. It was dry though and as her eyes became accustomed to the murky surroundings, she began to imagine how welcoming it must have been to Ben on that first night. The floor was piled high with bales of hay, and up above there was a separate floor with a ladder leading up to a trap door, well away from any possible prying eyes. This was where Ben would have hidden himself, climbing up the ladder, pushing the trap door open, despite it being very stiff and heavy from a lack of use, and then he would have bedded himself down in the piles of hay that he had collected from the floor. It would have been comfortable and warm and for a few brief hours he would have slept peacefully, away from the nightmare that his life had become. It was here that she too would bed down for the evening. It didn't really make any sense, especially as she knew that the more she used of her time, the better chance she had of finding her son, but it just seemed the right thing to do. So she collected enough hay to make a bed and climbed the ladder and opened the trap door. It was heavy and stiff, but she managed it and then she found a nice clearing away from the edge of the floor and made herself a bed of hay. It took time, and she wondered how poor Ben had coped, but eventually it became more manageable and soon quite comfortable. As she lay back against the hay, bits of it irritating her neck as it bristled against her, she wondered if this was the way it was all those weeks ago with Ben. Did he lay there and stare at the ceiling, spying through the cracks at the dark sky? Could he also hear the sound of a rustling beneath him as the mice went about their nocturnal habits? What about the almost silent cry of an owl somewhere above her, its luminous eyes bearing down without flinching? She wondered for what seemed like an age before the exertion of the day began to tell and she slowly and gracefully fell into a fitful, but deep sleep.

The next morning she made her way to the farmhouse a mile or so away. This had been where Ben had stayed for a few weeks according to the police and if he had been as hungry as she was now, then it was hardly surprising that he had made his way in that direction. As she approached she noticed that it looked virtually empty. There were no welcoming lights from the windows and most of the surrounding land was overgrown with weeds and bushes, as if no one had taken care of the place in a long long time. There was not a sound as she came to the large oak door that she presumed led to the kitchen. Was this what Ben did? The handle turned easily without a murmer and pushing the door open a little she called softly "Hello". There was no answer or indeed any sound so she pushed the door a little more so that it opened completely. She was greeted by the smell of newly baked bread, and at the far end of the room she saw the huge oven where it came from. It was the kitchen as she suspected and far from being deserted, it was clear by the pots and pans cluttered on the table that dominated the room, that this place was still lived in. "Hello", she called again, her voice trembling slightly, "Is there anyone here?".

"Hello"

The reply shocked her and made her jump, but when she turned toward where it had come from she saw a frail old woman, dressed in an oversize shawl, sitting on the only chair in the room staring at her. The face was instantly recognisable from the TV pictures, despite the shock of the bruising still visible around the eyes. Mary smiled warmly at the lady, stepped inside the kitchen and walked toward her. "I'm sorry to intrude but my name is Mary Fuller. You must be Hannah? I think we have a lot to talk about".

If Ben had known that his Mum was on his tracks, then he would surely have stopped and waited for her to find him, but sadly he had no idea. Each day had become like the last. He had walked miles and miles, sometimes in the countryside, occasionally coming across a small town or village. On those times he'd been extra careful so that no one would recognise him, as he was sure that he would get into a lot of trouble for stealing the money off Hannah and especially Arthur. In his child's mind, he'd done wrong and he couldn't see how anyone would take pity on him anymore, especially his mum and dad. He had no clear idea where he was going, he just kept on running. The money he had was enough to keep him fed, but as each day went by he became more and more scruffy and dirty, so that he started to attract attention. Once he tried to wash in a brook that trickled down the side of an imposing hill, but it wasn't easy and the water was icy cold too. His clothes were becoming ragged and rather smelly and so he eventually gave up the pretence of respectability and started to do what he had become good at…stealing. He knew how to enter a shop from the rear whilst the owner was busy dealing with a customer, and as a village shop seldom had more than one member of staff, it made sense for him to target those places. He soon found that creeping around the stock room he could help himself to food, drink, clothes, in fact anything at all. It was all a bit too easy and it never occurred to him that any other child his age who hadn't had the upbringing he'd had, would seriously struggle to survive in such an environment. Gradually he'd replaced his old clothes, and had actually buried them beside a stream, and soon he had a bag full of sweets, fizzy drinks, water and chocolates. A real feast at night when it became cold. In terms of his survival outdoors too, he had now become quite adept at making do with such things as empty barns, or discarded vehicles where he could creep into the back of derelict van and snuggle up amongst the old and musty carpets that had lain there for months. It was a hard life and one that he didn't understand as to why it had visited him, but he was coping. Coping as well as a boy his age could anyway. Maybe one day he would see his family again. Maybe one day he would see his mum again and she would take him in her arms and love him, but it seemed such a long way away that he now suppressed the feelings of longing and quite simply took each and every day as it came. The future would now look after itself.

If it had been possible to have known in advance the danger that was lurking for little Ben, then even at his tender age he would never have entered the pretty village of Little Hanwick. For him it was just another place he had stumbled across, somewhere else that had warm barns, inviting shops with unattended stockrooms and far enough away for him not to be recognised. There was nothing that he could perceive that would suggest there would be anything to cause him any pain or sufferance. If it were possible to listen to the woods and the trees, then he would have known not to have gone beyond the village boundary and to have turned back to whence he came, but no-one can really understand what is being said to them by nature. Even more so the creatures of the woods would have called out to him if they knew he would listen, but how is a boy to know that he is being warned by inhabitants of a forest? Would any of us listen to such a thing? It is doubtful, and with that in mind Ben's ignorance can be understood and forgiven. As he walked past the sign on the edge of the hamlet welcoming any stranger, he had no possible idea that he may never get the chance to walk back the other way. Such are the moments that dictate fate, and on days like these, there aren't really too many things that can be done to change it.

For Ben it was like most any other place he had seen over these past few miserable weeks. His now expert eye looked it up and down and immediately focused on the only shop in the village. It was like so many others he had stolen from, the front full of domestic items such as plastic washing baskets, brooms, dustpans and freshly cut flowers. Inside the store would sell virtually every item that could possibly be needed by the inhabitants of a village where a trip to the nearest town could be regarded as a pre-planned day out. There would be little that Mr Fairbrother wouldn't have in stock or wouldn't be able to get hold of. It was the only way that a shop in a village as small as this could possibly survive. Not that any of that meant anything to Ben. All he was interested in was how to get into the stockroom by the rear entrance, and so with the worldly knowledge that he had gained, not just from the housing estate that he had lived in during his now previous life, but also from the weeks on the road since running from the farmhouse, he darted unseen to the rear of the building and hid behind the high wooden fence that separated the back garden from the fields beyond. Spying through a crack in the panels he saw what was now a familiar and welcoming sight, the back door was wide open and there seemed to be no-one around. He waited a little longer, again experience had taught him not to be too hasty and that it needed a patient mind to finally succeed in moments like these. He waited and waited until he was totally certain in his own mind that the coast was clear enough for him to proceed. He silently climbed over the fence, making sure that it was strong enough to take his weight, and then darted to the back door, briefly stopping outside so as to give himself a chance of hearing if there was anyone inside. Again after a few moments he satisfied himself that the place was empty and so he crept inside. The sun had been bright that day so it took his eyes a few seconds to grow accustomed to the greyness inside, but once they had he saw that everything he needed was within a few feet of him. There were boxes of sweets and chocolates stacked on the shelves, cartons of fruit drinks stacked on the floor, bread, milk, water plus items of clothing which he needed badly. There were packs of underwear and socks plus brand new shoes of all sizes. There wasn't much time, although he couldn't hear voices from the front of the shop, so he picked up a huge black camping bag that had an orange 'For Sale' tag attached to it, and filled it with everything he could get his hands on. It didn't really occur to him that the more he put in the heavier and more difficult it would be to carry away, he just wanted to help himself to as much as he could. It was only when he heard a voice in the shop that he stopped filling the bag and decided to get out as quickly as he could. The voice was also heading for the stockroom. "I think I've got some in the back. Sit down Mrs Hutton and I'll have a look". It was a strong male voice and was clearly the owner, Mr Fairbrother. Ben gathered up the bag and heaved it over his shoulder and ran as fast as the weight would allow him out of the stockroom into the garden. On the way he accidentally kicked over a metal bucket that had been left by the pathway and it clattered across the gravel, spilling its contents of grey and dirty water all over his shoes and onto the grassy lawn, turning the green to a muddy brown. The noise was enough to alert Mr Fairbrother and he rushed out to see what it was, thinking that maybe a fox had wandered into the garden and was helping itself to cat's food left over in the tray on the doorstep. It took him a few seconds to comprehend what he was seeing, the sight of a young boy trying desperately to climb over the rickety wooden fence with a huge bag over his shoulder. If this had been in the city, then Martin Fairbrother would have realised immediately what was happening, but in the country life was a lot slower and free from the burdens of crime, so he stood and watched.

Then as Ben disappeared over the fence it was only then that he cried out and chased after him. By the time he had opened the unwieldy gate at the side of the garden and ran round to where he had seen Ben go, the boy had gone and was nowhere to be seen. His eyes scoured the fields beyond but there was no sign. In fact everything was as normal, no sounds except the cry of the starlings in the sycamore tree just beyond the hedgerow. Shaking his head he returned to the shop and after apologising to Mrs Hutton, immediately called the police. In his twenty-one years of living in Little Hanwick, this was only the second time that he had been burgled, and the last time the offender was caught within the hour. Shaking his head as he talked on the phone, he had no idea at that time that his phone call was about to set off a tragic chain of events.

Ben ran as fast as he could, considering the burden he was carrying. Across the meadow toward the familiar and comforting patch of woodland ahead until he was deep inside, well away from the prying eyes and distant cries of the shopkeeper. He traversed the glade, hopping across a running brook until he came across a clearing, large enough for him to sit down, and covered enough for him to be hidden from the outside world. It was there that he sat down, letting his bag drop to the floor and took a moment to allow his breathing and heart-rate to return to normal. After a while he opened the bag and spilled the contents onto to the floor. It was a sizeable haul and one he was proud of. There was food, water, shoes and new, warm clothing. Before he did anything he immediately got changed, replacing his now quite unpleasant smelling shirt and trousers with new ones that were a size too big, but still preferable to what he was already wearing. With new shoes and a feast of chocolate bars and coke cans, he soon felt like he was a new person and ready to move on to the next village. Strangely though he started to feel sleepy, something which he hadn't noticed before, especially before he entered the woods, and so for a few brief moments he decided to lie down on the soft and welcoming forest floor and close his eyes. It was comfortable and he felt a huge sense of well-being as he slowly drifted from the area of wakefulness to the slow and sleepy stupor before falling into a deep and restful sleep. He only meant to nap for a while, but soon Ben was completely lost to the physical and mental demands of his body and mind, both crying out for a respite from the life they now had to endure. It was deep sleep, the kind that only comes when total exhaustion is reached, and no matter what his intentions, there was no way the forest would let him awake before it was completely the right time.

# Chapter Twenty-nine

It was later, much later in the afternoon that Caroline stumbled across the boy. She had decided that the cottage was too stifling and her mind was beginning to shout to her, and she felt that it was time to take her regular walk through the dark woods that almost encroached onto the back garden of the cottage. It had beckoned to her earlier but her scream of defiance had helped for a while, but soon all thoughts of the events of the morning had drifted away and she had decided it was time to immerse herself in the dark and sometimes foreboding forest that she now knew so well. She had only walked for a while, aware that the trees that had been moving almost rhythmically to the sound of the breeze, had now taken on a statuesque quality, and the birds that had chorused for most of the day had now all but disappeared to a murmur. *No matter*, she thought, *I can make it happen if I need to.*

She walked deep into the woods, along the path that she had trodden so many times before. In the distance she heard, but could not see, a deer scamper away as her footsteps, no matter how soft, disturbed the gentle rhythm of the undergrowth. As she entered deeper it became noticeably colder, although Caroline was now oblivious to such things. She just immersed herself in the beauty of the surroundings. As she looked high above her at the forest canopy, she again remembered again the words on the plaque, and again reminded herself of the beauty that can be found anywhere you cared to look.

It was only then, as she was completely lost in her thoughts, that she stumbled across the figure of the young boy silently sleeping, with his head rested against the trunk of a large oak tree. It came as a surprise to her as much as it would have been if she'd come across a group of mad march hares. This was HER forest. No-one ever came through this way, and in all of the years she had lived here, she had never come across anyone in these woods. At first she stood and stared and wondered what to do. Who was this boy? He looked like he was well looked after as his clothes seemed quite clean and new, although a little mis-matched. His face was angelic, but his tousled hair and grubby features suggested that he had been out in the open for quite a while. Nearby was a holdall that had the unmistakeable sales tag attached that she had seen at the local store, and further away she saw a pile of old clothing that had obviously just been discarded, and then she realised. This boy didn't belong here, but was 'passing through' the village, helping himself to a few items from the main shop on his way. Caroline smiled to herself. This boy may be relaxing now and resting his tired body, but she knew he would never be able to leave now that he had entered the forest. *Poor mite*, she thought, *he really has no idea*.

For a while she stood a few feet away from him and just stared. In her mind she was formulating thoughts as to what to do. Then it became obvious. Her inner consciousness then grinned to herself. She knew exactly what she was going to do. She reached into her back pocket and pulled out a scrap of paper and scribbled on it: **'Follow the track back to the cottage and you will have a warm welcome. See you soon, Caroline'.**

It was enough, and she knew that he wouldn't be able to resist. There was a brief temptation to awaken him, but she chose not to and quietly returned down the path from whence she had come. *Let him sleep a little longer. He will need his rest.*

Later Caroline did the usual school rounds and picked up Adam and Shelley. Since the death of Lorraine, she had been forced to do this on a daily basis, and there was no denying it to herself, but she found it intensely boring. Standing outside the school gates waiting for her children, she studiously attempted to ignore the other mothers, some of whom occasionally tried to open a conversation with her. She would smile politely, offer a couple of words and then turn away hoping that it would deter any more contact. Soon the other mothers became aware of Caroline Bolton's reluctance to make friends, and after a while she was treated as if she wasn't there. On this day it was no different. After a brief wait she heard the school bell ring and within seconds the children came bounding out of the large red doors and into the playground, running toward the gates and freedom from another dreary day of mathematics and English literature. Ben and Shelley emerged together, both of them searching, as always, for their mother as they trundled out of the building. They were a typical mixture of crooked ties, satchels hanging off the right shoulder with socks rolled down to the ankles in a time honoured fashion. Neither of them smiled anymore, especially after they had heard about the accident to Lorraine, but as soon as they saw their mother's face they grinned widely and came running toward Caroline. She took it in good heart and bundled them both into the back of the estate, listening to the tales they both told above each other of their day. Eventually when they had calmed down, Caroline said. "Now I think we will have a nice surprise soon." Both Adam and Shelley looked at each other and smiled. "What mummy?". Shelley was the most eager to know. Like all children, they loved surprises. "Well, I can't tell you just yet, but if you promise to be very good tonight and eat all of your dinner and go to bed early, then we shall have a new friend coming to stay with you."

"Yesss", said Adam. A new friend coming to stay. Someone else they can play with. "Is it a he or a she mummy?"

"A nice young boy. He's staying with friends not far away at the moment, but he's promised me to come and visit very soon. Would you like that?"

"Oh yes," they both replied, and with that the journey back to the cottage was a pleasant one. At the front of the car Caroline thought and thought and thought and realised she was about to enter a new dimension as she continued to look for the beauty all around her. The smile came upon her lips once more and deep down she started to laugh. Life was so good now......

\*      \*      \*

Mary listened intently to the old woman. They were in the kitchen and she was sat opposite her across the huge oak table, cradling a hot cup of sweet tea after just eating the final remains of the freshly baked bread with strawberry jam. She listened to every word, occasionally allowing a tear to form in her eye as Hannah told of how Ben had been such a good boy and had helped around the farmhouse, making himself at home. She could imagine in her mind's eye her son dusting the sideboard in the living room and then putting out the rubbish after washing the dishes. The kind of domesticity that she had never introduced in the flat back home, and she had often wondered over these past few, painful weeks whether these were the reasons for Ben's disappearance. The woman was old, frail and maybe not completely at one with herself anymore, but there did seem to be a kindness about her. They talked of many things, including the abusive relationship she'd had with Arthur and how he used to beat her if she ever questioned his activities. She had become very lonely and so whenever they had had visitors, it had been her who had made them welcome. For Arthur it seemed he didn't mind as it kept Hannah's mind on other things whilst he went about his nefarious activities. He was now in police custody, so she wouldn't be bothered about him anymore, but sadly they had got no closer to the whereabouts of Ben. After a while Mary asked the question that had been burning deep in her soul for so long. "Did he never talk about me or even try to contact me?" she asked with searching and soulful eyes. Hannah looked up, her face a mask of regret and sadness "Yes he did Mary. He spoke about you all of the time. He missed you greatly and I'm ashamed to say that when he did try to contact you, by writing a letter, I promised to post it but instead I just threw it into the waste bin". Tears welled up in her eyes and she briefly looked away. "You see, he was such a lovely boy and I felt so very lonely that I couldn't bare the thought of him leaving me. I know I did wrong and I knew there was a mother somewhere out there thinking of him, but I just couldn't do anything else." She looked up and deep into Mary's eyes. "I am so very sorry. Could you ever forgive me?".

Mary looked into Hannah's eyes and could only see sadness and despair and almost immediately she felt an overwhelming sense of pity for her. "Of course I forgive you", and with that she walked around the table and took the old woman in her arms cradling her as they both sobbed quietly. "Of course I forgive you Hannah, you didn't know really, but I need to leave in the morning. I have to find Ben soon. You understand don't you?". Hannah nodded her head and allowed the months and years of pain and terror that she had endured to come out in floods of tears as Mary, someone she had only met a few hours ago, cradled and hugged her and gradually made it feel better.

The next morning she bid goodbye to Hannah and left wondering what on earth would become of her. She was a lonely old woman with seemingly no means of support, yet never was short of food. A constant supply of freshly baked bread and countless pots of tea meant that somehow she was surviving. Mary made a mental note to herself that once this nightmare had come to an end she would look up Hannah once more and try to offer some kind of help, although what she could do for someone else was always debatable. Maybe at some stage she could contact the social services and they could help? She'd always had a healthy dislike and mistrust of the people who worked in that field, but maybe on this occasion they could be of some use.

Off down the pathway leading away from the farmhouse, the sun was shining brightly and for the first time since she'd left the coach on the motorway, she felt a sense of optimism and almost excitement

at being re-united with her son. She couldn't tell where it came from
or indeed why it had appeared, but it was there nonetheless, and
she approached each step with a new vitality, almost singing and
humming to herself as she again followed her motherly instincts,
feeling that each pathway was leading her back to Ben.   There
was no plan or indeed method in Mary's progress. She had a deep
inner instinct that she just followed, almost literally. She allowed it
to guide her down unknown and strange pathways, through fields,
across glades and meadows and along main roads that lead to towns
she had never seen or heard of. Each turning she took she knew it
was the right way. Only once did she have a doubt and that was when
she came across a junction of pathways and bridleways that lead into
four different directions. For a moment she hesitated, but then she
closed her eyes and imagined which route her son would have taken
and in a flash she knew in an instant and immediately followed the
right path, happy in the knowledge that each step was getting closer.

*       *       *

Ben was woken with a start, the crashing sound of a tree either
falling or swaying too heavily in the now tempestuous wind. It had
been a deep, but not particularly restful sleep, and when the sound
awoke him, Ben found himself shivering as the wind howled and cut
deep into his clothing. So different from a couple of hours ago when
he had first sat down to rest. He immediately got up and gathered
all of his new-found possessions, quickly stuffing the excess clothes
into his bag. As he did so he saw the hand written note pinned to the
sales tag and realised that he had been visited whilst he was asleep. It
disturbed him, not the least the fact that the person hadn't bothered
to waken him, but had written the note and then left him be. His
young mind couldn't really understand why, but it did make him
wonder whether he should follow the instructions and go to see this
person called Caroline. As he stood and thought, he heard another
crashing from deep inside the forest, a heavy sound that seemed to

182

resonate from within, and with it came the howling of the wind, more active and menacing than before. With that he knew he had to get away from this place immediately and find comfort elsewhere. He craved the softness of a bed with crisp, clean sheets, just like at the farmhouse. In fact there were times when he craved the sanctuary of Hannah's place, and he often wondered if he had done the right thing by stealing and then running away from the place.

As he stood the wind blew so hard that he had to momentarily grasp hold of the nearest branch to steady himself. It made it difficult for him to lift his bag over his shoulders to carry, and he felt his mop of hair flap into his eyes, making it almost impossible to see. The howling intensified and he began to get scared. This was not normal as far as he could tell, and it was something he felt he needed to get away from quickly. With great difficulty he released his grip on the branch and edged away from the clearing, remembering to follow the brief instructions on the piece of paper that was still attached to the bag. He could hardly stay upright and it felt that no matter which direction he was heading, the wind would be full in his face, stopping him from making any progress. As each step was taken it seemed to get stronger, biting into his eyes, making them water and sting with pain. It became so difficult for him to walk that he had to devise a way of moving forward by literally grabbing hold of successive branches and tree trunks to enable him to move forward. The frustration became more and more evident in his face and at one stage in sheer desperation he shouted at the top of his voice "Mum!". He so wished she were here to help and guide him, and at times like this he missed her so much. Eventually Ben escaped the clutches of the forest, by following the directions left on the note, and by almost crawling on his hands and knees. It was only after he had cleared the last of the trees that he felt the wind die down and for the first time he felt the sun on his face. Blinking his eyes he looked ahead of him and saw the cottage standing just away from the last of the trees. How could the weather and elements change so quickly? Behind him was the tempest, yet here, stood only a few feet away, it was total calm and serenity. Straightening his hair and his clothes, he walked steadily now toward the rear of the cottage, which was surrounded by a white wooden fence, and hopefully a friendly welcome from this person called Caroline.

If he had known what was to come, the temptation to have turned around and retreat back into the foreboding forest would surely have been too great. Sadly for Ben, he had no ideas of the dangers that lay ahead, and it was this unconscious decision that would cause the pain and hardship that was soon to befall him. Such moments are made on days like these.

# CHAPTER THIRTY

Listening to the car radio on his way home, Tom couldn't quite believe what was happening. After everything recently, now there had been a terrible accident on the main A-road leading out of the village, where a young policeman had pulled out into the path of a fast moving lorry and had been pushed into a ditch. According to the news report, the officer was killed instantly and the driver of the lorry was in hospital in a state of deep shock. It was just incredible what had happened in such a short space of time, on the back of the death of Lorraine from the cottage nearby and then of course the young girl Sara after the dinner date they had shared. What made it even more incredible to him was Caroline's reaction when he spoke to her about it later. "Yes, he'd been here and was asking all about Lorraine. Such a shame, because he'd seemed like such a nice young man. "

"He'd been here and was asking you questions?".

"Yes, why?"

"Well, it's just that you never mentioned that the police were visiting you, and you seem", Tom couldn't quite figure out what to say or how, "...so unconcerned by it all".

"Well what would you have me do Tom?". Caroline continued laying the cutlery on the kitchen table with the plates and dishes. "It's not like I knew him you know...and besides why shouldn't the police come and see me? Lorraine was someone I was acquainted with."

"Acquainted with? She was your friend!"

"Oh stop going on my love. The policeman came here, asked a few unimportant and rather routine questions and then he left. Sadly for him he didn't make it back and I'm truly sorry for that, but it hardly has an impact on us does it?", and with that she went over to him and squeezed his stomach playfully before reaching over and kissing him passionately on the lips. "Now stop this and go and have your bath. By the time you're out, dinner will be ready and I'll send the kids to bed and we can have a few quiet moments alone."

Tom nodded meekly and made his way upstairs. For once he felt deeply troubled about his wife and couldn't really understand why. There was something now that Caroline wasn't telling him, and with his own deep secret, he felt he had to tread even more carefully than ever. As he walked past the children's bedroom he heard them screech with laughter and he made a mental note to himself to make an effort later to go in and read them both a bedtime story. He'd been neglecting them too much recently and had started to feel more and more guilty. He would play with them after dinner before the inevitable ritual of the evening with Caroline. He thought he'd heard another noise coming from the second bedroom, a kind of muffled sound, but thought nothing more of it as it didn't re-appear. *Probably just George settling down for the evening*. The dog was getting a little too old now and so was maybe trying to get himself comfortable before sleep.

Later, as he lay in the bed, he played the events of the past few weeks and days over and over in his mind. With the dismissive conversation he'd had with Caroline this evening, and with the secret of his relationship with Janet, it made him more and more uneasy with himself. He wasn't sure why, but he felt that there was something that his wife wasn't telling him. The question was, how could he find out the truth without giving anything away himself? These questions needed an answer soon, before it was too late.

\*　　　　　\*　　　　　\*

The back door opened and there had stood Caroline. She'd been expecting him and smiled broadly at the young boy stood before her. "I knew you would come", and with that she reached out to his arm and guided him into the warmth and comfort of the kitchen. "Sit down and I'll get you a nice cup of coffee". Ben did as he was told and sat at the large wooden table that was the centre piece of the room. He said nothing but just sat and took in his surroundings. In a way they were similar to the farmhouse that Hannah and Arthur owned, but this place had a different feel about it. Almost immediately he had felt it, the second he had walked into the cottage, but it was something he couldn't quite fathom. Caroline took his bags and placed them in the corner and busied herself with the kettle and filling a huge plate with all kinds of biscuits and savoury cakes. "I knew when I saw you asleep in the woods that you were coming here. Can't have a young boy like you sleeping rough can we?". Ben looked at her, really unable to say anything. She was incredibly beautiful. Even at his tender age he could see there was something special, almost magical about the woman who was fussing all over him. Her long blonde hair was cascading around her shoulders, and each time she brushed past him, he caught a whiff of the scent that she wore. If he knew what the word meant, he would describe it as intoxicating, but all he knew was that he liked this lady. He liked her a lot.

"Cat got your tongue then?" She smiled at him as she asked, and it made him relax. "No, not really. I don't really know what to say".

"Oh, you won't be shy with me you know," she said as she placed the coffee and biscuits and cake in front of him and then sat at the seat opposite. "I'm Caroline and I live here with my two children, Adam and Shelley. They are a bit younger than you, but they'd love to meet you. They're at school at the moment, but we'll say hello when they get back. "You're Ben aren't you?"

Ben was shocked as he'd never told anyone his name and he'd only just met this woman. "Yes, but how do you know?".

"I know a lot of things young Ben." She smiled at him and her eyes delved deep into his and he was captivated. "I know that you've run away from home and that your mum is looking for you…isn't that right?".

"I don't know", whispered Ben, putting down a chocolate biscuit as he felt the tears well up in his eyes. "I haven't seen her for ages……. and I want to".

"I know Ben". Caroline reached her hand across the table to his and clasped it hard. "You will though. She's on her way and while she is looking for you, you can stay and wait here with me. How would that be?".

"Yes" said Ben, choking back the tears that were beginning to form. "This is a nice place and I'd like to stay here."

"Good", replied Caroline. "…and so you shall. Now eat up your biscuits and cake and drink your coffee and we'll get a room ready for you".

With that Caroline disappeared for a full hour upstairs leaving Ben to sit by the fire in the kitchen eating his biscuits and cake. It was warm and comforting, away from the wind and rain that was now battering the rear windows of the cottage. In the silence that followed he heard the old grandfather clock chime. It was noon, midday and he felt very sleepy. Slowly his eyelids began to close with the exertion of the past few days and within a couple of minutes he was sleeping soundly in the old wicker chair whilst the flames of the kitchen fire warmed his body. Upstairs Caroline made preparations for her new guest, singing and humming a tune to herself. Her spirits were high, and Ben's arrival had confirmed to her that she was on the right path. Stopping briefly she looked at the plaque above her bed and smiled inwardly once more. If it ever meant more she was not aware. This was the moment as far as she was concerned….

…every now and then a person falls into a state of total despair. It can come about through many ways, but it is a state of such hopelessness and negativity that there is little the person can do to overcome it alone. Help is what is needed, but sometimes even that isn't enough. If a person embraces the goodness of their friends, their colleagues, and indeed any professional help that can be offered, then there is always hope. If that person chooses not to embrace it, then they will fall into the abyss of their mind, not knowing what they can do to improve their lot. Each decision becomes clouded with uncertainty and a lack of surety. Eventually they lose the ability to see through the fog of their mind, and after a while it all becomes too blurred, and the simple task of distinguishing between good and bad, right and wrong can be beyond them and eventually they become lost forever. It is at this moment that the human mind loses control and falls deeper than anyone would ever dream possible....

"So tell me...what is happening?"

"I don't know"

"You must"

"I don't"

"Well I suggest you sort out your mind and quickly before this takes over"

"I will"


If Caroline had ever known the depths of her sickness and depravity, then she had kept it a secret. Either that or she had been in a constant state of self denial. Whatever was happening in her mind, she wouldn't and indeed couldn't face it. It was happening and to her it was entirely normal. The beauty she looked for was rarely there, or as rarely the way she perceived it. For her, life was a constant search for something that in an average person's life just didn't exist.

# CHAPTER THIRTY-ONE

If little Ben Fuller believed that the misery he had endured in his short life was about to come to an end, then it was a belief that would be sadly disproved. What was about to happen to him would be far worse than anything he had experienced in his short life before, and certainly far worse than anything that should ever be experienced by any human being, no matter how long or brief there stay on this mortal coil. It was only just beginning.

His first memories of this unwelcome part of his life were cloudy and lost in a haze of fogginess that pervaded his mind. He awoke before opening his eyes and was immediately overcome by the powerful smell that attacked his senses. It seemed to reach deep inside him and the aroma made him feel almost nauseas. It was a stench he'd never felt before but one that suggested decay and something terrible. Opening his eyes he blinked in the darkness and realised that he was in fact in total darkness. Then he realised he couldn't move. His arms were tied above his head and he could now feel that they were bound together at the wrists, which in turn must have been tied to the top of the bed he was lying on. Trying to lift his head he immediately felt the thunder of pain in his forehead and slumped back on to the pillow. He tried to move his feet and legs, but again realised that they too were tied at the ankles and to the foot of the bed. What was happening? Panic overcame him and suddenly he began to shake violently. He tried to speak, cry out, but no words would come as if his voice had been lost. Gradually his eyes adjusted to his dark surroundings and he could see he was a small room, not much bigger than his old bedroom back home, but this was a dark and dank place. There were a few shelves on the wall immediately opposite with a selection of what seemed like glass jars, but it was difficult to distinguish in the haziness. Twisting his head slightly, ever so slightly to avoid the jarring pain that seared through his eyes, he could also see the outline of a lone chair in the corner, and what seemed like steps beyond leading to an entrance at the top. He was obviously in a cellar of some sort, tied to the bed, unable to move or speak and with pain invading his mind. He tried to calm himself, as only a young boy who had been through so much already can, and eventually controlled his breathing. How had he got here? He couldn't remember much apart from falling asleep in front of the burning log fire, while the nice lady Caroline was busy upstairs making a bed for him. He had a brief vision and recollection of being carried upstairs by two strong arms, and then the pain in his head. That was something he could remember. The heavy object that hurt him so badly for a few seconds and then nothing. Now he was here.... but where was here? How long had he been here? Was it Caroline who had put him here? He just couldn't understand and slowly the tears fell down his cheeks. At that moment he had never felt so lonely, so utterly bereft of any hope, so completely overwhelmed by the despair of his situation. Although no noise could be made, he sobbed until he slept once more, in pain in both body and soul.

\*　　　　\*　　　　\*

Janet woke that morning with a new feeling of determination and hope. She had desired Tom for too many years, and now that she had him, there was no way she would ever let him go. No matter what it took, she would make him happy. Even if she had to become a surrogate mother to his two children, she would do it. Standing in front of the bathroom mirror she looked at herself. True, she didn't have the beauty of Caroline, but there was something else that had always attracted men. She had a sensual attraction, one which she would always save now for the love of her life. She smiled at herself "You're not bad you know". The reflection looking back didn't disagree but just smiled. Now she had to find a way of dealing with Caroline. From what Tom had told her, the woman wasn't exactly the most stable of people, and anyone who demanded loving every night of the week has to be slightly unhinged. This could be a problem, more so than normal, but she had spent her whole life dealing with problems, and this was just one more. As she left her small flat for the office, she looked back and realised that one day she would have to leave it. This, her sanctuary, her breathing space from the world, but it would have to go. The one consolation was that it would have to go because of Tom.

If her mood had been good when shed got up, it was changed instantly she walked into the office. There was no Tom. He hadn't come in today and hadn't called. She was confused and tried not to show her concern when asking colleagues. "So he didn't call then?", she tried to ask as casually as possible. "No Janet, he didn't call". The dismissive attitude irritated her more than ever. She'd always disliked Amy. A twenty five year old who acted like she was still a teenager. Her clothes too tight, her hair too bleached, her womanly charms too open for all men's eyes. The woman was a pain, and she was enjoying Janet's obvious discomfort.

"He wouldn't normally not come in and not call"

"Well he has this time hasn't he?" With that a withering look as she tore her eyes from the computer screen which was probably full of holiday deals and chat rooms. "I really wouldn't worry. You can enjoy yourself without your boss looking over your shoulder". The word was boss seemed to be over emphasised, or maybe Janet was particularly sensitive. "In fact whilst the cat is away eh?"

"Well I'm sorry Amy, but as his secretary I have a responsibility to Mr Bolton and this department so I won't be playing as you put it..." She stared back at this slip of a woman who so annoyed her, making Amy blush slightly. It didn't disarm her though. "Well yes Janet you are his secretary aren't you?. Everybody knows that"

It was time for Janet to blush. The inference was clear. She stood and stared at Amy, who after meeting her eyes then turned back to the computer screen and started typing as if she wasn't there. Janet stood for a few moments and then realised that in fact there were a few people in the office who were looking in their direction, and so as not to cause any kind of scene, she turned and returned to her desk in silence, not daring to look anyone in the face.

She tried not to attract attention as she called his mobile. It was unanswered. She sent a text which was not replied to, and finally in an act of desperation, she called his home number. It had taken courage to do so, as the thought of talking to the woman who shared his bed virtually every night made her feel almost physically sick, but it wouldn't arouse suspicion. After all a secretary had to be aware of her boss's whereabouts. As the phone rang her heart beat stronger, and she mentally rehearsed what she would say, but after the tenth ring she knew there would be no answer, so the feeling was a return of dismay and concern. What to do now?

For the rest of the day she worried constantly about Tom. Trying not to attract too much attention from everyone else, she carried on with her work, making phone calls, typing quotes, filling in appointments and making excuses for Mr Bolton's unexpected absence to irritated clients, but all the time she could only think of Tom. She called his mobile every half an hour until the hopelessness of it all became too much and she disappeared into the washroom were she cried silently to herself. By mid afternoon she made a decision to leave the office early and drive to his house. It was risky, but she needed to hear from him. Her imagination was now beginning to gain a life of its own, and as always in situations like this, it conjured up the worst case scenario. In her now confused mind Tom had declared his undying love for Caroline, had promised to end the relationship with her and was now preparing a new life in another town. If it wasn't that, then it was even worse. Tom had been driving into work and had been involved in a terrible accident and was in hospital...or even worse. The uncertainty was making her scared and no matter how risky it was turning up at his house unannounced, she knew it was better than being totally in the dark. *"Tom, where are you?"*

*    *    *

The pain was instant. It awoke Ben with a start, and for a moment he couldn't breathe, or think or speak or move. In fact he couldn't do anything except silently scream. It was so intense, he couldn't imagine that anything could have felt worse ever again. The knife was incisive and ripped into his skin like a laser as he felt it delve deeply into his chest. He wanted to cry out to stop, please stop, but again there were no words that could come from his throat. He couldn't move to escape the torture but had to endure the seconds of sheer unadulterated agony. Why would anyone want to hurt him this way? He tried to look up at the body that belonged to the instrument of torture, but there was no way he could move without the searing pain in his head adding to the agony of the knife now deep within him. After a while, maybe only a few seconds, but to Ben like an age, the knife was withdrawn and the pain gradually subsided. It was such a blessed relief that he wished he could cry out with gratitude, but of course he could do nothing but lie there. He felt the shifting breeze of another brush past him, and felt the same sense of aroma that he had noticed before,, but he couldn't see anything. In the distance he heard the sound of a glass clanking and maybe the unscrewing of a lid, but there was nothing else that made sense. How long had he been here? He didn't know, but the nightmare had been too long. Then there was the sharp prick of a needle, and within moments he drifted back into the blackness and the void, briefly numbing the pain that invaded his body completely.

In the fogginess and darkness of the room the trained eyes of the torturer looked at the exhibit and smiled in satisfaction. This would be a good experiment but also a little messy. They would have to be careful, of that there was no doubt.

Later that night Caroline had a dream. It was like no other and invaded her senses almost completely. She was walking through her favourite wood and admiring the blossoming bluebells that had carpeted the forest floor. Some were flowering as she walked toward them, whilst others hummed an almost silent tune, that only she could hear. Above her, the forest canopy was bathed in an extraordinary sunlight, brighter than any day seen before, allowing the light to cascade to the floor, illuminating all the creatures of the wood. In the distance the fallow deer hopped and skipped its way to the hidden undergrowth, and somewhere in the distance she heard the lark with its insistent cry. The day was perfection, but then she felt a tearing in her breast…a pain that gradually intensified. She felt herself struggle to breathe and in an effort to relieve the pressure of whatever was delving deeply, she ripped away her blouse and threw it to the floor. It was the she noticed the scarlet blood on her fingers and as she looked down she could see her breasts, stomach and legs covered with blood. It was seeping from a wound that gradually got bigger and bigger, so that she could see deep into her chest. The blood then began to gush out and quickly covered the green forest glade into a reddish brown. Becoming weaker and weaker she fell to her knees, still trying to stem the tide of blood that now cascaded from her body. No one could lose that amount of blood and survive…but she kept on breathing. There was now no pain, but a numbness that overcame her and as she sank to her knees she felt herself drift into unconciuosness. In the distance she heard the lark singing louder and louder as if it was approaching, just as she fell into blackness, she saw the fallow deer approach her and smile……..at that moment she woke up. It was with a start and for a while she lay there gathering her senses and allowing her eyes to get used to the darkness of her surroundings. She was bathed in sweat, and beside her she felt the rhythmic breathing of Tom fast asleep. After a few moments she composed herself and smiled inwardly. She'd had dreams before, but none that matched the vividness of that one. It had startled her, but for the wrong reasons. In fact the dream had excited her and she felt alive within. It was then that she slowly climbed on top of her husband and gently woke him from his slumber.

*          *          *

Briefly during the evening Ben woke, but it was such a painful experience that he wished he would never wake again.

*          *          *

Janet's heart thumped hard as her car approached the cottage. All the way she had wondered and thought what to say should the door be opened by Caroline…or even Tom. How could she explain to her that she had come to see Tom, all this way? How could she explain to Tom that she had come all this way to see him? Surely that would be easy? They loved each other, but then why had he disappeared and not been in touch? If he really did love her as he said, then he would have called or something. The doubts had started to cloud her mind and the insecurities had taken over by the time the cottage came into view. Now what?........

*          *          *

The steps Mary took brought her closer by the minute. The sight of the cottage was the final step.

196

# CHAPTER THIRTY-TWO

*Three months later....................*

The charred remains of the lovely cottage that sat in the village of Little Hanwick had been a blight on the beauty of the area for too long now, and the vivid memories of what had taken place there were still too raw in the minds of the locals. At a community meeting one wintry Wednesday morning they had all agreed, to a man and a woman, that the site had to be cleared completely. It would cost money, and as the local council were clearly going to drag their feet in attending to the problem, then they, the villagers, would take care of it. They would all contribute and eventually the darkness that surrounded the place and the time of the cottage would be taken away.

PC Hemping studied the rubble and dust of the place he had visited so many times in the past few weeks. Each time he had stood there he had felt the terrible chill take over his body, no matter what the weather and no matter how strong the sun. The story of this place had so quickly become part of legend and local folklore. He was a thick-set man, not easily bowed, and had been on the force for over twenty years. In his time he had witnessed and dealt with many murders, horrendous crimes and incidents, and had felt that there was little that could shock or hinder him in his now desensitised occupation...not so. The last few months in this once quiet village had shocked not just the usually un-moved force he belonged to, but the whole nation. What had at first been a localised upset soon became a national horror story as the events unfolded. Now three months on, as the media had departed and the ghoulish onlookers stopped bothering the villagers, it was left to them all to almost literally pick up the pieces. As he stood there he silently remembered each and every victim. The horrors that had taken place deep inside the picture-postcard building were sometimes too much for anyone to contemplate. The deaths of a bright young couple and their two children, plus an innocent visitor who had been caught in the crossfire. These had followed the suicide of the young woman who had lived down the lane, and of course a colleague who had died in the car crash. How could so many things happen in such a short space of time, and in such a quiet country retreat like this? It was now down to him to try to unravel the events. He sighed to himself and turned away. Climbing into his car he shook his head in despair. Somehow all of this had to be explained, but where to start? As he pulled away he relived the events chronologically from the moment they had been made aware that there was something deeply amiss at the cottage.....

"Sergeant, get yourself down to Little Hanwick. We need to talk to this Caroline Bolton again. She was the last person who spoke to Adam Weston before the car crash. We need to establish what state of mind he was in when he left."

"Yes sir". The DC was sat opposite him at his desk, looking terribly worried. Adam Weston had been a protégé of his, and the loss was especially felt. A bright young star of the force, and so cruelly extinguished in a dreadful fashion. It had put a cloud over the force, and with the apparent suicide of Lorraine Ripley still unexplained, it had put a lot more pressure on him than anything recently. Add that to the fact that he was nearing retirement, and this was certainly not something that had been planned.

"I will get on it right away", and with that Andy Hemping left his boss's office and returned to his computer screen which was busy printing out details of Caroline and Tom Bolton. He felt sorry for DC Pemberton. A kindly soul who had always been there when there had been trouble, personal or otherwise, and had the greatest respect from his men. For this to happen on his patch just two months from his retirement was a real piece of bad luck, as most people knew that there would be nothing he would prefer more than an easy end to his career. This terrible car crash that had taken one of their own, the suicide of a popular woman in the village, and now the suggestion that the missing boy, who had been headline news a couple of months ago, was now likely to be in the area, meant a busy time for them all.

It had been more than a busy time, he thought as he swung the car out onto the main road, the one that had tragically taken Adam Weston. It had been the worst time. He thought of the day he heard the news, and the shock that had surrounded his colleagues in the office. He thought of Adam's wife and young child, and shuddered when he remembered that it had been initially down to him to inform them of PC Weston's death. Fortunately for him, he had been sent out to discuss a domestic dispute in the adjoining village, so it had been given to WPC Aston. She was older and more experienced in such things and he knew she would be able to make a far better job at handling such a delicate situation. It's funny how so many policemen and women 'go missing' when such a job is given to them. No matter how much training one is given in dealing with such delicate situations, it is never something that comes easily, and there isn't a single one of them that would volunteer for such a task, no matter how well loved the deceased might have been.

His mind then wandered to his first meeting with Caroline Bolton. She had answered the door, and he had immediately been taken aback by both her beauty and her manner. A visit from the police hadn't fazed her at all like most people, but it had seemed that she was quite used to such things. She had almost immediately, almost too quickly he'd felt, explained that her husband was out on an errand and wouldn't be back for at least an hour, and would he like a cup of tea? He declined, but accepted the offer of a seat on the spacious sofa that dominated the pleasantly furnished living room of the cottage. He had very quickly noticed the perfume she was wearing and wondered how Adam Weston had reacted to it. There was certainly a flirtatious way to her. A lingering smile that lasted just a little too long. Sitting just a little too closely, and a familiarity that seemed out of place with a member of the local constabulary. It was the kind of situation that could easily get out of control, but his years on the force, and more importantly his happy marriage, meant that she would be no more than a mental diversion, and nothing else.

Caroline answered the questions in a matter of fact way, but gave nothing new to the inquiry over Adam Weston's death. She blanched a little when Lorraine Ripley was mentioned, but again seemed very guarded by what she said. Strangely as he was leaving, she asked about the missing schoolboy, Ben Fuller. He had no idea why as it wasn't a case that had interested anyone at the station as it had been in a different patch at that time, but he told her he would make enquiries and if there was anything to report he would get back to her. It was to his eternal shame that he didn't pursue it and ask why she was interested in such a thing, but then hindsight is always a good thing....

That hindsight might have helped him identify the muffled noise he heard as he walked down the pathway to his car. He wasn't sure what type of noise or indeed whether it came from the cottage, but as he turned around to look back he saw Caroline staring at him in a rather unnerving way, and decided for once to forget what he had been taught all those years ago and walk away. He should have gone back and investigated. He should have asked Caroline Bolton if he could take a look upstairs where he thought the noise came from, but her stare and her flirtatious way had stopped him. It is decisions like that that can change a person's destiny, or indeed the destiny of many. He was guilty of that.....

It had been that lack of decision and commitment that allowed so many things to go unchecked by the force, and why it was now that a post mortem of sorts was being held, and not a pre-investigation. When the call came to the emergency services concerning a fire at the Willow cottage, there could have been no indication as to what it would lead to. The fire brigade had arrived within twenty minutes. Not a startlingly fast time, but having to come from the next town, it was a remarkable effort. Sadly it wasn't quick enough to save the $17^{th}$ century building or its occupants. Once the flames had been doused sufficiently, and rubble sifted, the charred remains became clear. The young fireman who discovered the first body found it hard to suppress his emotions and sat away from the scene quietly sobbing to himself. A comforting arm around the shoulders and a hot cup of sweet tea, helped, but the shock of the two young children wrapped in each other's arms would be a sight that would haunt him for the rest of his life. The next discovery was as harrowing. It was difficult to tell whether the person was male or female, but a few strands of hair had survived the inferno, helping the post mortem at a later date. Just a few yards away from the main area that was once the idyllic cottage, there was the untouched body of a dog, seemingly dying of a heart attack as it had tried to escape the flames. It was this scene of despair and tragedy that was now PC Hemping's to investigate.

It was established that Tom and Caroline Bolton were a happy couple, according to the villagers who ever met them, bringing up two young children in a cottage they had moved into a few years previously. Tom was a womaniser though and had numerous office affairs which, when she found out, had devastated Caroline. The move to the little hamlet was a way of 'starting again', but Caroline had found it hard to cope and also forget her husband's infidelity, and she had found herself becoming increasingly more and more dependant on anti-depressants, mixed with large amounts of alcohol.

The children were cared for in all material things, but in terms of schooling, they were very much left to their own devices. There was little interest or indeed love from Tom for his children and he could go days without even seeing them. Work was always his main distraction, and with his absence during the day, Caroline had slowly started to sink into the madness of her unstable mind. She had seen a psychiatrist but had stopped the counselling abruptly when it had been suggested to her that she had an unnatural obsession with her husband. According to the reports, she was on the verge of mental illness, and had a frequency toward violence, although there had never been any suggestion that it had been inflicted on her children, or indeed her beloved husband. What had been of concern though, was that the day before the fire had started, she had bought a very dangerous weapon from an antique shop in the town, and despite the shop owner's call to the police as a matter of course, they had chosen to ignore that information. The discovery of the badly melted sabre amongst the burnt ashes was something which was a worry to the police, especially as the deaths of the victims hadn't been entirely down to the fire.

The fire had been started deliberately, that was confirmed by the fire brigade within a few days. That was another reason why the police had taken a more than usual interest in the case. It would be a difficult few weeks, but Adam Hemping had been in the force for over twenty years, and with his crack team of fellow detectives, he felt confident it could all be resolved sooner rather than later.

# CHAPTER THIRTY-THREE

As he sat staring out at the unforgiving sea and its waves crashing against the barrier, he felt nothing. There was no emotion, and the glass that separated him from the inferno that nature was providing outside in a way signified his mind and his barrier and separation from the events of three months ago. He had not spoken a word since. There had been no emotion shown, no cries of anguish, no tears of despair, just silence. Each question was unanswered, except in his own mind. All he could do to block out the horror of the past was to empty his mind of everything. There was no-one left to help. He was now an empty shell.

She was different. The light-hearted nature continued. Everyday was like before. In her mind nothing had changed except it was her and him and no-one else now. Life was sweet and joyful and beautiful and there was so much to embrace. She would be his rock, his guiding hand, his companion and his lover. Nothing had changed at all.

# CHAPTER THIRTY-FOUR

"So let's analyse this properly". Adam Hemping sat down heavily on the thick set chair and planted two pints of Badgers Ale on the heavily stained oak table. Sat opposite was his working partner of five years, a gruff looking man, considerably older in both years and attitude. He smoked a pipe when not on duty, was a real ale man, someone who would happily travel the country in search of the perfect beer. They had known each other for many more than the five years they had worked together, and had been the best man at each other's weddings. Bill Freedling was a copper of the 'old school' and preferred to solve a case over a couple of pints in the pub, just like this evening. The pub in question, 'The Coach' had down the ages seen and witnessed many cases solved in this way, always in the evening in the comfort of the snug and nearly always with a heated discussion. It may not be textbook sleuthing, but it certainly worked.

"How else to do you suggest we do it then?" asked Bill, taking his first sip of beer, allowing it to slowly slip down his throat. It tasted good and no matter how many times he drank this particular brand of beer, it always gave him that feeling of comfort and pleasure. It was one of the luxuries of life as far as he was concerned, and one that he would never give up no matter what.

"Well, yes of course". Adam hadn't completely missed the irony in his good friend's voice, but had down the years got used to it and it had stopped bothering him. "What I meant was, let's take it chronologically".

"Are you cold?". Bill got up and walked to the only window in the room. It was closed but outside the rain was falling heavily, and with the wind blowing heavier than usual, it had sent a draught of chill into the room, which even the generously roaring log fire in the corner was having difficulty in counter acting. "What we know is that Caroline Bolton was an odd lady to say the least". He looked up at the curtain rail as he talked, it causing difficulty as he pulled to the heavy fabric that blocked out the outside world and its inclement weather. Walking back to the table and puffing on his pipe so that the aroma filled the air, he sat down and looked at Adam. "There was no emotion when she was asked about her friend Lorraine, and you said yourself that when you went to see her, she acted in a not very normal way. Surely that's where we start. If you really believe this fire was started deliberately she is the one we have to look out for...if she is still alive".

"I thought we had established that the body wasn't Caroline, but Mr Bolton's secretary?"

"Well, that is what we all believe, but this has been an odd case and all I'm saying is we should keep our options completely open. Especially as the post mortem has had so much trouble identifying the body, but let's go with the general consensus and say that it wasn't Caroline Bolton in the fire. That means she is still walking around, either in a state of complete despair, she did lose her two children remember, or she is the cold hearted murderess that the media are now suggesting."

"Hardly a scientific conclusion is it Bill?". Adam seemed disappointed at the ease at which his colleague had simplified the case. He took a large gulp of ale and eased back in his chair. It felt so comforting and there were times when he felt he could just close his eyes at moments like this and sleep the night. It had on one or two occasions even occurred to him, but the thought of Jenny at home fretting and worrying herself had deterred him. Still, he felt relaxed now.

"What do you want? There really isn't anything else we can go on. Yes there appeared to be problems in the marriage, and there is the suggestion from the friends of the deceased that there was a relationship taking place, but was that enough to set fire to the home, killing her children in the process? How many mothers could do such a thing, unless of course there was a serious mental illness… and that is something which we must surely accept now. This is a woman who showed no emotion over the death of her friend, who was indifferent to the car crash of a man who she had spoken to only minutes before, and we know that she was actively spying on her husband. If she survived the fire, and my belief is that she did, then she was responsible for it and the murder of three people, including her two children."

Adam went silent for a while as he listened. When Bill stopped talking he didn't say anything but sat and stared at the fire watching the flames leap and dart around the charred logs, engulfing the crackling wood. It gave off a pungent smell which was not unpleasant. It was hard to believe that something as spectacular and warming as fire could also be so destructive.

"I'll get you another pint". Bill had already finished his first and was thirsting for another. Adam quickly downed the last dregs of his and watched as his friend walked toward the bar in the next room and thought. This was not the world he'd expected when he first joined the force. He'd been seduced by the cardboard characters of the television, with their flash cars and clothing speeding from one crime bust to the next. It had seemed exciting if not necessarily glamorous. The reality was different. It was true this was the first really spectacular case that had taken place for a while, but the thought of the charred bodies in the remains was something that was haunting him now and probably would continue. He thought of his situation with Jenny and the sadness that had engulfed them when it was revealed that she would never be able to have children. It was something that had hit them both hard, and had almost seen the relationship and marriage end because of it. They had thought of adopting, but decided that it would be in their eyes a very poor substitute. A very selfish view, they had both admitted to themselves, but it had to be right and if Jenny couldn't conceive, then they would not try any other way. The sadness that had always followed Adam was tonight highlighted even more when he thought of the two young children found in the fire. How could anyone do such a thing, especially a mother? It was the one thing in this case that made him more determined than ever to find the solution.

The shrill ring of his mobile rudely interrupted his thoughts. He pulled it out of his jacket pocket and looked at the screen. It was Jenny. He knew it before he even looked, and it gave him a warm and soothing feeling. They had been married for twelve years, but the thought that she would still ring him when he was working late was proof of the love that existed between them. "Hi darling..."

Outside the rain came down even heavier, so that it almost bounced off the pavement. The wind was howling and only the hardiest would venture out on an evening such as this. Inside the pub the lights burned brightly giving out the welcoming glow and the regulars sat in their familiar places and enjoyed the convivial atmosphere. In the distance a pair of eyes, shielded from the heavy rain by a darkened hood attached to a heavy full length coat, stared directly into the windows of the snug. They had watched as the man had walked to the window and pulled the curtains, not quite meeting in the centre so that there was a shaft of light that escaped and a window to the inside was visible. It was this that the pair of eyes stared at, the lips and mouth mumbling obscenities to itself. There was a hatred in the eyes, a feeling of fear and evil. It was directed at neither the two men who sat and talked over a pint of beer, but at the folder that lay on the table between the two, clearly visible, and the picture of the beautiful blonde haired woman that dominated the open page. The men were talking about her and pointing to the picture as they spoke. The prying eyes couldn't see the picture fully but knew it was her. The hatred flared up and at that point if it were possible, the picture would be laid to bare for all to see, but in a more decisive way. They would have their revenge.

As he sat there Adam felt the presence, but couldn't discern it. It was like there was a pressure from somewhere and was pushing down on him, but there was nothing and no-one around. He waited for Bill to return.

"Does this place feel strange to you tonight?".

"What?" Bill placed the two pints of beer on the table in front of him, but not before taking a large gulp from his. "I think this case is getting to you".

"No, it's just that there feels like there is a presence of some kind...I don't know, maybe I'm getting odd in my old age eh?"

" Getting...?" laughed Bill. "Got you a treat...eat these", and he threw down a couple of packets of cheese and onion crisps.

That was Bill, thought Adam, always down to earth. Nothing ever fazed him. It comforted him, but also concerned him too. He'd felt worried about this case ever since the first visit to the site of the fire, and it was one of those things that he felt he wouldn't be able to discuss with too many people, especially Bill, and especially Jenny too. It was something he decided he would keep within him.

"Well tomorrow the pathologists report will be ready, so at least we should have a better idea as to who it is we are actually looking for. Drink up, I've got a shepherd's pie waiting for me in the oven"

The next day the report came out. There was nothing that was either positive or indeed helpful. The bodies of the two children were identified as Adam and Shelley, but the body of the woman was still unidentified. The charred remains were so bad that it was impossible to gain any kind of identity, even from dental records. The single strand of blonde hair that had somehow survived the inferno was not necessarily from the body alongside. It made the task of the police even more difficult. With the agreement of the fire investigators, they suspected arson but at the moment really had no idea who it was they were looking for. Their belief was that it was Caroline Bolton but there was no evidence to suggest that she had either survived or died in the fire. There was also a question as to where Tom Bolton was, and why hadn't he appeared after the terrible incidents. It was a complete mystery and one that seemed no nearer to being solved.

# CHAPTER THIRTY-FIVE

Three months earlier...

The sheets were soaking wet again, the dreams had been as intense as before and as such just as disturbing. Frank blinked his eyes rapidly and immediately the pain of loneliness and despair returned. The pain that had followed his every move and action since the fateful day was there by his side once more. The pain that at times was so real it almost physically hurt. It was at times like this that he felt the need to close his eyes once more, and let the respite of sleep take him away from it, in the hope that the waking hours would never come again. Not this day though. On this day he had a mission, a purpose, something to make things a little easier, something that will maybe make sense out of the whole grieving episode.

With a supreme physical effort he hauled himself out of his sweat filled bed and crawled into the shower, the hot spray waking him and touching his senses once more. Dried and dressed, choosing a pair of the jeans and a t shirt that Sara had chosen and Verity had loved...*aaahh dear Verity, I wonder how she is now*....he then made hot coffee and toast before leaving the apartment building and climbing into his Jaguar. He knew where he was heading, and he knew what he was doing. The plan had formulated in his mind for days now, becoming stronger and stronger each time he played it through. This was the only way he could find peace within himself and find a way of justifying his future presence on this planet.

As he manouvered onto the main carriageway, slowly accelerating to match the traffic, he found himself again returning to the dreadful moment in the hotel. The memories were as intense and as clear as then, and the pain hadn't subsided for one moment. The following days were as a dream, or to be more realistic, a complete mental nightmare. He had drifted through the questions, the comforting gestures, the kind words and the careful guidance of the young woman police officer who had been assigned to ensure he would be looked after. He had been very quickly been eliminated from their enquiries, especially when they had witnessed the level of grief that he had shown, and it had been decided that he needed careful attention. There was no question that Verity would have to be taken care of by the social services whilst a decision was made as to her future. Frank wasn't family, and he certainly wasn't in any state to take care of her. In fact he never saw her again after she was taken away by a kindly lady. All he remembers her by was the bemused and shocked look on the little girl's face as she was led to the car outside. As she walked away, she turned and looked at him, a little smile and a wave, and then she was gone. The thought of her intensified his grief, and the tears would always involuntarily fall. Maybe one day he will return for her? Maybe....

The drive to the village was one he had never taken before, but he'd guessed it would take a couple of hours. Ideal time to formulate his plan. The more he thought, the more he convinced himself that this was what was deserved. The hatred was one he could control, but not an emotion he would ever be able to be free from. What had happened to him, and the love of his life, should never have been allowed. This was his way of making sure her death would be avenged. With that he turned on the radio and allowed the strains of the 'Sunday-night' jazz to calm his senses. He drove the rest of the way with his mind at rest and in silence.

The cottage wasn't difficult to find. He'd seen it described on the internet as one of the five listed and protected buildings in the hamlet. It wasn't difficult to establish where they lived. Simple detective work that anyone could have done. Driving past slowly, he looked up the driveway and could see there was a light on in one of the downstairs rooms. It shone like a beacon on what was a very overcast and dull day. Soon it would shine even more.....Parking about half a mile away, down a lonely wooded lane he pulled the car into the verge sufficiently enough for it not to be noticed immediately. He had to take as much care as he could and not attract any attention to himself at all. He walked to the back of the silver car and opened the boot, and pulled out the rucksack that contained the tools of the day. It was heavy, and as he heaved it onto his back, he breathed a huge sigh from the effort. He crossed the lane and chose to pick a hole through the hedge into the adjoining field, instead of walking brazenly down the lane. It was parallel to the cottage and he was sure he wouldn't be seen if he kept to the edge, where his track was shadowed by large overhanging trees. The grass was muddy and wet underfoot, but he hardly noticed. His focus was directly in front at the cottage and its now bright light burning from the downstairs window. He thought he saw movement but dismissed it. Obviously he wanted there to be movement from within, otherwise his mission would be futile, but it was something that he didn't want to ponder on too much. Getting closer his heart pounded, so loudly that he was convinced it could be heard all around the village. His breathing became more rapid and heavy, either from the weight of the rucksack, or the weight of the knowledge in his mind. About ten feet from the white fence that surrounded the garden, he got down on his hands and knees and crawled toward the side of the cottage, ignoring the dampness of the ground and mud that splashed over his jeans and shoes. Once he had got near enough, he let the bag fall from his back and opened it to reveal the contents. It didn't take long for him to assemble them in the right order as he had thought this through day in day out for the past month, and in just a few minutes his task was accomplished. With a smile to himself he whispered *"now it's your turn"*, and with that he turned and made his way quickly back to his car, unseen by anyone. He jumped in, not bothering about his wet and dirty clothes and started the engine, wincing as it ignited with its usual roar. He couldn't afford to be spotted now. As he pulled away he glanced back and saw the light burning just a little brighter. Soon it would light up the overcast and dull sky and his job would be done. Soon they would also know the pain of grief and loss. Soon he would be able to rest in peace.

*        *        *

The cottage was empty when Janet had arrived. She had knocked on the wooden front door, the sounds matching the beating she could feel of her heart as the anticipation and fear gripped her. It became obvious though, and very quickly, that there was no-one there. No Tom and no Caroline either. She couldn't decide whether the relief of not having to face Caroline was overwhelming the sense of despair that she still didn't know where her lover had gone to. She was convinced he would be here. For a while she stood and thought, the silence of the village and her immediate surroundings helping her to rationalise everything. She knew that she couldn't just walk away and after a quick glance around to make sure she couldn't be seen from the road, she walked around the side of the cottage, not sure what it was she was expecting to see. Coming across a kitchen window that was half open, she prised it away from its lock without damage and rather inelegantly climbed in, crashing on to the floor below in a heap. A pair of sleepy eyes looked at her, sighed and then closed again. A lovely dog, but of course hopeless in these moments. It was the only thing that had made Janet smile all day, and she walked over and patted George on the head gently. The place was quiet and deserted and it gave her time to look around. It was wrong she knew, but she had to find where Tom was, and this convinced her that this was the right thing to do.

It was only after she had walked around the downstairs rooms, and admired the décor, that she heard what she thought was a slight murmuring upstairs. For a moment she froze. It could have

213

been Tom and Caroline, but after staying absolutely still for a few moments, it was clear they were not in the house. The murmuring returned, and she thought it had to be an old lady, or the radio or the television, and it was with an enormous amount of courage that she climbed the narrow and steep stairs, trying to avoid the creaking sounds that inevitably follow when you walk around a building of that age. It was only at that moment, when she had reached the top of the stairs, that she smelt the burning, and then within seconds she heard the whoosh and roar from outside. It sounded like the forest had suddenly exploded. It gave her such a fright that she immediately turned on her heels to run down the stairs, but lost her footing on the top one and fell backwards, head first to the bottom. The crack of her head against the wooden floor was final. As the blood slowly seeped from the wound, she felt herself become woozy and sleepy, and finally drifted into the welcoming blackness. Outside the flames started to caress the outer wall and lick the moss and planting that surrounded, so giving the fire more energy and passion.

From the wood Mary watched the flames erupt and also watched the man in the car slowly drive away. She had witnessed him and wanted to put a stop to it, but there was something that held her back. Even though she had no proof, she knew that dear Ben was not in that cottage, and there was something from the forest that was telling her that what she was watching was for the best. *Let it burn*, she thought. *Let it burn, let it burn, let HER burn.* There was no explaining it. She couldn't understand where the feelings were coming from. All she knew was that the force that had lead her this far in her search for Ben, was also the force that was stopping her from approaching the cottage and was also telling her that Ben was safe. She watched the Jaguar car drive away and felt a warmth for the man who sat in it. Whatever it was that had forced him into these actions must have been serious enough. Whatever it was, she felt total and complete sympathy for him. She also felt a complete sense of comfort and contentment knowing that Ben was safe. Soon they would be re-united.

\*        \*        \*

That morning she woke with a blockage in her throat. It wasn't physical, but it felt strong enough to be noticed. It was hatred choking her. It was the sensation of total hatred that left the feeling deep in her throat. Rising from the bed and looking at her reflection in the mirror, she no longer saw the beauty but instead the ugliness within. Her eyes no longer sparkled back at her, but had a dullness that offered the insight into her soul. Her mouth, now down turned at the edges, no longer smiled. It had that sneering suspicious look that had been thrown at unwanted presence so many times. Her body, a temple of beauty and sensuality, was now a sagging shell while her mind had stayed exactly the same. It continued its journey down the road it had taken many years ago, knowing that the end was near. Caroline stared at the person looking back and smiled. A wan smile. A smile that resonated nothing but hatred. The final solution would soon be in place and the result would be so satisfying. Turning to look at Tom she felt instant pity. He was a victim. There was nothing she could do about that, but she could continue to love him. Sitting down on the chair whilst her husband slept, she opened her diary once more and wrote.

"*The day no longer matters. The entry I write now is without title or in any way following what went on before. This is the way I feel now, whether it be connected to the past, or a portal to the future. I am what I have become, and I am what I want to be.*
*The children have gone. It is a shame, but deep in my soul it never really bothered me. They were a part of what we were, but now are a part of the past. What we are now is on a much higher plane, and my only sadness and regret is that they couldn't be a part of it. They will rest in peace and I will never forget them. My focus and life will now be devoted to him.*

*There can be no other. What is to come is inevitable, but the result will overcome and overwhelm all the beauty that has surrounded me in my life. The flames could have been started myself, but instead they were a gift to me. I could not have envisioned a better end. That part has gone. Now we have the future.*

It was only after she had closed the book that she felt the tremor in her heart. It was like an involuntary gasp. She knew instantly and pleaded for it not to be so. Her mother had died of a heart attack, such a rare occurrence in a woman, but there had never been any suggestion that it could be hereditary. *"Not now please. Not after everything that I have done. Please not now"*

Whatever it was that was about to visit her, it would not be welcome. After all she had achieved, this was no way for it to end. Caroline Bolton would soon say goodbye to the world she had created around her, and whatever was waiting for her would not be pleasant.

# CHAPTER THIRTY-SIX

The dream was explicit enough. So much so that when Mary woke she continued the vision. Ben had stood before her and smiled. The sweet innocent smile that he saved usually for her and her only. He had then turned and pointed. Pointed to the clearing in the forest, a place that she had seen already and one that was not far from where she was presently. The message was clear. Ben was showing her the way to go and how to find him. He was alive and she was going to find him. Her firstborn would be back in her arms soon. Getting dressed quickly she knew where to go. She knew how to find him.

In his damp and barely furnished room, Dale lay there and for the first time in months smiled. During the night his older brother had come to him in a dream and told him he would be okay. Ben was alive and they would be together again. He'd missed Ben so badly, and all of the taunts and the bullying of the kids at school would soon come to an end once he came home. Ben would always know how to look after him.

Next door, in the living room, Chippy lit up another cigarette and felt contentment. It wasn't a drug that made him that way as all he smoked now was simple nicotine. It was a deep knowledge that Mary would be coming home soon, and would bring Ben with her. The living nightmare was over. Life would improve and they would ensure that the future would be a happy one. The kind of life that so many others had taken for granted, but had so easily evaded them. The past didn't matter. The future would be different. With that he took another long and satisfying drag and stared out of the less than clean window and smiled. Above the tenement block opposite, the sun had broken through the clouds and was glistening on the pavement below. Suddenly, landing on the window ledge in front of him, a small red finch hopped from one foot to the other and cocked its head to one side as it looked back at him. Chippy couldn't remember the last time he'd even heard a bird in these parts before, never mind seen one. He watched for a while and then the bird flew off as quickly as it had arrived. It flew far into the now blue and cloudless sky, and Chippy kept his eyes on it for as long as he could, before the speck finally disappeared. Closing his eyes he then stood and allowed the sun's rays to float over him, giving him a warmth that now matched the inner warmth he felt. *"It is going to be okay"*, and with that he smiled once more.

If there was ever a doubt that a happy ending can be possible no matter what the levels of despair or unhappiness, then this can dispel it. One boy, a victim of circumstances, came through the sheer hell of his life and triumphed with a promise of a better future. These are the days that make it worthwhile. Days like these can happen, if only they are allowed to......

Dear reader. Thank you for staying with me this far. This has been a tale of despair. The despair of one woman who seeks her child, and the desolation of another who finds herself falling into an abyss. It has not been a happy tale, but suffice to say it is one that has a message for us all. The beginning of madness can be something that no-one can predict or understand why. At least this tale has had a suitably happy ending. So far at least. Unfortunately our tale has not ended. There is still one more twist of fate to befall our characters. A twist that will be told in the final chapter. For those of you who have come this far and would like to leave us now, I can only say thank you. For those who would read a little further, I say also thank you...but you will not like what you are about to read.

# CHAPTER THIRTY-SEVEN

"BEN!" Mary screamed at the top of her voice. "BEN, I AM HERE". Standing in the open clearing in the midst of the forest, the place she had dreamt of so vividly, she felt the howling wind buffet her and take those words and throw them away. Around her the trees swayed in a mad demonic rhythm, and in the distance she could see two large birds flap their wings in agitation and fly away. There was a screech and then a crashing through the undergrowth, making Mary tremble with fright, and then three deer came charging out into the clearing, not noticing her or caring for her. High above a thunder clap followed by a flash of lightning lit up the dark and forbidding sky for a brief moment, only to be overwhelmed by the greyness of the autumn day. The wind howled louder and louder and Mary screamed louder and louder. "BEN WHERE ARE YOU?. ANSWER ME PLEASE!". She looked around her in a state of panic. He was here, she knew it. He had spoken and appeared to her in the dream. He had shown her where to come, so she KNEW he was here…but why didn't he come? She ran to the edge of the clearing and stared deep into the forest. He wasn't there she knew that, but still she stared and shouted. "BEN". There was no answer and no sign of movement except the swaying high above as each tree clashed and crashed against each other, entwining their branches only to have them torn apart as the wind suddenly changed direction. Every living creature that had inhabited the forest was startled by the ferocity of the howling wind. Those that could left quickly, scattering in all directions, whilst those that couldn't just burrowed deeper into the ground not daring to turn their eyes to the carnage that was taking place.

Mary ran from one edge of the clearing to the next, shouting her firstborn's name, but there was nothing. She knew he was here, but still nothing. She screamed and hollered and shouted until her throat hurt and her voice became hoarse and then after what seemed like hours, but was in fact only minutes, she collapsed onto the wet and unforgiving floor, sobbing uncontrollably. "Ben, Ben. Where are you my love. Please come back to me. Please Ben...."

Below where his mother was slumped on the floor, some six feet at least where she was, lay little Ben. He was awake and alive, but no longer of this world. The pain and despair that his poor body and mind had endured had finally won through, and Ben lay there entombed with no knowledge of what was or what was to be. The six hard walls that surrounded him gave him little room for movement, if any at all, and the clean fresh air that had filled his lungs throughout his recent ordeal was even now deserting him. Replacing it was a stale and putrid substance. The darkness gave him no respite, and thankfully he was in no state of mind to understand his horrendous predicament. Whatever demons had driven his tormentor to end his ordeal in this way could never be understood, for here was a boy, on the cusp of manhood, with his life taken away in the most horrendous of ways. Thankfully for little Ben, he never heard the cries of his mother. Thankfully also he never really understood where he was, because if he had ever been given an inkling, he would surely have died anyway from the shock. No one could survive such a thing. Soon the darkness entered his mind too and then he rested.

Ben had never hurt anyone. He hadn't enough years on this planet to know what the reality of hurt really was. He had been brought up in circumstances that had been against him from the start, and when he found himself torn away from the family he had known all his life, there was no turning back. He was a boy who had potential, like most boys his age, but that was where it ended. There was no one who would be able to take him by the hand and lead him to a better place. The love of his mother came too late, and was not enough to stop the descent. The concern of his teachers was an occasional one, and couldn't ever lift him away from the gloom. His peers only saw him as a way of another trick to line their already criminal pockets. The only kindness that had crept into his life was with Hannah, but like the scorpion who can't help itself, Ben had too left with a deadly sting. It wasn't his fault, he just knew nothing else.

He thought these thoughts as he felt himself float above the forest. A now calm and serene forest where the birds tended to their young in newly laid nests that comforted amongst the branches. The tall and green trees swayed in perfect harmony, whilst down below on the gladed floor he saw squirrels, hedgehogs and fallow deer all going about their business as only they can. He felt himself float away from the forest at a speed that couldn't be judged and looked down on the face of the young girl who sat in a nursery cuddling her favourite teddy. On the table next to her there was a picture of her mother, a startling looking woman who had kind eyes but a sad and haunted expression. He saw as the girl was taken in the arms of a much older man. Rather shabbily dressed but with a smile that encouraged the love for her to flow out of him. She was safe, he knew that.

Then he looked down at the face of the young lady who had so badly wanted her love to remain. It was a sad face, but he could sense a feeling of satisfaction and nothing to regret. She had lived her life and for the last few months had lived it with the one she dreamt of. He looked down at the sad faces of two little children who had really had as little chance as he and he promised to himself that he would make their lives better when they eventually met. He saw the faces of the man, a shadow of himself, haunted by the horror of his life, and then the woman who sat by his side. He shivered involuntarily and saw the look of sheer evil. Her time will come, of that there was no doubt.

Finally he saw the face of Chippy and his brother Dale. Their sadness overwhelmed him and he hoped and he prayed for a better time for them both. The living room was just the same, but it was emptier than before. As he floated high above the trees, as high as the clouds he saw one last image. That of his mother. She was lying on the floor of the forest, her eyes closed. She slept soundly, but he knew and felt that she would awake to the sadness that had invaded her heart. With his final act before saying goodbye, he felt himself drift down and fall gently to the floor so that he lay next to the body of his mother. "It's okay Mum", he whispered as he put his arm around her waist and kissed the nape of her neck. "Everything will be fine. One day you will make another Ben and he will be big and strong like me. One day you will be proud of Dale. He will do great things and although I will always be with you, there will be a day when you will let me go. Goodbye mum", he leant across to look at her sleeping face. It stirred a little but her eyes didn't open. "I love you Mum".

## THE END

# Author Bio

Roy Calley is a BBC TV journalist working in London. Brought up in Blackpool he has travelled extensively and twelve years ago published a history of his local football club, Blackpool FC. This is his first novel, but has had numerous stories and scripts published down the years.

Printed in the United Kingdom
by Lightning Source UK Ltd.
120553UK00002B/10-21